About the Author

Jennie has worked as a primary teacher for most of her career, which began in the early 1970s in the eastern suburbs of Sydney, Australia. She later moved to the outback settlements of the Northern Territory, in the remote locations of Maningrida, Pine Creek, Lajamanu and Warrabri. Shortly thereafter, she taught in the western suburbs of Sydney. During that time, Jennie focused on her academic writing, children's literature, and, more recently, historical narrative.

Jennie is enthusiastic about teaching; her inspiration to write is developing as she works with young children. She credits this experience as having shaped her interest in social history and the lived experiences of the past. Her interest in memoir, history and philosophy becomes evident in her writing as her words contain stories about challenge and adversity.

This novel, *Tanami Desert Star*, is based upon Jennie's experience living in the outback of the Northern Territory. Her research into the early communities of regional Australia from 1860 to 1880 enabled her to reflect upon the difficulties that the early settlers may have faced. She is presently continuing research on historical fiction.

Jennie is married with three grown-up children and currently lives in the Blue Mountains of NSW, Australia.

Tanami Desert Star

Jennie Warren

Tanami Desert Star

Olympia Publishers
London

www.olympiapublishers.com
OLYMPIA PAPERBACK EDITION

Copyright © Jennie Warren 2025

The right of Jennie Warren to be identified as author of
this work has been asserted in accordance with sections 77 and 78 of
the Copyright, Designs and Patents Act 1988.

All Rights Reserved

No reproduction, copy or transmission of this publication
may be made without written permission.
No paragraph of this publication may be reproduced,
copied or transmitted save with the written permission of the publisher,
or in accordance with the provisions
of the Copyright Act 1956 (as amended).

Any person who commits any unauthorised act in relation to
this publication may be liable to criminal
prosecution and civil claims for damage.

A CIP catalogue record for this title is
available from the British Library.

ISBN: 978-1-83543-213-6

Some references to historical events, real people, or real places are
used fictitiously. Other names, characters, places and events are
products of the author's imagination, and any resemblance to actual
events, places or persons, living or dead, is entirely coincidental.

First Published in 2025

Olympia Publishers
Tallis House
2 Tallis Street
London
EC4Y 0AB

Printed in Great Britain

Acknowledgement of Country

The author acknowledges the Traditional Custodians of this Land. She pays respects to Elders past, present, and emerging and celebrates the diversity of Aboriginal peoples and their ongoing cultures and connections to their lands and waters.

Prologue

Lucy made an impact on others from the day she was born, but the influence that the Northern Territory had over her was greater. The song, dance, customs and beliefs held Lucy to this land. She had lived her entire life on this property in the middle of the Tanami Desert. Mandalong Station had belonged to her family for over one hundred and fifty years and would continue to inspire the Roddick family into the future.

Lucy had grown up hearing the dreamtime stories, had watched the dance of the waterfowl, and smelt the sweet scent of the desert acacia. This is her story.

PART I

Chapter 1
Napaliarri: The Seven Sisters

The dark sky enveloped them as their eyes beheld the Desert Star. It shone with great majesty, its brilliance seduced them forward, captivating them into its hold. Daniel held his granddaughter close, as he told her the story of the Seven Sisters and the Desert Star.

"The Napaljarri-wanu Jukurrpa is the story of the seven ancestral Napaljarri sisters. An ancestral Jakamarra man was in love with the seven Napaljarri sisters and chased them. In a final attempt to escape from the Jakamarra, the sisters turned themselves into fire, and ascended to the heavens to become stars." **(1)**

Daniel reached over and placed his arm around Lucy. "Our land," he commanded. "Belongs to this Indigenous community. The stories and traditions of these people are older than any we have made. They are the custodians of this great land and share with us our future."

Chapter 2
Tanami My Home

The didgeridoo rolled dimly into the distance. With each beat, Lucy took another stride, easing her way through the dense pandanus palms. She held back the branches as she followed the sandy track that led her back home. Her body had rested briefly earlier that night under the stars, but she knew there would be her family who fretted over her absence. Her pace quickened as she walked, gathering speed with each step. Lucy looked down briefly, as the sun had reflected upon something shining brightly within the sand. She stooped towards it and quickly picked it up. She did not have time to examine the object more carefully, but instead felt it between her fingers as she quickened her pace.

Lucy arrived breathless into the familiar station compound. It was now early morning. The sun was rising in the distance and the birds were singing their cheerful welcome as they flew from branch to branch following her. The chickens, too, ran around her feet as she tried to edge closer to the gate that enclosed her property. She pulled her small body up towards the latch, and then closed it carefully behind her. The lights were on in the kitchen, and she hoped her father had not discovered her missing. She climbed uneasily in through her bedroom window and lay down quietly to escape detection. It was not long before Lucy fell asleep, her mind returning to the place she had just been. She felt warm and content as her body relaxed into a deep sleep.

Within hours, Lucy had made her way to the kitchen. The

household had dispersed, leaving no evidence of their presence; the dishes, washed and stacked into the shelves, the floor swept, and the kettle was boiling on the stove. The young girl moved her chair closer as she sat at the old cedar table and examined the metal object she had found earlier. It was long and round and had a shaft within its encasement. Lucy placed the object back on the table and ate her bowl of cereal, before running outside.

Lucy was an independent girl for her age, but leaving her home overnight was not acceptable, and she knew there may be consequences. She pushed the fly wire door open and ran outside. Her father had left for work in the yards earlier that morning and her mother was tending to the washing in the back garden. The conversation with her indicated that all was normal. Lucy reached out to pick a couple of flowers from the side garden and ran towards the homestead. She loved her home because it was peaceful and a safe place to be.

Living in the outback was a constant challenge for the Roddick family. The land could be remote and at times, unforgiving. The challenges became, for some, too difficult to endure. The dust from the desert winds, the fires and floods, droughts, famine, pestilence, and plagues all brought a certain amount of turmoil. One had to be strong to brave the impacts of this landscape. For most of her ancestors, these trials just made them stronger. It was now 1975, and Mandalong had housed its fifth generation of Roddicks, a family blessed with making this land a productive piece of the Northern Territorian landscape.

Lucy stepped inside, flowers in hand. The kitchen would look beautiful, and she knew her mother would enjoy looking at them. Her home was a rambling stone building. The double walls were more than twelve feet thick, the vent between them creating a draft of cool air which made living in the rooms more achievable.

Each room contained a large fireplace and beyond the kitchen, dirt floors replaced terra cotta flagstones. Throughout the entire building, Lucy could find her mother's possessions, all of which made her feel at home: Persian rugs, oil lamps and earthenware, wrought iron beds, fly wire cots, and precious camphor boxes which housed the delicate tablecloths. A ceramic bowl and jug sat above the dressing table, and of course, the earthenware pot beneath the bed was invaluable, as the run to the outside pan toilet was always difficult at night. The family was most dependent on the fuel stove in the kitchen as it provided hot meals for the household during the day, and heating on cold desert nights. Lucy had watched her father chop the wood for the stove most mornings and her mother would always have a kettle and a camp oven on the top. The meal was made early and simmered silently as the household addressed their duties.

Young children from the local schoolhouse ran around outside as Reg, the gardener, raked the sandy soil. Reg lived with his two wives outside the compound. His new wife, Beth, was less than half his age and sat grooming herself against the wall of the outhouse during the day. Reg was also married to Martha, betrothed to him forty years earlier. Each day she would work as housekeeper to Lucy's mother.

Reg was elderly; a quiet man who would smile occasionally, however, out of respect, he would look down and avoid eye contact with his boss, Jack. He referred to Lucy's mother as 'Missus' and respectfully fulfilled her wishes around the property. He adjusted his belt which held up his uneven and baggy trousers. They were his favourite, as he religiously wore them most days. Reg worked as he smoked his pipe, very often stopping to add tobacco. He would push the fragrant mixture down inside the bowl and tap it lightly. He'd then use a match to light the tobacco and return to work, the pipe hanging awkwardly to one side of his mouth.

Reg was proud of his garden, regularly leaning over to tend to the groundcover below. At times, he would look down and shake his pipe over the stonework alongside the garden wall. The old tobacco was at last removed, together with the spit that had accumulated in the stem. Reg was patient. He knew his garden as he had worked at the homestead longer than anyone. He enjoyed his work as he could achieve more when not interrupted. Although he remained stiff with arthritis, his achievements at the homestead were noticeable.

Reg would spend a great deal of his time sweeping away the pine needles which had collected on the dirt paths and gardens below the big oak trees. He knew the barbs would make the soil acidic and that should be avoided at all costs. Reg would then collect the pinecones that would fall and give them to Lucy who would decorate them. 'Mandalong' is an Aboriginal word meaning 'where the forest oaks grow' **(2).** Known as desert oaks, these trees appear in groves and inspired the Roddicks as they offered a source of protection from the hot sun. They were tall trees, growing up to sixty-six feet, so Lucy and her friends would often be seen climbing up into the canopies.

When Lucy was not climbing trees and picking flowers, she was inside her home, very often tended to by Martha, the house-girl. Lucy often lamented the times she and Martha spent together when she was a small girl. She knew that this woman would always be an integral part of her life. Her mother, distracted by running the homestead and all that it entailed, left Martha and Lucy to enjoy each other's company. Martha spent the morning preparing Lucy for the day and then taking care of home duties.

The morning regime was predictable as it centred around Lucy, and she enjoyed this attention.

Martha would place Lucy upon the kitchen table to perform her daily ritual; to disrobe her and then place her small body in the large wrought iron bath. She had not conceived children of her own, and she often thought that Reg had married a younger version of herself so that he could have the children she had not provided. At times, she felt inadequate as she knew motherhood had been something that was expected of her. Martha would then smooth down Lucy's blond hair as she brushed it against her scalp, and then carefully lift her into the bath water, stroking her limbs as she cradled the soap. Lucy loved these times as she could feel the tepid water roll from her body, cooling her with its magic. Lucy also knew there was something special about this woman who sang to her. The words were foreign, but always familiar.

Today would be different. Martha stood before her, comb in hand. Lucy stood, gazing up to Martha, and awkwardly explained to her that she wished to start washing herself. She noticed disappointment appear on Martha's face, so she stretched up to her, before giving her a big kiss. After dressing, Lucy ran out of the door for school. She hoped that the few hours of sleep would be enough to last the long day ahead, and that her friends would not make too many serious demands on her time. Her day seemed to move quickly, especially after obtaining an early mark for being industrious.

Lucy had transparent blue eyes that sucked you into her gaze. Blond ringlets scattered from her brow to beneath her shoulder line. Lucy's smile was warm, as she engaged with others naturally in a conversation. Mary would cover her regularly with sunscreen to protect her fair complexion, as she was always too eager and energetic to wear a hat. She was impulsive at times too, as she had so many things to achieve. Her enthusiasm was magnetic, as she charmed both relatives and friends.

Later that day, Lucy sat by the fuel stove to complete her homework. She was not talkative, as she knew if she completed her problem-solving, she would then have the weekend to share with her friends. Mary, her mother then proceeded to ask Lucy about the barrel she had left behind on the dining room table.

"The barrel that you left behind has been missing from our clock for years. Where did you find it?" enquired her mother.

"Outside, near the gate. It was in the sand," answered Lucy.

"Your father will be overjoyed, but I can imagine Daniel will be the one who will be especially grateful, darling," Mary added.

Lucy soon found her grandfather sitting at the table under the old oak tree in the kitchen garden. He kissed and thanked her for finding the missing part to the mantle clock. He then paused before he continued. Her grandfather would often remind Lucy of her heritage.

"The mantle clock was one of the only items brought over by William and Kathleen Roddick. Finding the barrel enables us to wind the timepiece again. This clock, is an important reminder of our ancestry and connection to history," he declared.

Lucy climbed up onto the chair to sit with her grandfather at the kitchen table. Daniel had his big mug of strong black coffee that he drank at this time, every morning. It was in a potter's mug, made by his wife, Gladys, when they were first married. It had his name on it, and he treasured it, as he had very little to remind himself of those special years they had together. Lucy leant over to be closer to him. Daniel then took a deep breath and began to read from an editorial in the 'Northern Territory News' on cattle stations in the district. He cleared his throat and held her hand as he read the text.

"Mandalong is 137 hectares and is situated 543km north-west of Alice Springs and 930km south-west of Darwin, close to the Hooker Creek Settlement (Lajamanu). There are about four thousand head of cattle; about one thousand and six hundred brahman breeders and the remaining cattle are short-horns and brahman cross," Daniel read carefully.

"…Although, with your father's management, it could increase in number within a short space of time," Daniel confessed.

Lucy looked up at Daniel. She adored him and felt important when he shared the Roddick history with her. Daniel knew that Lucy absorbed his every word, and this loyalty became a feature of their relationship for years to come.

That night, a veil of darkness descended upon the homestead. Dingoes wailed in the distance, while frogs chortled near the jellybean well outside the front door. Its waters held minerals, gifts to the soul. Lucy was snug and warm under the rugs, the air being cooler now as darkness had approached, but the howl of the wild dogs made her feel uncomfortable.

It did not take long before Lucy ran to her mother's room. She jumped heavily upon her parent's big bed, and snuggled into her warm body. Lucy would often catch her mother, feeding Eliza, her sister, propped up by big pillows. She could hear her mother breathe heavily as she allowed her baby to suckle. Eliza nuzzled into her mother, noisily drinking as she held her mother's breast with her fist.

"Why is your breath shorter than mine?" Lucy enquired.

"My breaths are shorter than yours, because you have a longer life expectancy, and so your heart needs to pump faster," her mother explained. Lucy looked up into her mother's eyes, and for the first time in her life, she realised that she may not have her forever. She knew then, that she had a limited time to learn everything she needed from her mother.

Mary placed the baby beside her and gave Lucy a tight squeeze.

"Everything will be all right, darling," she reassured her quietly. "Whatever might happen in the future, you know I will always love you." Lucy reached up to her mother's face, touched her cheek briefly, and replied, "And I will always love you." With that, she jumped back down onto the floor, and ran outside to find company.

Lucy woke the next morning to the smell of toast drifting through her door. She pushed the bedclothes aside and ran down the hallway to look upon her father and his team cooking breakfast on the open stove. Rashers of bacon and dozens of eggs were simmering slowly, as the kettle whistled its impatience for service. The jackaroos and station hands, known sometimes as 'The crew', clambered over each other as if there was no time to lose. Each smothered salted butter over their hot toast and sat down to eat their hearty meal.

Jack thanked Lucy for bringing the barrel from the clock back to the homestead. The small key attached to the barrel made it possible to wind up the clock, but the key to the face was still missing, so Lucy promised to be 'on the lookout'. She was grateful that she had made her father so happy, as it had meant much to him.

Lucy stood by the window and watched a mother hen quickly pick up speed, as she gathered her chicks and made haste. The sun would be up soon, and she knew she would have the day to herself. Mary, her mother, stumbled past and apologized for her lateness. Lucy looked around. The men were finishing now, and Martha removed the dishes and began clearing the bench. The noise then shifted outside as Lucy's dad, Jack, loaded the utility with fresh supplies. He announced his departure with a kiss and Lucy returned his affection with a big hug. She loved it when he went to the bush because he always brought back stories that he would tell her before she fell asleep. He would cover her up carefully below the huge fan and snuggle in beside her. Then he would reach in with his arm and place it behind her head. He would then whisper quietly, and bring the bush to life with his tales. She believed that he should have been a writer, because when he spoke, he stole her heart with his imagination.

Jack wore a blue cotton safari shirt, and khaki trousers held up with a heavy leather belt. His slouch hat tipped to one side, covered his forehead to the bridge of his nose. He was quite charming, and was considered, by those who knew him, to be a gentleman. He did, however, spend a considerable time each morning attending to his ablutions. His most noticeable feature was his dark moustache. Tapered at the ends, it accentuated his good looks and fine bone structure. Mary always contended that her husband spent longer grooming himself than any member of the family; in fact, she boasted that she could coordinate the family, pack their bags, wash up and all before he had left the bathroom.

'Lightning Jack' as everyone called him, walked as if he was impatient to get to his destination. His heavy leather riding boots were noticeable as he walked, for his long strides were made with definition as each step had an intention. When Jack walked into a room, he would remove his hat with a cupped hand, his hair then falling into thick curls around his face. He then would deliberately scoop the offending strands and flick them back and out of the way. He would then sit by the door and casually roll a drum cigarette. He was careful to smoke outside as he knew that it was not polite to smoke indoors.

Today, Jack moved with limited ease and grace, his large boots hitting the floor to announce his departure. Within minutes, the engine misfired, and 'the crew' lifted their arms and hollowed, and then they were off. A short cough of smoke left the vehicle and then it fired up, sending them off into the back paddock and beyond. Lucy knew now she would not see him again for days.

It was early, and Lucy sat at the kitchen table as she always had since she was small. The clean plates were on the counter, and her school bag sat beside her with the books and lunch within. Martha was a woman who shared her smile and warmth generously. She was understanding and compassionate, quiet, and only spoke when it was necessary. She moved slowly but with exaggerated conviction. Martha carefully brushed Lucy's long blond hair, tying it up as she braided each side with ribbons. Then, she cleaned Lucy's face with a warm washer to remove the remnants of breakfast and Lucy happily jumped down from the table. She held onto Martha's hand as she said goodbye, and took her school bag from the table as she ran out of the door. *Mother should be out in the garden*, she thought to herself. There, before her, defined by her big straw hat, sat Mum, in the sunflowers, weeding with passion. It was not yet light, but she had already managed a sweat, the perspiration dotted above her eyes and falling like streams along her brow.

"School already?" Mum asked.

"Have to meet Winnie before school starts," panted Lucy. The two hugged and exchanged a quick kiss.

Lucy ran off into the bush to find her friend. As she did, she reflected on her mother and how much she did for her. Her friends believed Mary to be dependable and trustworthy. She could also contain herself in tricky situations, delicately avoiding subjects that prevented her from speaking her mind. Lucy adored that her mother had a wicked sense of humour, as she often enjoyed recounting comical events from her past.

After studying literature and languages at a university, her mother aspired to teach overseas. However, this goal altered when Mary met Lucy's father, Jack; they fell in love and got married. That arrangement took her to the Territory where she had remained ever since. Mary had a passion for cooking, painting, and gardening. She occasionally entered artworks in competitions held at the Alice Springs Museum and Art Galleries of Australia. On one occasion, Mary was awarded 'Most Commended'. When her mother entered a room, Lucy noticed that all eyes were upon her. Her dark angular features attracted the attention of others, as she stood statuesque and confident. She could hold a conversation with a variety of people, as her interest noted on a diverse range of topics. She also enjoyed talking about politics and the challenges of democracy.

The rains were coming, and wildlife had a way of announcing the change. Black cockatoos swept from the acacias above and into the blue sky. The swish of their black wings was noticeable as they arched their way into the blue heavens. Black and majestic; they appeared as royal as one could be out there on the outback plains. Then calm! Nothing moved! The cool breeze that followed, stirred the willy willies of the bush from their roots below the surface. Then quietly, the soft droplets of rain from above speckled the red dust below her feet. As she looked upward, a clap of thunder announced its presence and with it, an ear-piercing jolt as lightning struck, bringing along the torrents of rain. The insurgence would pierce the landscape from December to January. The black inky blue sky would indicate the storm was approaching. Falling with tremendous power and blocking every sound in its wake, floods of water pierced the landscape with an unforgiving force. Lucy ran as fast as her legs could carry her to a place of safety up in the red hills above. There, she could rest before looking for her friends, Maisie, Jimmy, Winnie, and Red.

That afternoon, Lucy played in the bush before running home from school. She noticed how the rains had turned the landscape green overnight. Her friends assisted as she gathered flowers from the lily pads, and collected berries to eat later with hot damper and golden syrup. They then ran around the trees and found honey in its branches. The sun streamed down as she swam in the waters under the fast-flowing waterfall above. The torrents of water washed away the dust from beneath her feet, and worked to clean her tired hot body with its surging current. She climbed the steep cliff above the waterfall and rested under the shade of the overhanging acacia trees. Lucy then gathered spinifex grass and threw it down upon the rock, above the waterhole. Her friends were not far behind. She turned around to hear giggling, and there, beside her, were her companions. They had been friends since they were young. Everyone had the freedom of the wide-open spaces and the time to enjoy what it offered.

Running barefooted upon the dirt, Lucy later made her way up the path, and past the sandstone rocks that were bordering the garden. She looked up towards the veranda. It was open and encircled the homestead. Her feet at last, rested upon the wooden boards that formed the floor. As she stepped forward, the boards moved slightly. She then jumped up, onto the stone step that marked the entrance to the property. Noticeable dips in the stone made over time, was a reminder to those who entered the property, that others had been there decades earlier.

Lucy entered the kitchen. The kettle whistled, a high-pitched song of attention. Its steam had choked the windows, and the vapour extended throughout the room, clinging to the surrounding walls. A door banged behind her as she saw her mother run into the room to remove the offender from the stove. Lucy let out a long sigh. She felt comforted at seeing her mother, who later reminded her that it was bath time.

The scorching summer had made it necessary to spend the cooler evenings catching up with the chores around the property. Jack and his family flung the wire door open as they entered the kitchen at midday. They looked around for a place to sit and cool off. Mary brought in sandwiches and cool drinks as they sat under the fans.

"The herd is finding it tough, love," Jack briefed her. "The heat is so unforgiving! For every tree that stands alone in the paddock, there stands only a handful of cattle, gaining whatever relief they can muster," he continued. Jack dozed off briefly before slipping back out with 'the crew'.

An old wives' tale and one that Mary's mother would often recount was,

"A man's heart is through his stomach." This advice was given in the best of good humour, as the two would often reflect on the importance given to mealtime.

Her thoughts were justified, as Jack's first words, as he walked through the door that evening was, "What's for dinner, love?" Mary thought it was puzzling that sometimes, we are expected to balance everything within the home; wash and iron, provide for the children's needs, balance the books, pay the bills, manage the staff, and yet the menu becomes the topic that is foremost on the agenda. She laughed to herself as she started to cut the onions and rinse the vegetables. She would be making fried rice tonight, a staple in their house as she always had plenty of these ingredients. The meals at the homestead were varied, and Mary was adept at turning whatever she had, into a feast everyone could enjoy.

Mary was resourceful. Not only did she have the home and her responsibilities for the station organised, but she managed to instruct the girls about those things she considered important. This would include preparing the girls for a trip in the bush to find 'bush tucker'. They were also taught the importance of stocking up on food and water, and acquiring maps and a compass for the trip. Each of them felt they knew this land, but they also understood that places in the bush could very easily resemble one another. An essential item when travelling was petrol, as their mother had warned them that they need to be ready for any emergency.

Mary knew that the best way to instruct her girls would be to take them out for a trip into the open desert country. They enjoyed being able to escape the confines of their home to find adventure outside. Very often, Lucy would help her mum find wild food to take home.

"Duck shooting is my least favourite hunt though, Mum," Lucy would say.

Mary understood this far too well as she had gone duck shooting with her father in Queensland, where the birds were fatter and made an easier target.

"These beasts are smaller by comparison to the birds on the more fertile plains north-east of Australia," her mother replied.

Mary helped the children to understand that killing animals to eat was acceptable in these parts. "If we are not brutally killing for sport, there should be no harm," she would say.

"And we definitely do not kill any animal that is endangered!" Mary emphasised.

Mary always took her girls 'out bush' when Jack was away. They would go hunting, and the girls enjoyed watching their mother, as she instructed them on the safe handling of the weapons. Lucy relied on the strength from her mother as the shotgun was heavy and her hands were small, therefore, lining up targets was difficult. Mary was aware, that for them, needing to know how to load and reload a rifle may be a matter of life and death. Years later, the girls would personally value that lesson.

"You may thank me one of these days," advised her mother.

Jasper, the dog, ran 'like the wind', catching the birds as they fell from the air. He had been a constant companion over the last few weeks, and belonged to Red. The shot rang out as the gun fired, taking with it three of four small birds at a time. When the ducks had been collected, Mary and her daughter would pluck the feathers from their small bodies and prepare a dinner for all. The jackeroos would love these meals and sit at the table afterwards, licking their fingers.

"Great tucker, boss lady!" they would call out in appreciation. She loved it when they were happy as they worked hard, and she valued their efforts.

At other times, the girls would hunt rabbit. These beasts were pests, so Jack would always be happy when he had rabbit stew for dinner. It would be prepared that afternoon in the hotpot. The stewing would tenderise the otherwise tough meat. One knew he did not particularly like the meal, but he never 'let on' as one rabbit in the pot was one less rabbit he would need to trap.

Red and Jimmy often surprised their friend Mary, with a supply of fish from the Tank Stream. This bore-water ran across the property and became a reliable source of water supply for the locals. Whenever the fish were in short supply, the locals knew, that the water was not suitable to drink.

"Mrs! Caught desert rainbow fish and yabbies upstream. You got a hot pan ready for your tucker?" Jimmy would enquire.

"Gee!" Mary would exclaim. "You lads are both so generous. If it were me, I would eat them all!" They would all laugh. This happened regularly. Mary always knew she could depend on Red and Jimmy when the fish were biting. Further out, in the deeper flowing waters, they caught barramundi, but they needed to travel a long distance to be able to bring these monsters home.

Recipes varied, but beef from the station was the most commonplace, with chicken, pork, rabbit, and fish served occasionally. Sometimes, the beef was not available, and this created problems for the locals. These prized cattles would leave Mandalong, to be sent to the abattoir in Katherine. The meat was then packed and sent to South Australia to be inspected, to then returned by road train back to Katherine. The locals often questioned the validity of this procedure, and wondered why inspections could not take place at the station. This meant that, at times, access to this fine meat was in short supply. Occasionally, these jackeroos would take a calf and lean it up against a tree to dissect it into its various parts. Mary would take a share from them and freeze the pieces, but not before salting the briskets in brine in her large enamel sink. It would sit there overnight to be packaged up the following day and frozen with the other meat.

Mary received a test that remained topical for some time. It arrived with the impromptu visit from Dr Coombs and Professor Stanner, who were dignitaries from Canberra. On this occasion, Mary was ill-prepared as there was no available meat to cook for the guests that evening. The beef had not returned from the abattoir, and 'the crew' were indisposed. This meant, the family could not supply alternative 'bush tucker'. Jack and Mary would just have to do what they could, to make their guests as comfortable as possible, and this meant, cooking horse meat.

Jack and the visitors spent the afternoon with the Elders, shortly after their arrival, to discuss current issues before returning for the evening dinner. One concern remained high on the agenda. Earlier that month, Jack had called an unofficial meeting, as he had been concerned about the amount of unwanted personnel presenting themselves at the station. Once Jack had related his displeasure, the conversation relaxed somewhat.

Later that evening, Mary busied herself in the kitchen, occasionally bringing out bowls of salad and vegetable dishes to arrange on the dining table. The girls sat and listened to the men continue their conversation while they waited for their meal. After a considerable length of time, Professor Stanner turned to face the girls and asked them about their education. The girls spoke in glowing terms about their school, and at times, briefly explained how they fish in the local river. The guests were generous with their attention to the girls and Lucy became quite attached to the professor.

The family finished their meal that evening and then the men resumed their discussion. Eliza, Lucy's sister, enjoyed having visitors and spent the rest of the evening trying to add a comment. Although she had only just begun school, she was able to listen carefully and convey an opinion. Lucy found her sister annoying and once she had excused herself, made her way to her bedroom.

The visitors returned to Canberra the following morning, leaving Mary embarrassed at having to serve a less than appetising meal of horse meat to her guests. She would regularly use this event to emphasise the importance of preparedness and organisation.

The following day, Mary travelled to the piggery at the station to bring home a large sow in the back of the utility. She had been left shocked and embarrassed by the previous evening and would now rectify things by selecting an animal that 'the crew' would cut up when she returned.

Mary approached the pen with the girls. The sows were seated in the mud, as it had been raining the previous evening. A litter of piglets had attached themselves firmly to their mother, to drink what they could, as the barrows ate from the trough not far away. Cabbage leaves, carrots, and apple cores, lay in a pile alongside the freshly laid straw. The sows were content to sun themselves all day until a visitor appeared. Each of them would then noisily grunt, as they ambled to the fence to investigate any intrusion. Lucy chose a large barrow and the attendant assisted as it was lifted into the tray of the utility.

On her return trip, Mary would pick up supplies from the local co-op store. Canned and frozen produce, a bag of flour for baking bread, and sunshine milk were available for her to take home. Mary was thankful that she did not need the vegetables, as they were expensive and in short supply. She was appreciative of her own garden, as this meant food was always on the table.

Living in the bush was complicated at times. Your survival depended on whether you had access to road or air transport. Unfortunately, sometimes drivers of road trains had to abandon their load on the bitumen highway. This happened in times of flooding, or when large corrugations and potholes appeared on the surface. The drivers would, on these occasions, leave a voice message on the two-way and drive on.

The family often made a long road trip to Katherine to buy

produce. Every eight weeks, this five-hour trip was made, and Lucy remembered it vividly.

"Dad, why does the cabin stink of petrol?" she would ask her father.

The truth was, and Mary knew the reason; that Jack syphoned the petrol from a long hose, and the smell of petrol would then consume the cabin as they drove in the heat of the midday sun. That, and the flies, made the experience quite uncomfortable. She would watch as he stretched the petrol cannister from the back of the utility to the petrol hold within. To get it started, he would suck the end, and then, turning to face the ground, spit out the residue to make an unbroken link from the canister to the vehicle.

Most of the time, Lucy enjoyed these adventures because there was always something different happening, and she did not know quite what to expect. She remembered the time when they were bogged two hundred kilometres west from Katherine. The truck they were travelling in, coughed its last breath, and then sank into the brackish mud, which eventually claimed it completely. Lucy looked on, fearing that if she ventured forward, she too, may sink below the sand.

On another occasion, her father used a tree as a winch, to pull their vehicle up, clear of the muddy terrain. Lucy volunteered her help when she could. She stepped down from the vehicle, the dirt under her feet often turning to mud. Lucy wrestled with a winch while being ankle-deep in water. After hours battling the terrain, Jack finally let out a scream of relief when the Land Rover released its hold in the sinking sand. The tyres of the vehicle would then become anchored to a branch, which would catapult it towards the clearing. Lucy and her dad were content to be following the track towards home after their ordeal. They would then retire for the evening, recounting the adventure to anyone who would listen.

Jack and Lucy enjoyed travelling the road from Katherine to home. She remembered one time with fondness. The mist ahead temporarily blinded them as they drove into the light. The air was crisp, and the magpies were singing sweetly. Salt bush outlined the corrugated road, which served tired travellers who were travelling east. The air was getting hotter now, and Lucy noticed the steam rising beyond the freshly laid bitumen ahead; it moved with the light and mirrored it. Hot, musky air rapidly overtook their senses, as a stiff carcass lay motionless beside the road. The air was still, the heat rising. Red kangaroos jumped quickly before them, and Jack had to react quickly to avoid a collision. The black cockatoos travelled noisily above them, in search of food between the mulga bushes. Then, the landscape changed to flat and undulating plains. On either side of the road, green ant mounds surrounded them, eagerly surfacing as if to collect their last meal. They picked at the food, devouring the contents within minutes. Lucy's body glistened with the heat as it was late afternoon, and this was the hottest time of the day. She opened the car window to gain reprieve, but the air was hot and stale. Lucy took a deep breath anyway and turned her attention to the landscape beyond. In front of her was the corrugated dirt road which would extend for forty kilometres before reaching home, her Mandalong.

Her spirit heightened as she looked beyond to the plains and above them, to the range of mountains ahead. She remembered these mountains fondly, as she and her friends would often take the track to the foothills, and there they would play until the sun gave notice that it was setting. Then, they would return home before the light had left them. These adventures were special to all of them. Lucy knew that home was close-by, and soon she would be able to rest her weary body and cool down with the tank water, that served her family so well.

Chapter 3
Brolgas Dancing

Lucy was growing up fast. She was adventurous, enjoyed the open air and kept busy, always making use of her valuable time. She made friends easily, and like her father, enjoyed the company of others. Her friends believed she would follow her dreams and lobby for 'freedom of opportunity', a topic which was close to her heart. Lucy believed that this would mean years of study at a university in one of the big cities. She did not want to leave her home, but understood that if she made this sacrifice, she would come back to represent those who needed a voice. The chance of her friends accompanying her to receive a degree, however, was unlikely, as her friends were highly under-represented.

Jack's life was busy as he had to share his time between his family, his work managing the station, and the staff, who worked for him in the stockyards. Occasionally, he would sit on the ground with the Elders under a shady tree to hold a meeting. Here, they would discuss ongoing business, and the management of Mandalong. These meetings were important as they documented the employment and training of staff at the station. This official documentation would then be sent to Canberra, to become a record of the business, and attest to the education each of them was receiving.

Jack often quoted Gandhi, *"Education must be a great equaliser in our society."* Lucy agreed with her father.

When Jack was not consulting with the Elders, he was busy

with jackaroos in the cattle pens. His preoccupation with sorting the stock was essential, as it determined the value of his cattle and the future of Mandalong. In the first yard, there were five hundred stock, who were lashing their tails and horns wildly. The thunder of the herds as they came crashing down every minute, was deafening. The object was to get one hundred or so of the cattle into the adjacent yard. The mighty stock whips set the beasts retreating towards the centre, then the men made a line behind; shouting, yelling, and cracking their whips to drive the stock onward. Jack hollowed, excited by the urgency, and held his breath.

The remaining cattle entered the second yard, where there were two lines of stockmen with more whoops cracking, and bellows. So, it continued until forty or fifty were secure in the third yard. This area was a long, narrow holding yard with a gate at the end, leading into the final division. The last selection were prime creatures, ready for the Sydney market and breeding purposes. The battle was eventually over, and the animals were placed into approved divisions. Jack breathed easier now.

The dusk had fallen tenderly over the garden and the paddocks that evening. A white star or two came out and blinked up away into the high heavens, but the heat was so intense, that it had turned the daisies, and as their hearts sank, they fell onto the dry ground underfoot. The pampas grass stood bravely against the sky as the white arms of the ghost gums stretched to the moon. The pungent smell of wattle awoke the senses as one brushed past, and this was, Lucy feared, the fearless scents of summer. Jack and the jackaroos assembled and decided to make it a night. It was not long before Jack was home and ready to retire, after what had seemed a very exhausting evening.

Lucy woke from her sleep the next morning with a jolt. She heard bushes rustle outside her window and then, whispering. She removed the bedclothes, got up out of bed, and leaned out of the window. There, before her stood two of her best friends, Red and Winnie. Red, had been named because of his tight black curls, which glimmered red with the dust of the desert and Winnie had the biggest smile, even if she had nothing at all to be happy about. They looked startled as they turned to Lucy, their deep black eyes filtering the light that held them transfixed to her image.

"What's up, Red?" Lucy asked inquisitively.

The two shook their heads, raised their arms, and pulled Lucy from where she stood. Her long white nightdress trailed after her as she slid from the bedroom window, becoming snagged on a branch in the confusion. She wrestled with the fabric briefly before tearing it away to catch up with her friends. She then ran out onto the sandy enclosure as fast as her legs could carry her. A twisted bough reached out, as if to catch her as she ran past. Something must be up, and it was Lucy's job to find out what it was.

Holding hands, the three remained intact as they stole across the campsite. They ran through embers of fires lit the previous evening, lifting filaments of ash onto the encampment. No one was there to greet them, only startled cattle dogs, and a couple of noisy chickens. The commotion they had stirred was deafening, but very soon, the three friends appeared in a clearing. They steadied themselves before gaining pace, choosing to duck behind a spinifex bush. Providing little cover, Lucy realised that her untidy frame and dusty nightdress were now on display. Lucy's heartbeat was loud, thumping madly within her and following, the pace of drums off into the distance.

The land was open ahead, save an occasional stringy bark. The sand was hot as the sun had been up for hours. A large throng of people had gathered, all spread out into an open circle. Within this enclosure, there was another throng of tribal members who surrounded two young boys.

"This is an initiation corroboree," whispered Red.

Lucy turned to Winnie. She was still smiling; her familiar face had not lost its sparkle. "I must go now," remarked Winnie.

"Why?" Lucy enquired.

"See that old woman over there. Eyes gone, Lucy! She, no, see this," Winnie answered.

Lucy stood transfixed as she interpreted Winnie's quick rant. Did she mean that the woman had her eyes removed because she saw too much? Red elaborated further.

"Women and girls are always forbidden at an Initiation Corroboree. When that woman was a young girl, she saw 'men's business'."

Lucy understood that the old woman's punishment was the law. Lucy looked around to catch Winnie, but she had gone.

Lucy knew she was taking a chance, but as she was with Red, she knew she would be safe if she kept the whole adventure a secret. The didgeridoos kept pounding, and the dancers in the inner circle kicked up dust and sand as they chanted. Inside this chamber of veteran Elders, sat the teens who would undergo circumcision. They would then need to survive in the bush for weeks. Upon their return, they would be considered 'a man'. Lucy could not see the performance, as the men in the inner circle were trying to provide the necessary security. Lucy felt like an outcast as she did not belong. She shielded her eyes and turned around.

With the tribal ceremony finished, Red took Lucy by the hand and pulled her away as the crowds began to disperse. They ran, now faster than they had before, through the trees that surrounded the creek. They raced up the dune that seemed to hold onto their legs as they ran. Then, as they approached the summit of the sandhill, they collapsed to drift down to the other side. In time, they reached the ridge; there, confronted by a fence which kept wild dingoes and foxes out. They tumbled into small tufts of grass, laying there together as they caught their breath. They both stood up to survey the land ahead. Lucy and Red then quickly separated, swearing that they would not speak of their adventure to anyone. Lucy now needed to clean up before Martha saw her attire. As she climbed up to her bedroom window, she reminded herself that her lips must remain sealed, as she did not want to get Red or Winnie into trouble.

Lucy loved athletics. Her long legs could run quicker now than anyone who dared to challenge her at the school carnival. She always brought her ribbons home to her mother. Lucy enjoyed showing them to her father too, who was often unable to watch her compete as he was out with 'the crew', fixing fences, or driving cattle. Lucy had come first in her aged race. After her athletics, Lucy very often cooled down by the water hole on the northern reaches of her property. On this occasion, Lucy ran to her favourite place to swim, collapsing before the water's edge, and then tumbling quickly into the water. The cool liquid adjusted her body temperature quickly and she smiled with pleasure.

Winnie and Red had been there earlier, together with all her classmates and friends, stirring the mud from the depths beyond and jumping from the rocks that cradled the water from within. With her friends now gone, Lucy stood up to examine the trophies. She lay among them, stretching her aching limbs on the warm rocks below.

Lucy gazed beyond at the darkening sky and slowly closed her eyes. She ached all over, her small frame savagely beaten by the onslaught of heat. Suffocating air pinned her frame to the water's edge. Then, leaning towards the body of water, she reached over to gain relief. The steam rose sharply from her skin.

Without warning, a sharp bleat rang out above her. She lifted her head and turned to see the silvery foliage of two brolgas dancing before her. Their bodies, coated in lustrous white and blue feathers, captured the sunlight. As they danced with precision, they held their heads erect. This was a classical ballet performance, Lucy thought to herself. The breeze rustled past them and played with the reeds at the water's edge. The song it played as it vibrated past, announced the performance had begun. Lucy watched intently, as the birds continued to move in a routine that she imagined they had memorized and practiced regularly.

Time stood still. The dark sky enveloped Lucy as she reached out towards it, the vibrations of the reeds escalating with each movement of the dance. Lucy, suspended in promise, held her arms upward to catch the stars above. Then, without warning, a soft gust of warm air shifted past her, as if to murmur a mystical chant from the bush. The magellanic clouds of stars now appeared low in the sky. Millions of stars appeared from two galaxies and began to fall from above. These stars reminded Lucy of a Dreamtime dance, where a girl enters the sacred ground of the brolgas who live in the wetlands of Arnhem Land. She plays, mimics, and discovers, the sensual and magical nature of the environment, but she must learn to respect the secret brolga knowledge. A flock of brolgas joined in to protect her on the journey of learning, as she prepares to become a woman. She walks between the brolgas as they teach her. She surrenders herself to become one of them in an alliance of understanding and a sense of belonging to her own dreaming. **(3)**

Lucy opened her arms and reached outwards with all her might. She imagined heaven was within her reach. She smiled as she remembered the stories of Dreamtime. The chant of the bush became clearer now. Lucy fell to her knees. These men of the 'Never-Never' were in touch with this land, this wide open and spiritual land. She felt that she had quietly touched the spirit world, as she believed in the stories and the song of the ancestors of this dark and mystical place.

Storm clouds gathered overhead as these blessed birds gracefully took to the skies. Lucy thought for a moment that they had paid homage to her before leaving, but upon reflection, believed that she may have been imagining it. A piecing sound of lightning rang through the skies above, and the clouds let out a thunderous applause. The rain fell with such force that it beat against her skin with needle-like precision. The 'Big Wet' had begun.

Lucy lay there for a time, before opening her eyes. Rain washed down her body, the cleansing, fragrant water, now touching her skin. Above her, shone the stars, but they seemed more distant and out of reach. She recollected her impressions of that night. The dream-state that she had experienced appeared to be real, yet, she wondered if the brolgas had given her a message; that she should not have stolen a place at the Inner Circle. Lucy sat upright with this thought and uneasily made her way home.

In the quiet of that evening, Lucy sat with her grandfather, Daniel and collected her thoughts. She remembered in detail the events leading up to the appearance of the dancing brolgas. Daniel listened carefully to her recount and elaborated further on the stories of the Dreamtime, and the significance they had for Indigenous peoples.

Chapter 4
Standing Tall

From the day she was born, Eliza had made herself noticed. Her mother had a philosophy about births; that a child who 'demonstrated their importance during labour', would very often make similar protests during life. Lucy often reminded her sister about this, as the process had been an arduous time for all.

The Royal Flying Doctor Service took five hours to arrive after the call, so it was plausible, that by the time the service had arrived, Eliza had already entered the world. The flight, coordinated from Katherine, relied upon the medical staff and the provisions to board before flying two hours to the destination. Dan, a Jackaroo at the station had not delivered a baby before, but was on hand to serve as always. On the evening of the 18th of April 1972, Dan became a hero in the community, as he delivered a baby girl. The pair was later taken to Katherine hospital for further medical attention. Soon after, it became obvious to the staff, that both mother and daughter were not well. They would spend the next three weeks fighting an infection, but further medical intervention became available to Mary and Eliza in South Australia.

When the convalescence was over, Lucy was so delighted to have her mama and baby sister, Eliza back home again. The family made changes as they knew life would be a little slower for a while. Martha helped more by arriving earlier in the morning and prepared the evening meal before retiring for the night.

That period was uneventful, apart from the time when Charlie Ireland and Dan, who were Aboriginal trackers, discovered a snake track through the homestead. They both knew it to be a king brown which was common in these parts, but after investigating further, discovered that before exiting, it had slithered under the fly wire cot where Eliza lay sleeping. The snake could not be located, but Charlie assured everyone that it would not return.

That night, Mary reflected on how much she appreciated this enclosed cot, as it had protected her young infant as she lay sleeping. Mary looked down at her daughter and kissed her lightly on the forehead as she slept. Eliza seemed quite unaware of the commotion that her family were experiencing that evening.

As Eliza grew, her stubborn will and independent streak became more obvious. It was the summer of 1977, and the Sunday School Picnic was a major event for the year. Mary delighted in treating the girls and this event warranted a 'dress up'.

"Come girls!" she would call to them. "I have the most glamorous dresses for both of you. See them."

At the time, Lucy preferred her casual clothes to the satin, velvet, and lace, but her mother knew better. She would have her girls looking unrecognisable at least once or twice a month, no matter what!

On this occasion, Eliza and Lucy showed up to the Sunday School Picnic in dresses organised by their mother. The family had left home early in a convoy of trucks, loaded up with all the paraphernalia essential for the races and the picnic that followed. Their friends were unrecognisable in their zinc cream and hats, covered appropriately from neck to knees in clothing, except for

Lucy and her sister who were presented to the crowd in fashionable party dresses. The girls jumped from the truck, embarrassed as they greeted their friends. They had frilly dresses and lacey socks, patent leather shoes and thick blue ribbons holding their hair in braids. But the most noticeable feature was worse than any dress could offer. The damage was instant! Her friends, particularly Red and Jimmy, rolled over laughing at the paper flowers that adorned their hair.

"Look at Lucy! She has a garden in her hair!"

Lucy could not find the funny side but felt like she was having the most terrible day ever, until the first race started. Lucy threw her patent leather shoes aside and ran bare-footed the whole distance. She worried less about the stones against her feet than letting a remark like that get in the way of her having fun. She won her race, and from that moment on, Lucy forgot what she was wearing and enjoyed her day. Eliza, on the other hand, after a tantrum, gave way to despair, and sat under a tree to read a book for the entire day. No one noticed her until pack up time.

During the event, the men from the area liked to play catch up with their walkie talkies, signing in and out with catchy names and humorous anecdotes. They eventually assembled at the marque, purposely built for these occasions. The crowd would disperse and then gather again when the horn would announce the next race. The children ran in the 'egg and spoon', the 'three-legged', and finally the 'aged' race. The last race was particularly exciting, as the parents and grandparents would be racing against each other. The flying doctor, the town publican, the local nurses, and the teacher, would join in too. The Elders did not partake in the events but sat back and watched the progression of competitors with equal good humour. The picnic itself was memorable as each family was responsible for their meal. The

Roddicks enjoyed the mulberry tarts, corned beef, and pickle sandwiches they had made that morning. Picnic Day was, and always had been, an enjoyable occasion, and was a topic of discussion for some time before and after the event.

The family washed the food down with homemade ginger beer. Daniel had recently made this batch from his ginger beer plant. The plant was made of ginger, sugar, and yeast; a little broken off at a time, and set in a vacuumed bottle with water. There had been many occasions when an explosion was heard from the back of the house, and then splinters of glass scattered throughout the back rooms. On one occasion, all the back windows were blasted out.

That summer, life had been quieter, and the family spent longer reading to each other during the day, and telling stories on the veranda in the cool evenings. Jack appreciated his family, and knew that if he did not protect them, life would not be so simple. All that changed one morning. The radio phone rang off into the distance and Jack marched across the compound to answer it. This form of communication was for all the locals to use in case of an emergency, and was situated in Jack's office at the corner of the homestead.

The news he received left Jack anxious. He dropped the phone, leaving it to hang in the air until his assistant picked it up and placed it in its cradle. Both men stepped out into the open. Jack nervously gave directions and went inside to his wife to explain his departure. She was speechless.

The compound became busy, with Jack's voice heard above the clatter and bangs as the staff loaded the four-wheel drive. Something was happening, but Lucy could not tell what it was. Mandalong was in the centre of the Tanami Desert and, two to five days from Katherine. It depended on the weather, the dry was easier access, but the wet season meant flooded roads. If the weather was favourable, air transport was possible. Earth machinery occasionally would make the road easier, as the pits and corrugations in the road surface would then, be less noticeable. It was now between seasons, but Jack was ready to take the chance. They loaded the winches, chains, ropes, water drums and cans of food to the swags, that were already present. Cattle dogs would complete the load and then they were off again, driving into the dry blue yonder, kicking up dust behind them.

Not everything went according to plan on Jack's bush trips. At home, Mary had to run the house; and this included, making sure everything was the way Jack had expected. Within days of his departure, Eliza had not been drinking and was so dehydrated. The medical staff at the local hospital had warned Mary, that if Eliza did not drink within the next couple of hours, they would have to admit her. Eliza was her typical obstinate self, her body fighting against any intervention as she became noticeably weaker. She showed signs of fatigue, the dark rims below her eyes mirrored the fight she was having with her body. Her parched mouth could no longer protest as it did not open, and her cracked lips continued to hold fast in defiance.

"Help me! Hold her, Lucy! If we do not get her to drink something, however little, she could die!" panicked Mary.

Mary and Lucy fought on for a frustrating couple of hours before Eliza gave in, her will at last broken. She accepted a little water at first, enough to slightly wet her parched lips, then a mouthful, a long pause, and again a sip until, at last, she sank into a deep sleep. When she woke up, she drank quickly, the liquid noticeably pressing hard upon her burned and bruised tongue. It took a day or so before she experienced a full recovery, but she soon returned to herself as expected.

Jack returned to Mandalong the same way he had left it, in a trail of red dust. He was glad to be back and looked forward to spending time with his girls. Lucy would look forward to these times too as they were always special. She would learn more about him as he revealed his secrets and told her stories. They were fiction, she believed at first, but her inquisitive mind questioned this as she listened more intently. Jack spoke of the time when the miners cut into this land. He painted pictures with his words, about how heavy machinery had impacted the hills and cliffs on either side of Mandalong. He told her stories about how the native wildlife had disappeared as the streams and water holes became contaminated.

Jack was a hero to his Aboriginal brothers because they had faith in him. They believed he respected their customs, beliefs, and their values. He had spent years studying anthropology and sociology and knew their language and dialect. Jack understood their clan system well, although not completely. He appreciated how close they were to one another, and how they valued their land because they had a spiritual connection. Jack believed the 'white civilization' had things to learn from these old men of the land. Their customs and beliefs 'pre-dated time', at least in these parts. Her father told her the story about a government who backed the mining rights of big companies, in place of those who did not have the power to speak out for themselves.

In his story, he claimed that Indigenous men and women spoke of 'men with tin hats' who had claimed ownership of this land, killed native animal life, and made traditional landowners homeless. They 'pulled jewels out of the land', and took their plunder back to their homes. Then, they became greedier, wanting more territory and control. She used to like his stories, but this one was not one of those. This story had made her worry and gave her nightmares. Jack's philosophy was simple; governments need to stop talking about what needs to get done, and just do it!

One evening, Jack sat in his chair in the lounge room, surrounded by his family. He spoke about his mission. There had been claims from locals that outsiders had enclosed the area along the boundary to Mandalong. These 'intruders' had been menacing in their behaviour, throwing bottles out of their vehicles, boar hunting at night, firing rifles at targets in the bush and making their presence known. Lucy knew that her father had again shown his resilience, as he approached these hoodlums and sent them on their way. She could not have been prouder. It was now 1977, but she was aware that there would be more trouble in store for the residents of Mandalong. Lucy knew her father would do his best to represent these people because his position, as station master, meant that he had to serve them. He would take this matter further, and present their case to the government. She knew that he would do all he could to curtail this oppression.

That evening after dinner, and as dusk was approaching, Jack sat casually, as he often did, in his lounge chair to strum his guitar. He held the instrument with ease, as he began to strum it contentedly. He had often dreamed as a small boy, that his talent would see him singing to earn his money, but that was not to be. Whatever those dreams were, for now, he was happy to work hard on the property he loved. He sang more noticeably now, as Mary walked over. She grabbed a shawl, placing it around her shoulders as she joined him. The girls joined in to sing the final chorus of 'Hang down your head, Tom Dooley'. The song had probably never been sung so well. The family continued singing throughout the night, the lyrics of the chosen songs becoming louder as the night closed in. The couple then turned and looked at the girls. They were fast asleep. Jack and Mary laughed quietly as they carried the children to their rooms, before finally retiring for the night themselves.

By April, the heavens proclaimed the wet was over and Lucy and her friends decided upon a bike adventure. Bike trips were common between these friends as she was now seven. Today, being a little cooler, was the perfect time for an adventure, and Winnie, Maggie, Red, and Jimmy would accompany her. The jackaroos had arranged to take the children for some of the distance so that the trip would not be too exhausting. Jimmy lifted the bikes up onto the Land Rover, while the children then climbed on board. The crew took them to the outskirts of the ranges where arrangements were made for a pick-up at sundown.

With friends in tow, Lucy began her ride, following the winding track to Mount Herbert. Known for the rocky cliffs that towered above the valley below, this place was the perfect location for a bike adventure. The track ahead was easy, as it consisted of compacted red sand, extending its way to the mountain range beyond. The desert pea and cacti decorated its borders from the firm base of the mountain. Most noticeable were the paperbark trees which lifted from platforms to the side of its face, as if reaching sideways for a special look at the open horizon. The valley floor was deep and undulating, as it previously had been an inland sea. Lucy looked around her as they reached the steep face of the mountain. She then turned around to look below her at the red soil plains. Very soon they would begin their ascent.

With satchels on their backs, they sped off as fast as they could, towards the hills before them. The troop pushed onward in single file. Then, Winnie turned around to notice that Jimmy, who had been holding up the rear, was missing. She whistled to them all, a system they had in place to halt any action. Each of them stopped suddenly to retrace the ground, looking for their friend. The children knew Jimmy to be close by and continued their search for some time. At last, they found him under a honey tree. The tree held his interest because, within its branches, there was a hive with bush bees. Loaded with a primitive method of attack, Jimmy would use sticks and fire to take a portion of the liquid gold that sat inside the hive. Climbing capably by using his feet to push his way up into the canopy above, Jimmy then settled himself in the fork of the tree to pull out his tools. Lighting a fire from above was an arduous task, so he did not use the traditional methods, but a lighter to make the job easier. He would smoke them out and then use a stick to push part of the hive down below. Jimmy was fortunate as he did not wear battle scars following his escapades. He was jubilant as he slid the whole way down the trunk below, to then pick up the wax and honey, and run with the others to safety.

After a long bike ride, there was nothing better than to sit down and open their satchels. Inside was a damper, kept moist with a wet tea towel. They would place the sweet-smelling honey on top of the bread, and watch as it fell from their mouths as they bit into it. The crunch that the crust of the damper made, became even more enjoyable as they reached the honey-soaked bread that sat below. Cannisters of barley water quenched their thirst, but it never seemed to be enough. They completed their feast with apples fresh from the compound. Ancestors had planted the trees long ago at Mandalong. Reg made sure that in drought time they would not suffer neglect. The children bit into the hard, sweet flesh and ribbons of liquid ran down their faces as they ate.

The friends continued their ride together, bravely climbing

the rough terrain on their two-wheelers. At last, they reached the foot of the mountain. Mount Herbert's peak looked down on them. It was hard to imagine that this was to be their destination, as it appeared so formidable. The children then started to climb the rock face together. They stopped for a brief rest before recovering again on the precipice above. Within a short space of time, they reached the ridge that jutted out to frame the view of Mandalong.

Lucy could make out the compound, the trees beyond, the stockyards, and one of the sheds, although not in detail. She imagined her father looking briefly at her as she stood there waving from her outpost, but then realised that this was indeed impossible, as he was too far away. They followed, in single file now as they pulled each other to safety above. It would be hard to imagine how they would climb back down the precipice, but Lucy did not want to think negatively and proceeded with all her might. She had made this flag at school with her friends. It was a symbol of the friendship they shared, and she hoped that it would remain on top of the mountain for years to come.

Lucy's idea came about when she was studying the explorer, Edmund Hillary at school. He and Tenzing Norgay demonstrated their feat, by placing a flag on the summit of Mount Everest. Jimmy had come with her, but the others could not climb any further, so they chose to rest below. Lucy leant over at last to push the flag down between a gap she found in the rocks. She held on carefully as there was a strong wind. The altitude here was noticeably higher, and the air appeared to make it more difficult to breathe.

The final descent was much more difficult, as the pain from their calves and thighs was extreme. The children knew that it would be challenging, but now, they just desperately wanted it to be over. They eventually met up with their friends halfway down the incline. They pressed on. At one point, Winnie slid down the face of a cliff, getting up eventually to reveal broken skin and cuts to her arms and legs. Lucy was stoic as she continued without complaint, only once losing her balance, but held onto Jimmy to regain her composure. Once on the ground below, the friends hollowed, their cooee. It was thrown against the rocks above, and then resounded across the wide-open spaces before them.

Bikes in hand, they led each other to the track that twisted and turned between the rocks below the mountain. Forming a single file, they leapt on their wheels and ushered their bodies forward. They darted between these ancient rocks which hurtled around the base of the mountain. The outcrop was majestic and solid, burnt orange in colour, featuring the rust of bygone years. These towering cliffs carried the secrets of birth and death, had seen the ancients move below and heard their varied cries.

The cliffs rose sharply as the children chased one another along the paths of sand that lay ahead. Like a maze, these rocks were endless and the chance to play 'hide and seek' was always on the cards. The narrow crevices rang out with their laughter as they rode fearlessly along its corridors. The paths twisted and carried them unseen into each dark passageway. The fortress housed the secrets of generations and forbidden trysts made over time. The wind would often rush through the corridors of dust and bring the red earth with it as it travelled. The children held on tightly to the handlebars in front of them as they pressed forward, marvelling at their speed and endurance.

The daylight began to disappear around them. They needed to head home before the sun set, as tracks to get home would then be impossible to follow. Then, without warning, Lucy heard a scream. It sounded like Maggie, and she seemed to be far away. She and Winnie were missing. If only they would yell again, Lucy and others may find them. Jimmy and Red called out, eager to get directions. It was no use; the sounds were missing, and there were no answers or leads. They told Lucy that it was getting dark, and they needed a plan. Jimmy would stay with Lucy to look for the girls, while Red would try to follow the trail back to the homestead to get help.

The night was closing in, and Red had been gone for hours. Lucy and Jimmy kept calling as they climbed around the rocks. Occasionally, they saw a wild hare dart in front of them and Lucy at one point met up with a scorpion. She was too tired to take notice and trudged onward, knowing that with each hour, safety for her friends was more of a concern. The air was cooling down now, the night temperature could fall below freezing as this was a desert country. There was a growing concern between them as Maggie was the youngest, but Lucy reassured herself that Winnie was brave, and that she would be keeping Maggie's spirits high. But where were they? She thought that to hear Maggie's scream they must be close, so there had to be only one answer. They must have found a place between the rocks to hide. She thought there would be two possibilities; either they may have been stuck, or one of them had fallen and become hurt.

Lucy heard the yell again. She and Jimmy followed the calls. They climbed along ledges and into caverns below until at last, they came upon an entrance to a dark opening. This forbidding entrance surrounded them, but they knew their only hope was to enter. They called again and heard nothing but the echoes of their voices that hit against the walls of the opening. They moved within, sheepishly at first, but then at a quicker pace as they gained ground. Then, without more effort, they slipped over on a wet patch of rock below. Regaining their composure, they lifted their heads to see a light beaming above them. To their delight, the glow outside was filtering between two ledges, above their heads. As they turned around, they saw to their left, Winnie and Maggie huddled in a corner. Winnie was comforting Maggie as she whimpered softly under her arm. Lucy stepped forward to give a hand to Maggie. All four were together and safe at last! But where was Red and would he bring help?

It was then that it happened. A brief glimpse at first, but when they made use of the available light, it became more obvious. They stepped forward in bewilderment. There, in a cool, dark, dry place above them, painted high above, were images of animals. The paintings were in ochres, so Lucy knew it to be an authentic cave painting. This would be memorable and significant. It could top any of the stories her dad had told her. Lucy realised that the rock paintings above, would not be unknown to Red, Jimmy, Winnie, and Maggie. She knew that the mountain was a sacred place, and its secrets were only revealed to the initiated. Each of them held hands as they waited for help to come. The winds blew up from under them as if they were being watched closely. The children felt safe as they knew the ancients, would look after them until their release.

All was now dark outside. There was nothing to do but try to keep warm at the entrance of the cave. The children began to sing as they waited for the help to arrive. As the air became colder with each passing hour, hope too, began to fade.

Back at the camp, Red had sounded the alarm, but not before the crew had alerted Jack. The jackaroos had been concerned that the children had not shown up at sunset, as arranged. It was a relief when Jack later discovered that he would have police and emergency workers on hand, as they had been called to a disturbance at the general store some hours earlier. Search lights were ablaze over the compound, and motorbikes, utilities, and four-wheeled drives were loaded. There was scurrying all around, as Lucy's mother took supplies out for the volunteers who had offered their assistance. Camera crews from as far afield as Katherine were there to represent the press. Helicopters circled overhead and the local police vans, all two of them, sat waiting to escort the convoy to the mountain. Lucy's father looked unphased, but deep down others knew, he was apprehensive as this bizarre incident had not happened before on his watch.

Reg had been a tracker in his senior years. Lucy was not aware of his age but had referred to him as being in his seventies. He had been the primary tracker when George, son of Max Tyson had wandered off into the bush in '72. They reached his body in time before dehydration had set in, but hyperthermia during the night had made a considerable impact on his long-term health. Since then, Reg had tracked some red bellies, including the infamous one that slid his way through the homestead some years before. He had also tracked a runaway convict in Mandorah, outside Darwin in the late 70s, as a result, his reputation was significantly highlighted in the police force. So, it was understandable that Reg volunteered himself on this occasion. 'The crew' collected him in the utility and made their way to Mount Herbert post haste. He would lead a group of trackers who had been rounded up from the area.

Mary, Lucy's mother, threw in rugs into the back of one of the Land Rovers in the hope that it might bring the children home, safe and warm. She considered herself close to Lucy's friends. They had spent hours together playing amongst the trees at the back of the property. Sometimes they would paint, or make a brief appearance in a play that they wrote together. They would have the audience bring chairs and then magically appear in front of sheets for curtains and make everyone laugh. They loved to dance too, and Lucy had learned dance steps from her older friends on these occasions.

It was midnight and, it would take at least two hours to find the track that lay ahead. The spotlights marked the path and helped, but trackers would find their trail when all else proved too difficult. Red remained in the compound, exhausted, and dehydrated. The troop set off; the expedition made in haste as night had indeed now set in.

At one point, the trackers led them to the honey tree. They knew they were close, but still had some way to go. Red had earlier reassured them that they were playing at the mountain when the girls went missing. The trackers were methodical in their approach to this mystery, as they claimed that you can never be sure. The night air was freezing, and the topic of conversation was the girls and their ability to withstand this ordeal. They believed the girls would keep each other warm and stay positive.

At last, the trackers came upon Mount Herbert plains. The landmark preceded the larger mountain beyond. They pulled their convoy against the outer ridge and unpacked in preparation for a long night ahead.

The emergency services men prepared themselves for the night with torches, and lightweight apparel. They took cannisters of water for the girls, blankets, and sugared energy bars. A soft rain fell on the posse as they climbed, their footing sometimes becoming unsteady as they held onto the vegetation. In time, they were on the track that Red had described to them. They knew they were close, so they called out. There was nothing. The megaphone was a last hope. Swiftly, Lucy sat upright. She heard her father's voice. She knew her night was over and that he would take them all home. Lucy used all her remaining energy to stand, reaching forward, as she walked with urgency outside to the open. She called, but her voice was faint. She called again, and there, in front of her stood her father, with his strong arms reaching out towards her. She ran to him, and he held onto her for a time.

"Oh, Daddy, I am so glad you are here. I thought you would never come!"

She turned towards the opening and took him inside. As they entered, the emergency services were taking the girls. Placing them on stretchers, they made their way down the mountain side. The cameramen were taking videos and asking questions before they closed the doors to the vehicles. Lucy remained behind with her father. She had not finished. Even though she was tired, she knew that what they had observed above them in the cave that night, was more exciting than any missing children.

"Red and Jimmy say this is a sacred place to them. Their ancestors painted these walls, and they tell a story. Aren't they special, Daddy? Shouldn't we do something about them so that others can hear the legends too?" she pleaded.

Jack looked above as directed by his daughter. He was momentarily speechless as he saw the paintings with the help of his torchlight. *This find would be significant*, Jack thought to himself. He considered the possibility that the expedition to find his daughter would be memorable for many reasons. He believed in his heart, that everything would be different from now on for the Tanami community, and for Mandalong.

That night, Lucy stepped outside into the courtyard of her home. She was jubilant that all her friends were safe and that for now, Daniel would be pleased to hear about their discovery.

The Desert Star sat above Lucy that night, its beams cradling her with its blessing. It held her transfixed in its gaze, then moved upwards and back into the open sky. Lucy bowed her head and said a prayer.

Lucy found her grandfather in the garden shortly after. He hugged her, holding her tight as she recounted the day's events. Before she had finished, however, she turned to her grandfather and asked, "Gramps, how do I know if I have seen the Desert Star?"

"The Desert Star," offered Daniel, "is a heavenly being, that reveals itself to the chosen, to receive messages from the light source. If, as you say, you beheld this great star, then you are a believer, and protected by the light."

The two spent the evening reflecting on the day's events, and then, as tiredness set in, returned to their rooms to sleep more soundly than they had ever slept before.

Life at Mandalong seemed constantly busy, as a wave of correspondence continued from various departments in the government. Jack received approval from the Indigenous leaders of the community to manage negotiations with the government authorities and he would also hand some of his manual work over to the station hands. He then spent most of his time consulting between factions of the government, scientific personnel, and the media. Mandalong station was featured in the news for weeks as anthropologists completed studies at the site. Journalists then arrived to interview the residents.

The events of the previous weeks heavily impacted the people of the Tanami. The cave paintings, found to be over sixty thousand years old, were a cultural site and sacred to the Indigenous community. **(13)** Jack had insisted that Lucy accompany the representatives of Mandalong as they consulted with the government. The terms were not clear at this stage, but provisions would be made for the Tanami people due to this finding. Lucy, soon after, boarded a plane with her father and the Elders from Mandalong to Katherine, and after staying there overnight, made the trip of a lifetime to Canberra via Darwin, known by locals as 'The Top End'.

The touchdown was smooth as Lucy and her father held hands, but they had a turbulent flight earlier as low-lying clouds fell heavily upon them mid-flight. Jack had held his daughter tightly, accepting her reliance upon him, as something that he treasured and respected. Lucy looked heavenward and thanked the mighty spirit dancers for their protection and guidance.

Lucy was escorted by her father from the plane, and Jack knew both had never been happier. The flight attendants then took Jack and the Elders to the awaiting reporters. Lucy accompanied her father as she wanted to be a part of this historic day. Lucy became startled as bright lights flashed into her eyes. Microphones appeared, and questions were posed by the incoming press who were hell-bent on getting information. Then, some reporters asked Lucy for her view on the find. She was startled by the bright lights but remained transfixed on the interviewer, each one appearing more aggressive than the last. She eventually let out an answer, the tremor in her voice noticeable as she responded to the question. Lucy explained that the site belonged to the Indigenous people and that they would decide whether it would become open to the public. As young as Lucy was, she had become aware that politically, this topic could be quite divisive.

The following day, Lucy saw the headlines; her impassioned plea, on behalf of her friends, documented together with photos of Mount Herbert and beyond. Jack knew that life at Mandalong could now become more financially secure for their Indigenous brothers and sisters, should they wish to go ahead with tourism.

Some months later, the Northern Territory government responded. The Aboriginal Protection Authority would now collaborate directly with Aboriginal custodians from this land should they wish to seek a commercial venture. **(4) (5)** There were promises from the government of a **(6)** windfall for the residents, with money promised to boost education, health, and housing.

Lucy relaxed her taught muscles as she heard these words. She knew now, that the spirit people had indeed protected their own. A final trip to Darwin with the Indigenous Elders sealed the legal deal and Lucy then returned to Mandalong with her father.

The light of the stars now seemed to burn brighter as they gazed out into the heavens. The dance of the spirit people had created a rainbow of light. Mandalong had a new beginning, and Lucy knew this place would continue to be her home.

Chapter 5
The Shadow

It was the summer of 1978, and life could be exacting at best; with one emergency after another taking priority on life. That was until cinema night approached. For the audience at large, a little Clint Eastward or John Wayne was always a special event. With eskies loaded up with refreshments, the audience would then walk with deck chairs to the airstrip to view their favourite movie. One did not care if it had been the third showing this month, the priority was, that it was entertaining. There was a huge screen permanently erected, and it would be from here, that everyone would brave the elements to view their favourite movie stars.

Lucy had planned to collect her friends after dinner, but Jack and Mary had already left and were sitting in front of the screen with 'the crew'. As the night air became colder, crowds pulled up the rugs and opened their thermos. These people knew how to enjoy themselves and make the best of what they had. Saturday evenings were a special time on the calendar.

It was late Saturday afternoon, and Lucy was excited. Tonight, they would be showing James Bond and she and her friends were so excited. This evening, Jimmy, Red, Winnie and Maisie were coming to her house to pick her up. Her bath was warm and soothing as her day had been very tiring. She grabbed the towel and tied it closely to her body. She knew at this stage that she had minimum time to pack a picnic basket before she left with her friends. She dressed quickly and ran out of the bedroom door.

Lucy ran across the timber floor, her barefooted feet carrying her lightweight body with ease. Then, in an instant, her small frame became airborne as she stubbed her toe on the stone's uneven surface. Her fall was hard, her face had hit the surface of the step abruptly, and she lay there stunned and motionless. Blackness filled her head, and, in an instant, she felt a lightness that overtook her body and mind, and then she fell into a peaceful slumber.

She stirred. Her eyes, half shut, her mind foggy; she was sore and confused. She smelt burned sugar and knew that Martha must be making toffee. She opened her eyes slowly at first and looked around. The room seemed smaller, dwarfed by the large open fireplace up ahead. The firewood was crackling, letting out its last breath as it became consumed by the heat and light. Embers rose above it like white spirits, moving swiftly with the stifling air to separate themselves from the body of fire, as if in a ritual, and then become transported heavenward.

She slowly pulled her body upwards and turned to assess the room as she moved around it. She was not viewing the room that she remembered, but a more stark and empty space, devoid of the comforts she knew so well. Her breathing became laboured as the confusion consumed her. Lucy began to shake uncontrollably. She was surprised that she should be so unsteady on her feet. She was a little dizzy and unusually thirsty.

She stood at the door to the kitchen and there, standing before her, was not the woman she knew so well, but a large presence with a penetrating foreign accent and the body to match. Her focus was now on this shrivelled old woman calling out from her cauldron which she stirred upon the open grate. The old woman licked her lips as she turned her head around. Her face was entirely sunken beneath her cavernous mouth. The smell of toffee became overwhelming now, as she stirred it with furious intent.

"Abigail!" she yelled. "I have been calling you, lass. Where 'as you bee'?" she sang loudly. Her voice was not pleasing to the ear, but it had, she accepted, a melodic tune. She stood there aghast at her predicament. They watched each other, and the old woman did not question her arrival but appeared to recognise her, it seemed, as Abigail. Who was this woman and where was her Martha? There had been a mistake! This was not to her liking. For the first time in her life, she felt scared. Lucy began to despair as her family was no longer available to her. The question was now, how could she reclaim her family? Then, without effort, a small gust of air broke through the kitchen door and pushed her back down to the floor.

Abigail shook her head from side to side. She could hear children playing outside the door and they were calling out to her.

"Abigail! Abigail! Come here, sister dear. We will count to ten, then you will appear!"

Her mind had gone cloudy, but all she could think about was how much she wanted to join them outside. They were playing with chickens, ducks, and geese before the slaughtering at Christmas. Abby ran outside and began to skip with the other children. There were seven of them: Kathleen, Ruby, Arthur, Thomas, Millie, Simon, and Elizabeth. They were the children of Samuel and his wife Brigitte. Samuel, it seemed, ran the house, and Luke was his leading hand at the station.

Abigail later learned that Samuel was a capable and just man who led the congregation in Sunday prayers when the local pastor was not available. It was a customary practice that the leaders of the community held worship, and they would welcome a visit once or twice a year from a priest. People in these remote parts were thankful for simple blessings. Each visit would provide its members with baptisms, weddings, and updated church records for Mandalong. These documents served as an itinerary of births, deaths, and marriages, viewed by travelling clerks who would make a record of the entries for prosperity.

Abigail ran like the wind, for she knew, her friends would now be playing tag. Blindfolded and sometimes leg tied too, the chosen catcher would hobble around the courtyard in search of a prisoner. Sometimes the game became confusing as the catcher might find instead of small limbs and flinched skirts, a loud cache, and a bunch of feathers. Chickens, often caught in place of her friends, were part of the game.

Later that day, Abigail had been busy raking the straw outside in the yard when she noticed the station hands exercising one of the horses in the long paddock. Her attention was diverted as the stockmen moved towards a noise in the harness room and ran towards what they perceived, as imminent danger. To the contrary! There, sitting in a corner was a little, wet figure standing over a great bucket of soapy liquid. Sounds were heard to her left and without flinching, Abigail turned her head long enough to see a little pup shivering in the corner.

"Great heavens! God bless my soul!" one of them yelled.

The little boy was dripping as he stood looking wretched and cold. The boy's attention was drawn elsewhere as the stock hands laughed, but the pup was shaking with so much terror, that they decided to deliberate no longer and rescue the poor mut from further torture. There was quite a collection of dusty boots in one corner of the kitchen when all retired to the homestead for a game or two of pool and a laugh.

Abigail fell into life at Mandalong as if she had lived with these folks all her life. Her memory was blurred and for the moment there seemed to be only the life she knew here with Samuel. Abigail enjoyed the days she shared here. Her favourite pastime became collecting. She loved to sort, categorise, analyse, and systematically place in order her collections; the data was recorded in a miniature notebook given to her by Samuel. It was bound in leather and, carefully strung together with string between its pages and the binding. Her name was embossed on the front cover with the date, 1878. Abigail made ledgers inside to document her findings. Her collections comprised of a variety of materials including rocks, bark shavings, shells, marbles, wooden dice, pumice, and plinth. The latter were bases of stone pedestals and had been stacked away by Samuel in the shed. His interest in stone masonry, however, had long since diminished; but as a young man, he had experimented with this art form regularly. Abigail had found the pumice stone locally. She admired it for its texture and its ability to smooth a rough surface into a delicate one.

Abigail spent hours amassing her hoard together and then placing collections in rolled up cloth, tin, or in a wooden box. She would then take these treasures out into the bush and bury them in the sand below the white cedar tree. This was one of three one-hundred-year-old trees that grew near the riverbank between the homestead and the border of their property. The plinths, however, remained stacked in the shed along with her tools that she had claimed for herself.

When Abigail was not collecting, she was happily playing with her friends outside in the courtyard. They loved playing 'Hide and Seek' together. Today would be special as the family would be preparing for Christmas. The lunch bell rang at last, and Abigail carefully removed the blindfold from her eyes and ambled to the kitchen. Long trays of toffee stood before her on the table, cut into pieces. Boiled lollies of every shape and colour sat in jars on the cupboards afar and out of reach. Abby knew that preparations were becoming less secretive. She picked up her bowl and stretched it out towards the stove. Inside the pot above, was a hearty soup of vegetables with wild herbs, a tasty treat they enjoyed each Sunday before church. Beside her on the table, a damper was set in round pans. She pulled the crisp bread apart and ate her hearty meal. Millie sat beside her on the bench, swinging her legs wildly as she ate her broken bread.

Once all had risen from the table, they made their way to the horse and cart outside. It consisted of a tray and bench seat above two draught horses. Aunt May and Claudia sat on the bench above and the children piled into the back of the tray. Then, holding on with all their might, the vehicle took off to everyone's delight. Samuel and Luke would be waiting for them at the small church, erected fifty years before.

After the service, Abigail walked around the small fenced-in yard alongside the building. She noticed a small grave beside her and read the inscription. *'Bunty, taken by angels 1875.'* On her way home, Abigail asked Samuel about Bunty. Samuel took a deep breath and in a composed but affected tone, explained that one evening at the homestead, Beatrice, or 'Bunty' for short, reached for the candle above her on the bureau. Within seconds, she slipped silently from the chair, her nightdress in flames as the fire took hold of the dining room. 'Bunty' died weeks later from an infection as there was nothing they could do, but apply butter and bandages to the exposed skin. Bunty was much loved. They missed her long flowing curly blond locks which adorned her sweet and innocent face, and the homestead was never the same.

Since that day, the food was eaten in the kitchen, this being a new custom which would have been abhorrent to the Scottish ancestors of the past. "Traditions always need changing to accommodate our clan," Samuel used to say.

The ride home was slow, and it was evident that Abigail had brought back the past to haunt Samuel. All these events had happened years before, and all the family had since, tried to move on.

That morning, Abigail had played with Samuel's children for hours when a mighty storm approached them. Knowing the season to be changing, Abigail told the children to run to the nearest shed. Here, they would wait out the storm and play quietly until it was over. Abigail was content here with her cousins as her parents had sent her to live at Samuel's place while they visited the home country. In the meantime, Abigail grew accustomed to her Uncle Samuel and enjoyed living with him in these parts.

The light outside was now dimming, as Abigail returned to her room. She shared this with Millie and was becoming quite attached to her. Millie was younger in years, but they had a great deal in common. At night, they would giggle as they made up funny stories and shared secrets.

The following day, the girls would be visiting 'Old Jim'. He was in his nineties and had been a staple for the men at the station. Born James in 1851, Samuel's older brother was known for his expertise in the bush, his knowledge of cattle, the weather, and life in general. His advice was always forthcoming, hence his name. Unfortunately, luck was not on Jim's side of late, as he was having bouts of madness, rambling incoherently, and making rash decisions. Jim lived above the top paddock. His dwelling consisted of one room with an open fire. It was Millie's job to bring the water and Abigail was to take him his supper. Abigail hurried Millie as she had become distracted from her duties. Abigail reminded her that Samuel would not be pleased and grabbed Millie's hand to lead her quickly forward, but noticed she had something within her small fist. There, between her forefinger and thumb, Millie had been rolling a marble, white and blue in colour. She held it firmly for a time, before placing it away in her pinafore pocket.

Abigail moved fluidly along the pathway that led to Uncle Jim's house. Her full skirt touched the ground as she sped quickly forward, leaving the tails of her slip red with the dust below her. Upon entering the door, she placed the food on the table. Millie reached over, to place the heavy bucket of water there. Flowers that had adorned the vases days ago, now hung with wilted heads, bowed in defeat. Each of the girls took a stool from beside his bed. Uncle Jim greeted them briefly and began reading to them from an imaginary text. His eyes were wide, having sunk within their sockets months earlier. The story was based loosely upon his own life as a small boy, although, it was difficult to discern his speech, as he often wandered in and out incoherently and then would speak in Gaelic. The girls sat upright, smiling at him as he tried to convey his message. Abby empathised with Jim, as she knew him to be suffering a separation from his loved ones as he often dwelled in the past. His state of being, transported him to an almost unconscious state, a friendless and unwelcoming world. Occasionally, without notice, Jim would become aware of his audience and speak coherently in an audible fashion. Abigail reflected on Samuel's explanation about Jim's experience.

"Death is like a tree; the branches give the greatest plumage before expiring totally and with little notice. So it is, with Uncle

Jim; as he awakens briefly, he has clarity, and then, that notion abruptly departs. Transformation occurs when his outer body changes, leaving but a chrysalis behind. His spirit is then, at one with his Maker."

Abigail reached forward and touched Jim's hand. The old man now fixed his 'new' eyes upon Abby. Then he prayed 'The Lord's Prayer' and gave up quietly. Abigail knew his spirit was no longer with him. The girls sat with their heads bowed for a time, before walking back slowly to the homestead to pass these facts onto Samuel and the family.

Later that evening, Samuel took his place at the head of the table. The children sat around him, eager to begin to eat their supper. He read quietly from the Book of Job and then said grace as he did each evening at this time. At one point, Samuel stood up in protest. His wife, Brigitte, chastised one of the children as they began to eat from their plate before grace. The children sat with their heads affixed on their father, as Samuel resumed his position at the head of the table. The children began eating beef stew, and washed it down with lemon mint and myrtle water. Samuel sat quietly without eating, and when the children had finished, he requested they listen to him.

Samuel thanked the girls for their countenance during their uncle's passing. He encouraged his family to be mindful of his words as he was deliberating on the path forward. He explained to the family, that it had been the fortitude and courage of their ancestors, that had allowed their family a future at Mandalong. Samuel then expanded further by saying that just as Jim had made his mark upon the station, so too had his ancestors.

"The strength of family spirit still lives on, and is present in all of us," he said. "The Roddick house is a proud house, and the heritage of their great ancestors lives on within us." Samuel likened this gift as the Tree of Life. His message was clear and resonated with Abby because she knew him to be a wise man.

The children played peacefully outside. Amy and Sebastian had joined them the previous morning. Uncle Luke had brought them over to meet their cousins. They had been looking forward to the promise of a picnic at a river that flowed directly from Katherine Gorge. Amy and Sebastian had joined Samuel's children, and were excited as they could go paddling near the shallow end, and would make paper boats to sail between the rocks. Sebastian was six years old but Amy, his sister, appeared older than him as he had a birth defect which affected his growth. The family did what they could to make him appear older, which included dressing him as an adult. He wore a vest and a tie knotted in the front of his long-sleeved shirt. His long trousers covered his legs amply, and hid his scuffed, lace-up boots. His condition meant that adults gave him a little more leverage, and he seemed to get away with more than the other children. This meant that he was objectionable and defiant in the extreme; a condition that Samuel found unacceptable.

Wicker baskets held their lunch. There were Cornish pasties, a selection of cheeses and fruitcakes wrapped up in towels to keep from spoiling. Bottles of lemon water would quench their thirst and broad-brimmed hats would keep each of them shaded. Aunt Mary, May and Uncle Luke would replace Samuel who was away. Each of them took the children to the wagon. The adults climbed on board and sat in the front with Claudia, Kathleen, Ruby, Arthur, Thomas, Millie, Elizabeth, and Abigail who all sat in the tray below, swinging their legs as they sang their favourite songs. They were excited at being able to escape Mandalong and Uncle Luke had recently taken his boat up there for outings such as these.

The day was warm, but a fresh breeze made their trip more pleasant. The children were singing 'Frere Jacques' and 'Sur le Pont d'Avignon' with a selection of Scottish ballads. After a lengthy ride, the children reached the water. They jumped out, hollowing loudly as they ran down the embankment to the water's edge.

Aunt May and Mary picked up the baskets from the back with rugs to spread out on the ground. Uncle Luke unsaddled the horses to take them to the water's edge to refresh them after the long ride. The animals looked appreciative as Luke handed them carrots. Abigail ran over to help him as she loved draught horses and had always wanted to ride one.

"I love them, Uncle Luke. What are their names?" she asked inquisitively.

"Toby and Tom," he replied.

Luke looked upon her face as she stroked their manes and kissed them briefly.

She opened her arms and hugged them as he asked, "Would you like a ride one day?"

"Oh, yes, Uncle Luke. That would be wonderful! Can I really?" she pleaded.

"Yes, come down to the stockyard tomorrow morning and I shall arrange it," he answered.

Abigail was so excited that she forgot about the picnic she was going to enjoy soon and could not wait until the morning. She returned to the others with a smile that was bigger than any seen at Mandalong. Abigail made her way to her friends to find out what they were doing. She passed her aunts on the way and distracted herself helping them to set up the meal. They were very appreciative.

Abigail rang the bell to call everyone to lunch. The extended family sat down to a scrumptious lunch. When they had eaten, they sucked on boiled lollies as they began to play games under the trees. The adults lay down in the shade with hats over their heads.

During the early afternoon, Luke decided to get up and drag the boat to the water's edge. The boat was tied to a tree on the high side of the embankment as it was feared it could be dragged down the river during the floods. The children took off their boots and climbed in, three of them to a seat. The aunts balanced on either side in the middle and Uncle Luke at the stern. Mary and Amy were very capable rowers and Uncle Luke was quite impressed. As the boat moved, the children continued their singing, this time more enthusiastically, laughing at each other as they experimented with pitch, tone, and rhythm. Millie and Thomas had impressive voices, at one stage opting to harmonise together while the others listened.

Uncle Luke then called to them to turn around and that is when they started splashing. No one was dry as adults and children together had so much fun being together and enjoying the moment.

Sebastian, recklessly decided to stand. It was then that the balance of the boat became compromised and began to sway in the water. The children began to scream, and the adults looked nervous as they held onto the boat and tried to grab a child. Luke then calmed the children by jumping overboard to bring the boat into shore. The event was frightening, and everyone knew how close this had been to total disaster.

The late afternoon turned to dusk, and Luke began to collect the family for a departure. Abigail returned briefly to the water's edge to pick up their belongings, but she became momentarily distracted.

'The song of the bush became increasingly intense as it played a melodic chant, announcing an arrival. Appearing from the East, it came, bringing with it a white light, illuminating its surroundings. The Desert Star sat above Abigail in the sky, its beams, it seemed, were arching over her with its blessing. It held her transfixed and, in its gaze, then moved upwards and back into the open sky. Abigail once again, bowed her head and said a prayer.

That night, Luke owned up about the adventure to Samuel. Sitting at the table with the family, he spoke about how they had managed to come home safely. Without protests, the family spoke glowingly about how Luke had made the day so enjoyable. The family appreciated his concern and care for them during the day. Surprisingly, Samuel made no comment, but continued eating his meal. When he had finished, he placed his utensils together in the middle of his plate.

He looked up at Luke and cleared his throat before commenting, "Luke, I compliment you on your action, making the picnic possible. No doubt, you managed to bring them all back safely. They all speak positively about their experience."

Sebastian jumped down from the chair and as it was quite a distance, fell over. He quickly got up to his feet and laughed. He was quite a character and what he lacked in height; he gained in personality. The children were often inclined to make a fuss of him, but he did not appreciate the attention. He would laugh along with them when they thought he was funny.

Luke was a generous man, always thinking of others. He was Samuel's favourite brother and had never married. He loved children and would spend countless hours showing them how to manage the horses. The older children appreciated the lessons as they knew they were in the hands of a master. Abby had her day in the saddle as promised and learned many skills from Luke as she reappeared for lessons repeatedly.

When Luke was not available, Abby found other interests to keep her occupied. Millie and Abigail would enjoy drawing. Abby found Millicent to be an exceptional artist and always admired her work. She had drawn portraits of all the family, cleverly revealing their character in each painting. She positioned each of her subjects in front of the Australian bush. Samuel looked tense, but in charge for his sitting. His outfit was his Sunday best; his suit, fashioned in a heavy linen that looked becoming, his pocket watch and chain attached to his vest, and an uncollared cotton shirt and coat. His deep-set eyes were prominent against his fine features. His white hair and beard appeared untamed which posed a sharp contrast to his personality.

Below her chin, Amy had a lacy veil, her black pinafore dress fitting her body comfortably with a satin sash. Her hair plaited above her head outlined her delicate bone structure. Mary was more severe; her personality was at times overbearing and this showed in her solid frame. Her hair, cropped tightly above her head featured a bonnet which held coloured paper flowers, unfortunately not softening her looks as she had hoped. Her tight-fitting blouse held her large body in shape and her full skirt made of crimplene rustled as she walked. Millie noted how her small feet contrasted noticeably with her body shape. Each image appeared in the hall for the family to admire.

On the first Sunday of the month, Samuel would seek out the congregation for the pastor's visit. Samuel would then assemble the horse and carriage for Luke, who would bring the pastor from the township to the property. Samuel would then prepare the pastor's room so that he could stay overnight. The following three Sundays, lay preachers would lead, one of them being Samuel himself.

Sunday was an important occasion in the Roddick household as everyone, including the station hands had to front up to church in their Sunday best. Once seated in their pew, they sat quietly until the service began and then, bellowed out the hymns and followed the order of service. The pastor would deliver his sermon and the attendees would appear satisfied as they strolled within the church grounds afterwards, but there were few who considered the message a second time.

Samuel was a creature of habit, as he regularly spent time with his beehives on a Sunday, as a lead up to Sunday lunch. He would bring his equipment and cover himself appropriately so that he could collect the tea tree infused nectar for all the inhabitants at Mandalong. He would then bottle it in the shed and distribute it as often as he was able. The pastor left the homestead quite content the following morning with an abundant supply of the sweet nectar.

Dinner at the Roddick household on a Sunday was an elaborate affair, a roast with crispy potatoes and garden greens. The children of the household liked the formality of the occasion as it was what they expected, and this made them feel secure. Samuel was the head of the household, as his wisdom, they believed, could protect them for ever. The formal part of the day began as Samuel read from the scriptures. The pastor would acknowledge Samuel's lead and would bow his head in prayer. It was not long before Samuel would then give his daily devotion to the family and no doubt impress the good pastor with his knowledge and forbearance. Samuel had always wished to become a man of the cloth but as the head of the family, ran the station. Instead, he treated his family with regular Sunday devotion so that their place in heaven might be more available to them. The evening went ahead as expected and Samuel lead the family in prayers, and this followed with the family meal. The children then played outside until late evening.

One Sunday night, Abigail lay between her bed clothes, remembering the special day she had with the children. She closed her eyes gently. All at once her, body was down by the river. She lifted her heavy white skirt and pinafore. The petticoats were heavy as she ran towards the water, but she kept the fabric high in front of her legs so that she could 'run like the wind'. Her warm toes dug into the cool white sand while the refreshing water lapped up at her ankles as she spun around in circles. The refreshing water splashed around her. She turned suddenly and stopped, then bounded up the riverbank to untie the laces around her waist, and pull away the clothing from her body, only leaving her bloomers to cover her.

Abigail felt a satisfying sense of freedom as she dived into the river to swim below the surface of the water. Her body ached for this; swimming deeper than she had ever thought possible. As she touched the sand below the water, she felt the floor of the riverbed fall before her. It sucked away at her arms. As if not completely satisfied, it pulled her further as if it wanted all of Abigail. It was all Abigail could do to pull herself out of the suction that was enveloping her. She struggled impatiently to free herself completely from the quicksand below. Her body was losing, and she felt she might not be able to come up for air. As exhaustion set in, she released her grip and as she did so, the hold almost immediately became less noticeable. Abigail floated to the top and quickly inhaled the air above. Her gasping was noticeable as she coughed away the water and sand which had lodged into her lungs. She made her way up onto the beach and sat quietly. Abigail spent time in the solitude trying to regain her strength and confidence.

After a time, Abigail made her way back to the edge of the water. She knew she wanted a memorable swim, so this last attempt would be the treat she had expected. It was here that Lucy observed her body in front of her. She saw it dive into the pool of water and head towards the bottom. Her body moved, becoming the rhythm of the swim; it arched and rippled its way through the water to gain maximum speed.

Abigail manoeuvred her body, keeping her feet together as she brought her legs forward and back to gain maximum uplift. She then carefully dodged the open shells of crustaceans that were fixed to the walls of the rocks beside her. Abigail then observed her body change direction. As she swam, fish appeared in all directions. They were of all colours and sizes, and surrounded her to help her make a quick exit. A sea turtle then appeared, larger than most in these regions. It gracefully swam beneath and carried her the rest of the way. Abigail had been in awe as the sea animals took her to safety. She gained ground at last, digging her feet into the sand as she sidled up the bank. Here, she would rest before leaving. The swim had allowed her to reflect on why she enjoyed the river here, and everything it had to offer.

Abigail looked before her as she stretched her arms over her head and yawned. She opened her eyes and to her amazement, Abigail was in her bed and at home. What she had experienced had been in her subconscious. Abigail took no time to realise that the murderous, humanoid fish-maidens had tried to claim her, and that it was the spirit animals who had come to rescue her in time.

"There is something to be learned from everything we experience," Samuel had sometimes advised.

Abigail knew that she would not have come to the surface without these spiritual creatures, and she was in debt to them.

If only these creatures had words, she thought to herself, there would be so much to say.

Her eyes became enchanted by the bush. She felt alive and at one with nature, as it continued to reveal its incredible hold upon her.

Abigail and Millie spent the morning, talking about Abby's adventure the previous evening. Both of them were unsure if the experience held meaning, but both agreed the spirit animals of the deep had connected with Abigail.

Today they would have their own adventure. They would take lunch away with them, so that they could share their time painting and reading together in the shade. Cold corned silverside sandwiches with fresh bread, pickles, and freshly churned butter made their lunch special. Mrs Child lived up the road and the girls would walk to her property every alternate day to pick up supplies. Mrs Child made the bread daily and owned a dairy cow so that milk was available for a small fee. Her house was small as it consisted of one room. There was a fireplace with an oven, two small wrought iron beds in one corner and a wooden table in the centre of the room.

Mrs Child had raised all seven of her children, and she was fortunate to have brought them all up in this dwelling. Unfortunately, Mrs Child had the responsibility of raising her family on her own, as Mr Child fell from his horse when the children were young. He had been incapacitated for some time until he finally succumbed to his injuries. Since that time, Mrs Child had made ends meet by selling bread and milk, sewing and mending clothes, and occasionally spinning yarn to make jumpers from the angora goats she kept at the back of her property. Millie loved visiting Mrs Child as her youngest son, Billy was her age, and they would often play marbles on the old wooden floor of his home. They made a loud noise as they rolled them against the uneven surface. They planned openly how to execute a new tactic to win the game.

Millie enjoyed life. She was always happy and longed to make others feel the same way. She learnt to read quickly, often reading a favourite book to Billy Child whenever she came over. Books were scarce, but Mrs Child had a collection as her father had been a librarian years ago. Rather than play with her friends, Abigail preferred to assist Mrs Child in feeding the animals at the back of the property. Before the girls left the property, they would run to the rope swing in the backyard. The three children would take turns swinging as high as they could. For fun, they would scramble in front of the swing as a dare. This became a customary practice, until Mrs Child stopped the play because Billy had, on one occasion, fallen to the ground as he was approaching the swing. He recovered quickly, but he was fortunate to have escaped injury. The girls ran home, arm in arm. They were content because they enjoyed each other's company, and their kinship bonded them forever.

Millie had a tight regimen each evening. She would open her drawer to her dressing table and take out a jar in which she had filled oatmeal. She would mix this with water every evening and apply it to her complexion. She also wore Vaseline over her hands and feet, covering them with socks overnight. This routine was followed regularly every evening without question. Ribbons of all descriptions were coiled beside the face creams with a small, coveted tin of face powder that was inherited by an aunt long ago.

Millie had now thrown herself upon the old dusty armchair in front of the lounge room fire. Her tired legs sprawled sideways, she began to kick the beaten arms softly. She started to read from Francis Bacon, unaware of the author, or his contributions to philosophy. She occasionally stirred as she turned the pages, acutely aware that the folds in them made it difficult to decipher the text. The chapters were short and made her think more deeply about complex issues, her favourite one being 'of truth'. Unfortunately, the read did not satisfy her as she wanted to follow a plot. She picked up 'Wuthering Heights' and 'Pride and Prejudice' and attempted to choose between them. Her attention was momentarily distracted by the 'pop' of the fire as air escaped from the logs which Luke had placed recently upon the coals.

The heat from the open fire was intense now as it gained momentum. The sound of crackling could be heard as splinters of wood toppled into the cloudy inferno. It was then, that Millie imagined the fire which had taken the Roddick family some years earlier. Samuel and Luke had been out riding and spotted the plumes of smoke in the distance. Making their way to the small cottage, the men jumped from their mares in time to retrieve young Marcus from his bedroom window. There was no sign of the remaining members of the family, the fire had been too intense to escape. Their bodies were all found in the loft above the kitchen the following day. It was believed that the fire started when a log rolled out from the fireplace below them and onto the hardwood floors below. Samuel would always lecture his family about having the grate open and the screen in place whenever there was a fire. After the disaster, the flames were said to have covered the sky from one end of the horizon to the other, turning the backdrop a deep purple. In the foreground, the belt of black trees stretched motionless, with arms reaching into the opal background.

When Millie heard the story, she never forgot the words of Samuel. "Nothing stirred. The air was still, and the world, appeared forsaken!"

By now, Millie had lost interest in her book and placed it with care on the small table beside her. She then jumped up and ran to the hallway, with arms outstretched, so that she could hit the walls in a rhythm from side to side. When she reached the kitchen, she let out a whistle that was so shrill, that the cook and housemaid both scolded her. They then grabbed her by the arms and dragged her to the laundry. The copper chugged as the heat from under it unsettled the water. Steam shot into the air and condensed quickly as it hit the outer windows. Millie wiped the sweat from her brow, as she lifted the cane-washing basket in both of her arms. It was heavy as it held sheets from most of the beds. She began to trip as she lifted the huge weight and stubbed her feet on the uneven cobblestones. The house-girls' punishment for making a noise in the house was hanging out the washing, and Millie was used to this procedure as she was often in trouble.

When the morning was complete, Millie addressed her father, Samuel, at the dining table, apologising for her behaviour by reading from the Book of Ruth. Samuel found that appropriate as she needed to be reminded that she needed to adjust her thinking to the Roddick rules.

When she started from the passage, "...And your people shall be my people..." Samuel intervened and continued. "...And your God, my God." As Millie held her breath, Abigail reached out from beneath the table, to hold her hand as she slowly exhaled.

The following morning, both Abigail and Millie were assistants as the starching of the linen garments was taking place. Placing a pail on the table in the laundry, the girls set about making the starch. It was their job to mix one tablespoon of corn starch to every two cups of cold water. They would dip these in at the clothesline and leave them hanging to dry. The iron would be warmed on the hot stove above the fire in the kitchen, and then used by the house-girls to press the linen until crisp. The linen press adorned these fine linen and crocheted garments, many of them having been brought over by Kathleen Roddick herself all those years ago.

Being the senior house-girls, both complained of poor circulation and knee trouble, as the girls occasionally earned themselves a place scrubbing the floors. They both made it an enjoyable event though, as they used many suds and slid from one side of the cobbled floor to the other. Fortunately, these flagstones did not extend into the hallway, much to their relief. They both had been reminded how important it was to remove the suds before they were finished, as Luke had once fallen heavily upon the slippery surface. Both the girls were nervous that Luke could hurt himself again, so they never forgot to clean up. Luke always smiled at the girls as they went about their chores. He was the kindest of all as he swept them up into his arms and placed them back down with a kiss. He was caught by Samuel quite often as he giggled at their playfulness. Upon seeing his cover blown, Luke would remove his smile to one of indifference within seconds. The girls often reminded each other that they were fortunate to have each other, and that the family they shared were unique and loved them very dearly.

The cattleman's ball was an annual event held within the

Katherine Centre. The locals would spend the year deliberating the logistics of the event. Councillors would record meetings, designating aldermen and organisers to schedule the timeline of events. At home, the women would muster up the courage to sew the patterned dresses that would adorn the women of the household for such an occasion. The district was in earnest, each one aiming to make this event more memorable than the last, and the locals spoke of nothing else for months.

All the young ladies could speak of nothing but the upcoming event. Ruby was one who, being eleven, would be attending her first ball. She was, by all accounts, now a mature and capable young lady. Ruby was born with palsy and had managed to compensate for her affliction by enabling others to share her love of poetry. She had initiated a group of her friends to meet every month in a club called 'Poets Corner'. It was made up of children who loved to read and write verse. Ruby would offer tuition in oratory skills to her attendees, as she herself, had gifts in this subject, having had elocution lessons at an earlier time. The appreciation of the locals in general was noticeable and it was for this reason that Mrs Murdoch, the local seamstress, was chosen to make Ruby's frock for the ball.

Ruby shared her good looks with her sisters, who, having dark hair and the fairest of complexions, set many hearts aflutter. The colour of the material for the dress had been chosen as a royal blue taffeta, and would, Mrs Murdoch believed, highlight her pale blue eyes.

The night of the ball began with a shower of rain. Wagons and carriages edged carefully between the ruts in the road to avoid a bog. There had been many rainy days preceding the official event, so long dresses, trains, boots, and pantaloons became etched in red ochre.

Samuel escorted Ruby himself to the ball with instructions for Luke to collect some other stockmen from the huts on the way. He left a spare place for Andy, the stockman on the sulky. He had full eyes protruding as he lifted his dusty-looking hair back into place after his ride. His sun-dried skin and unkempt beard illustrated his poor attempt at grooming. His brown corduroy pants and jacket would not, it could be assumed, claim any interest or charm from the ladies. He stepped down to open the carriage door for Ruby. He picked her up in his strong arms and made his way to the entrance.

The hall was full of patrons, all dressed in rich colours and smelling sweetly of imported lavender and musk. Abigail believed she smelled wafts of opium being smoked out the back as she entered, but she paid little attention. Flasks had been filled with homemade rum, and the ladies wasted no time drinking the sherry provided by the organisers. The men lit up their pipes and sat back to look at the dance floor.

Ruby finally entered the room. She was sitting upon a chair rigged out with wheels borrowed from a perambulator. Her braided hair was tied up, and she wore a locket of the finest silver filigree. All eyes turned as her two older brothers carried her into the room. Her eyes were laughing as she beheld the crowd of people. Her gaze was steadfast, as she beheld Ernest who was standing in front of her.

"May I have this dance?" he pleaded.

Ruby extended a small, white hand and he shook it warmly.

"Of course!" Ruby answered cheerfully.

He pushed his hands into his pockets and paced the floor with anticipation. He was unsure how to raise her on his own. He pushed his hand forward, instead, gloomily looking at his boots.

"Come on," said Ruby, pulling onto his sleeve. She stood up, uneasily holding his arm which was held towards her. Ernest led Ruby to the centre of the floor.

Ruby remembered for years to come, how he looked on that evening. He was dressed appropriately, with a cummerbund sash around his waist, a cuffed shirt with ruffles, and a vest that held his grandfather's watch and chain. His boots were made of snakeskin, and he clipped the floor as he took his place with his partner. The orchestra started, and the dance floor soon filled with patrons, eager to take their first dance. Ernest picked Ruby up and held her tightly around the waist, her body falling limply below her. They both moved to the sound of the music, their eyes, only for each other.

When the music stopped, the musicians took to the refreshment table and by then, Ernest and Ruby were deep in conversation. Sitting at their table was Millie with her cousins. Abigail also joined in the discussion, and all spent the next hour exchanging ideas for their forthcoming poetry group. The roast fowl and duck tasted good, especially as apple tarts followed and ginger beer completed the feast.

After the dishes had been collected and washed in the adjoining kitchen, the older station owners had collected outside at the big trestle tables to drink and play cards. The night had been successful, their stomachs were full as they were content and relaxed.

They all returned that evening, earlier than expected and Elizabeth, Millie's younger sister, ran out of the carriage first to fall among the cushions on the lounge room floor. The wind had swept through the gum trees, sweeping her curls to one side, and flushing her face. She had been upset at not being able to attend as she was too young. Mrs Hill had looked after her during the event, so she had been crying all the way home. Her eyes were all red and swollen, and she was still sniffing inaudibly, as she had her face covered into a pillow. Millie, white-faced and dry-eyed, ignored her sister with ungracious intent.

Samuel was extraordinarily upset by this occurrence, walking stiffly towards the door when he noticed Elizabeth's titian hair arranged within cushions on the floor; and thought how much she looked like 'Bunty', who they had buried in the churchyard, some years before. He kissed her beautiful head and comforted her with his soft words. He felt the wind that was blowing in through the curtains and realised that it had brushed past the old church cemetery only moments before. Samuel always remembered the little figure lying illuminated by sunlight. Her death had made all his children dearer to him and helped him display affection a little more.

That night, as Abigail faired Millie a good night, she pulled the covers over her head and said a little prayer. In the space of a week, she had felt that she had grown up a little more. She felt confident that she could contribute as much to the family as her relatives had before her.

Abigail closed her eyes tightly and prayed hard. All at once, she saw a light before her, a blinding light that appeared translucent. It shone in front of her as her body ached from within. As she lay there transfixed, her body lifted slightly into the air above. Abigail looked down and there, in front of her, she saw her lifeless shell, appearing to look right up at her, eyes closed. It was then, that Abigail sensed the love around her, a warm glow filling her being. From that moment on, she was not afraid.

Geese squawked outside as she rolled over in her bed. The air was still and warm, and her hair stuck to her forehead as the sweat streamed down her face. It was going to be a sweltering day. She should get up and begin her chores. She opened her eyes abruptly as she was aware that two hands were holding each of her shoulders. There, in front of her stood her sister, sweet Eliza, looking extremely perplexed and troubled.

"Lucy," she called. "Please wake up, we all have been so worried you would never open your eyes again."

Lucy coughed out the words. "What do you mean, Eliza?" She sat up carefully as she tried to regain her balance.

Eliza then explained to Lucy that she had been in an unconscious state for a time, and that the flying doctor had come. After weeks in the hospital, and her leg in a splint, cuts and bruises to her face and arms, Lucy had come home to be a patient under her care. There had been a dark time, she assured her, when they all thought they would lose Lucy. The sisters hugged each other. They had never felt so close as at that time. It was then, that Mary and Jack entered the room in response to the commotion. Within minutes, Martha was there too, all of them forming a welcoming circle for Lucy.

Lucy thought quite often about her near-death experience. She felt much older than her years, and considered the unravelling of history was having a profound effect on her. Another thing struck her, and that was that she was thinking more deeply about things. She felt that for once in her life, she had more purpose and direction. Her family meant everything to her, and she knew she would strive to make each day count. Lucy began to walk with conviction. Although still a little shaken, each day gave her the confidence to continue to get well.

Lucy knew that her adventure had been a timely event and could not, however much she wished it to be, revisited. It had happened by chance. She would not talk to anyone about this encounter, except Daniel, of course. She believed, however, that her relationship with those she loved was significant. Lucy understood that while it was hard to believe, she too had made an impression on her ancestors. Daniel had referred to this encounter as being able to 'Take away memories, but leave footprints'.

Chapter 6
Revelations: The Dance of the Lights

Daniel spent his days at the back of the house. His living quarters were situated alongside the pool room where 'the crew' would spend their evenings together, before returning home to their families. Daniel did not mind the noise they made, as he said, they were having fun together. There were altercations, but overall, he felt they were well-mannered and polite because they respected the boss and did not want to jeopardise their situation. Daniel's area consisted of two large rooms, one of which housed his records and ledgers and the other, his bedsit. Since retiring from his work on the station, Daniel would spend his days recording weather patterns in the district. Ledgers were a testament to his commitment to this task, as he had detailed the findings for three generations. He made records from the rain gauge and the weather balloon, which was directly in front of his bedroom window. He also masterfully recorded the financial accounts for the station and then paid the suppliers.

Lucy's favourite part of the day was sharing time with Daniel. She called him 'Gramps' for short. She would be employed when she was younger, to do his filing and she made a name around the household as 'Daniel's little secretary'. They would then both use the ledgers to collect rainfall data and analyse the findings against previous months and years. Daniel would then show her how to predict patterns for the future. His system helped scientific teams in the cities as regional areas, he informed her, have significant contributions to make towards a national study.

Daniel was always a numbers man. His interest in mathematics began when he was small. Even when he began working on the land, Daniel would retire to work on his accounts long into the evening. Lucy enjoyed his company as he taught her so many abstract problem-solving formulas. The most rewarding observation for her was watching him at work. He was the wisest person she knew, except for her father, of course. Lucy always looked to Gramps for advice. She became invested in spending time with him as she felt protected and understood.

Daniel often shared with Lucy, the memories he had of his grandmother, Rebekah. Born in Germany, she came to the Northern Territory as a young girl, with her Lutheran pastor father and family in 1902. The family travelled to the Hermannsburg mission which had started there two decades earlier. She too, had encountered mystical images in the Australian bush, and respected the sacred association the Indigenous people had with the spirit world, and with their land.

Rebekah reminded Daniel as a small boy that there would be someone in their family who would, at some point in the future, connect in the same way, with the bush and its people. Daniel believed this to be Lucy, and after the stories his granddaughter had told him about these encounters, he had become convinced that she was the one his grandmother had prophesied about all those years ago.

One summer afternoon, Lucy made her way out to the northern reaches of the property. Her day had been long as she had completed a set of endurance tests at school and her body needed to cool down. She collected her horse and challenged him to gallop the distance, as she was excited at the prospect of cooling down. When she approached the water hole, Lucy collapsed from her gelding to stand before the water's edge. She then tumbled quickly into the water. The refreshing liquid adjusted her temperature quickly and she smiled with pleasure.

Lucy looked beyond, and there, among the reeds before her, bird fowl of every description sat quietly on the edge of the water. These wild beasts bathed silently, as if to prevent a scheduled flight into the orange sun. Then magically, without reason, Lucy became airborne as a cool stream of air took hold of her. She whimpered slightly as the chill of the cool breeze hit the sweat on her tired body.

For that brief time, it seemed to Lucy that her spirit body became raised and then placed gently back down again. She stepped upon the bank and sat quietly to watch the wild creatures before her. The smell of the bush was clean now and sweet smelling. The honey and the nectar of the foliage became noticeable as bees and dragonflies surged forward. Wild ants scurried around her feet, carrying supplies on their backs with ease and vigour.

An open sky lay before her, deep and dark and full of mystery. Magically, the sky displayed an array of dazzling lights, the colours of which she had never seen. Her arms felt heavy as a cool dry wind swept her body temporarily upward.

The chant of the night played mystically around her. Lucy reached out beyond the stars and leaned forward to take the dancers from their stage, opening her hands to then close upon them as their bodies leapt heavenward. There, encased by the protective sky, Lucy beheld the Desert Star. The light from this heavenly body reached down, protecting her. With her body reinvented, she moved into its light and held onto the magic.

Later that evening, Lucy reflected quietly upon this magical appearance. It seemed that the mystical creatures were blessing her as she stepped into the unknown. She believed in her heart that the Desert Star would be her guide as she made the journey into the future. Lucy sat and talked with her grandfather that evening as they had many things to share.

It was November, and the Roddick family joined the locals to sit on the oval above the schoolhouse to wait for the 'cracker night' performance. Large crowds would gather with their chairs and eskies. When the skies were dark enough, powerful explosions would begin. Leaves of colour would then fall from the sky, and puffs of light would hurtle towards the ground until at last, instantaneously, they would disappear. The family shared in the fun, lighting tom thumbs and catherine wheels, but the bigger crackers were left for the bravest and most entitled member of the family.

The friends sat together, ready with their bungers in hand. They were so excited, laughing often as each of the crackers let out a frightening sound. Lucy was seated beside her father and for this reason, decided to keep her burgers for later. Instead, she sat on the edge of her seat, her feet firmly planted on the ground. For although, she was excited, the shock of each explosion held her back, as her heart would jump out of her skin with each eruption. Her father would then place his hand gently on her arm when her body jumped in fright. He smiled at her and pointed to the sky ahead of them. The spears of light ricocheted towards them, and then disappeared quickly into the abyss. When all was quiet, the crowd would gather their possessions and return home, leaving the darkened sky, and the acrid smell of gunpowder and smoke behind them.

"The black skies provide a backdrop to this spectacle, but," Jack reminded her. "Nothing can compare to the colours of an evening as the sun sets in the west. The Tanami sunsets are something to behold," her father claimed.

When Lucy was home that evening, she pulled from her pocket a sparkler, which she had smuggled away earlier. She lit it and signed her name with fine silvery lines against the darkened sky.

'Lucinda Heming Fenn Roddick'

Lucy was seldom reminded of her official name. She moved her wrist in sweeping motions against the sky as she scripted the text. 'Heming' had been Kathleen's surname, and 'Fenn', Kendrick's. She knew it was a 'mouthful', but she paid homage to her roots.

The stars held her name fondly, finally taking the image from within and dispersing it throughout the heavens. Lucy looked down as she ambled back indoors. She felt tired now and knew it was time for sleep. The front door to the homestead was open, as if it were expecting her arrival. She closed it from behind and crawled into bed. She prayed that her Uncle Rick would arrive in time for Christmas, as she had missed him recently and knew that he too deserved time with family.

Lucy woke up early one morning on Christmas Eve, 1983. She had looked forward to this time for months. In previous years, Christmas lunch was delayed until the evening due to the heat of mid-morning. Both the children had made decorations for the Christmas tree, and had assisted in the kitchen as her mother made the traditional pudding. It would be very spicy, and the additional rum would help the Christmas spirit. Alcohol was a significant problem in these hot dusty parts of Australia. The isolation could make some of the strongest relent and join in the ritual of drinking after a gruelling day at work. It is for this reason that her mother rarely used spirits in her cooking. This event was an exception, she believed, as it marked a special occasion for her family.

This Christmas would be challenging for Mary, as she was reminded that she would be the new matriarch of the extended family. Her mother had recently died, and she felt a huge hole that could not be filled by any family occasion. As for Lucy, her uncle's visit was more exciting than Christmas, and he would be arriving the following day. *This occasion would be important to the family,* Lucy thought to herself, *as it would help them to move forward.*

In the past, Mary had enjoyed receiving mail from her mother. Whenever a motor could be heard from above, hearts would stop, as Mary would join other members of Mandalong in racing to the airstrip. Mary would also miss the conversations she had with her mother by radio telephone. This technology was a special link with the real world as mobile phones often had transmission problems in these parts of Australia.

Lucy had spent the night thinking about the special things she would show her uncle, and she knew that the next couple of weeks would be exciting. It was early morning and Lucy ran into the kitchen. She knew it would not be long before her uncle's arrival on the Conair flight. She hurried to eat her breakfast and ran with her parents out into the field beyond, and to the landing strip. Moments later, they could all hear the roar of the engine above. The air was hot as the morning sun had been awake now for hours. She stared into the sky, covering her eyes to view it without glare. The plane prepared for landing by circling above. The wheels then fell from the undercarriage and within moments, the craft hit the ground with a sudden force as it travelled with speed down the runway.

The air felt thick as Lucy composed herself and waited for

the door to open. The stairs fell out onto the tarmac. Uncle Rick appeared to be a little older than she remembered, but she ignored this thought as she rushed to the gate. He arrived in a fanfare of commotion. Mary ran to her brother with open arms and they both held each other tight for a long time. Then, Rick tried to pick up Lucy and Eliza, but realised immediately they only needed a hug. They held each other closely for a time, and then her uncle reached over to pick up his luggage from the tarmac and place it on the trolley. He then cradled them in his arms before beginning the short walk back to the house. Eliza followed closely behind.

Rick was a large man who was much older than his sister, and his patience was apparent as he sat down to his nieces and listened. Whenever all three were together, they would laugh away the hours. The wonderful thing about their uncle, was, in cuddling up to him, the bristles from his unshaven face often tickled. Then Rick would laugh loudly; his voice being as deep as it was strong. Lucy felt safe in his arms because he held onto her tightly and spoke softly when she sat on his knee.

Lucy and Eliza giggled as the maestro played 'honky tonk' music on the piano each evening. Lucy would lift her skirt and skip and swirl, pirouette and arabesque on tippy toes. Uncle Rick would roll around with laughter when he played, as he knew he was delighting the girls. Both the girls were exhausted when he finished playing, as he used every key in front of him to charm and elicit their response. The snake charmer would have provided his magic, and the girls would then kiss their uncle goodnight and run to their room.

Dancing gave Lucy a special feeling, like the one she experienced in the saddle. She would move with the wind in her hair as she imagined she was flying high above the ground. The music from the piano helped her to dream and be carried into the land of her imagination.

Tonight, as she danced, she visualised being on top of a mountain, then dancing down the slopes with the music holding her heels above the ground. Laughing loudly, Lucy played in the long grasses and then tumbled down the incline. She then lifted her head and arms through the air to pull herself up, whispering silently to herself. Her mind was temporarily clouded by her imagination, so she lost her footing and fell clumsily to the ground, hitting her head on the lounge chair. Lucy lay on her back for some time as her uncle and Eliza helped her to the chair. Her uncle then resumed his place in front of the piano to continue playing for Eliza as Lucy recollected her thoughts.

Lucy's mind was playing tricks. She was aware that when she hit her head, she beheld a vision. It had been Millie, swirling her flouncy skirts as she held them up high, lifting her feet to dance between the long grasses. Millie's face was soft and smiled briefly. In an instant, the breeze began to catch her, and then this ethereal vision disappeared in the mist above. Lucy believed Millie had come to her so she could place a message in her heart. Lucy would treasure this moment in time forever. She spent some time sitting, before she could join the others.

The days slipped into each other and before long, they had spent weeks together in the homestead. There had been so many things to talk about, and Mary and Lucy treasured the special times they were having together with her uncle. Lucy enjoyed showing her uncle her sketches. She had spent hours sitting outside in various locations to sketch the scenery. Lucy had amassed a great collection and rarely showed anyone, but Uncle Rick and Daniel were the exception.

"Uncle Rick?" asked Lucy one afternoon. "I have something to show you."

"Why! Of course, mistress Lucy. Anything for my favourite oldest niece!" He laughed.

Lucy took her uncle out into the fresh air. She sat with him in the shade and carefully opened her collection. She unfolded the paper which had protected the drawings inside a bound safety folder. The collection of paintings was protected with waxed paper, and a ribbon separated the pages within. Her eyes then became fixed upon one of the sketches. Lucy's head was swimming as she travelled back in time. There, before her, lay a sketch, carefully drawn with soft pencil, a specimen of rocks and marbles defined by order and position. She noted the proportions of the objects.

This is not my work, but how did it become part of my art collection, and why is it familiar? she thought to herself. She knew she had no time to question this any further, so continued her conversation with her uncle. She knew she would have time to investigate afterwards.

Later that evening, Lucy reflected upon her time spent with Samuel and his family, particularly Abigail. She remembered everything as if it were yesterday. Her memory of collecting objects came to her in an instant, and she realised that the painting was Millie's.

"How could this painting have become part of my contemporary art collection?" she asked herself.

She pondered over this for a time, but there seemed to be no answer, just more questions. With her mind running around in circles, she drifted off to sleep. Her paintings were safe again and she reminded herself not to show anyone, in case they may find out that she had met Samuel and the ancestors. She feared what they would think of her as she could not explain the event herself.

Lucy and Eliza spent the next afternoon collecting fruit from the large apple tree. The cane basket was overflowing, so they both decided to return to the kitchen. The tradition for children in the Roddick family was to share toffee apples on birthdays. Eliza was now nine and was looking forward to dipping the fruit into the sweet-smelling hot liquid. Mary helped them both place the sticks inside the core of the fruit, and again, as they dipped the apples into the gooey mixture, to rest them on trays. They would share the toffee apples with their family and a slice of birthday cake at the party that afternoon. Lucy could not describe it, but the smell was familiar to her. Not only did the smell of toffee hold memories of past birthdays with Eliza, but it began to transport her to places less familiar.

That night, Lucy drifted into the past. She visited Samuel's family in her dreams. They appeared ethereal and distant, but she embraced them all the same. Her body was not present, but she could look down on her loved ones and connect. Millie was sitting in front of her at the dining table. She was painting and talking as she worked. Lucy struggled to define what Millie was painting; her heart charged with adrenaline as she tried to find answers.

Lucy then woke with a sudden jolt. She was lying in a room of darkness. To her astonishment, Lucy realised that not only did she have Millie's artwork in her possession, but her dream featured Millie's painting the very same piece. Her discovery may have answered one question, but others followed. She tried to understand, how she could have been able to view herself in another lifetime. She was Abigail and Lucy, yet each, it seemed, in a parallel universe. She remembered Daniel's advice to her on one occasion.

"Lucy. You must remember that we are not in control of the

unknown," he advised. "The Germans believe in a doppelgänger **(12)** which is a replica of oneself, and when viewed, can enlighten," he continued. Abigail, she considered, was her doppelgänger.

Lucy understood that the stimuli for her was the smell of toffee. This smell had become a powerful trigger, that the memories transported her into another world. There was a powerful connection that she had with those who had lived in the past, revealed to her once again, this time in dreams.

Lucy shared her bedroom with her sister, the two of them often waking up together to the noises of breakfast. The men from the stockyard had gathered again around the kitchen table. Jack would be off with all of them for days. This time, Uncle Rick would join them, but they all knew they would be back for Christmas day. The men were gone before Lucy had time to say goodbye, but she knew she had things to do before they returned. She had decorated the Christmas tree last night and her uncle had helped her. She stood on a chair to reach over, as he handed her each hand-made item. They enjoyed placing them on the tree. The branches, taken from a wattle tree outside the shed on the western side of the property, were bare, so decorations kept the room looking colourful and festive. They all believed it to be the most magnificent tree they had ever seen.

Christmas had finally arrived, and Lucy was so excited. The house woke to the smells from the kitchen. Everything was ready and waiting for the celebrations. The roast was in the fuel stove much earlier in the morning as it had to feed all the men from the muster. 'The crew' would be returning in hours, and the Christmas plum pudding had been prepared weeks earlier. A boiler of smooth vanilla custard sat on the top of the stove. The eggs, collected from the free-range chickens, had conveniently laid twice daily. Mary stirred the mixture to make it an ideal consistency.

All was a bustle in the Roddick household. Charlie Ireland stumbled in first, and then it was a group of them, placing their knapsacks at the door of the kitchen. Jack followed, looking wearier than the rest. He moved aside and made his way into the house to find his family. Fly screens secured the windows to prevent the blow flies which collected outside, and plastic streamers hung from the door to let drovers in but bugs out.

The jackaroos began with a beer or two and made a great deal of noise as the Roddicks gathered in the lounge. It was now time to open the presents and Lucy and her sister were excited. This year would be special because they had Uncle Rick to share the festivities. The adults sat in the grand lounge chairs. It was a splendid feeling, falling into the chairs as they held onto one's body snuggly, and although there was a broken spring or two, the lounge was large enough to allow one to find a more comfortable corner. Lucy was first. She stood up to pick her gift. It was for her father, Jack.

"Although I am no longer a smoker, this lighter will come in handy when I am 'out bush'," he mused.

Her mother, Mary was next. She was so excited! Her brother had brought up her mother's Irish linen and embroidered tablecloth. It would fit her kitchen table for special occasions, and she reminded him that she would use it later that day. For her brother, Mary returned the thought by handing him a flick knife.

"I found it in the co-op Rick, and immediately thought of you," Mary offered.

Her brother was delighted and listed occasions he might use it, including cutting saplings in his garden. Uncle Rick was, one could say, a keen gardener. He would do the digging and pruning, while his wife, Sandy, would do the weeding and planting. She was not available this year as her own mother had taken ill. Their home in South Australia was always decorated with fresh flowers, filling their home with the sweetest perfume. For Eliza, her family presented her with some books from great authors, including Hemingway and Austin. Then it was Lucy's turn to receive.

Lucy had already noticed the big parcel below the tree. She opened the gift, wrapped in newspaper, and tied together with a big blue ribbon. Lucy smiled briefly as she realised the present would also serve to tie her hair in those unseemly braids. She handed the wrapping and the ribbons to her mother. They exchanged smiles, as each knew what the other was thinking.

"These will look beautiful in Eliza's hair, won't they, Eliza?" she remarked. Purely a rhetorical question perceived by Lucy.

She returned to her gift and opened the remaining tissue paper. New shoes for swollen feet, a new dress to wear on Sundays, and a diary for 1983. She thanked her family and helped to tidy the room before she ran outside for a brief play.

All the men had left, having carcases to take away. They would return at lunchtime to celebrate with the family. Cut vegetables were cooking slowly in the oven. There were two full trays of them. Above the stove, the custard was ready, but the peas, peeled earlier, needed more time. Mary took the roast out of the oven. It was heavy, but she managed. Now she would transfer the meat to a platter and make the gravy. Plain flour, added to the goodness of the meat, would make the rich gravy that her mother would always prepare. White wine and stock would follow. She stirred consistently to make sure there were no lumps.

Mary then set the table with the help of the family. Jack had returned to the truck to unload. The dishes arranged alongside cutlery and glasses, the jugs, and sauce and plates. There was also cranberry syrup which Mary had made herself. She had her brother bring the berries up from down south and had made it days earlier to freeze for this occasion.

Mary called everyone by ringing the gong above the hallway clock. It was high above the linen cupboard, and she had to stand on her tip toes to reach. Jack had often commented that he should make a little shelf to house the gong, but time had prevented him from doing so. As it rang, 'the crew' pushed forward and sat themselves down. Now this table could seat up to twenty-four people. Luke Roddick had made the table, and as it was so big, the extended staff and stock-hands could celebrate with them. Later, the jackaroos and stock hands would leave the homestead to share left-overs with their own family and add that to the bush-tucker they had brought home from the last bush trip.

Everyone was genuinely excited. The aroma was noticeable and permeated the house. Jack stood at the head of the table and cut the meat and placed it on a platter alongside the roasted vegetables, minted peas, and gravy. Now it was time to 'dig in'. Glasses of wine were shared amongst the adults, while the children had pineapple juice with ice blocks to follow. Most had seconds, and Uncle Rick once again, was amazed at his sister's cooking.

There was a knock at the door. Charlie Ireland was there. Work had distracted him, and he had not shown up for lunch. He had something, it wriggled and squirmed beneath a rug, but secure between his arms.

Charlie called out, "Missus! This is for you!"

Mary stood up and pushed her chair away. She came forward

and looked beneath the woollen blanket. There, beneath the folds, with its arms and legs outstretched, lay a little joey.

"Mother is dead! Needs home!" he announced with certainty.

Lucy sprang to her feet.

"Oh, Mum, can I please, please, please keep him?" Lucy pleaded.

"I don't know, Lu!" she replied.

"A joey is so hard to look after. You will need to feed it hourly, and… We had a joey over at the school years ago, but it broke a leg because it would slip on the polished wooden floors."

"But, Mum, the joey will be fine here as I will look after it, and it will feel right at home!" she retorted.

"Oh! Very well then," Mary responded with little coaxing. "I think he should be incredibly happy to have you as its mother. Just remember, if anything should happen to him, concentrate on the brief time you have had together rather than at your loss," she advised.

From that day to the next and for months to come, Lucy held her baby joey who she had called 'Rufus'. She had named him after a king who ruled England. Her grandfather had told her stories about kings and queens, and she sat spellbound as he described the times and places of old. Lucy read avidly, hoping to claim any history book to call her own. She was fortunate because her uncle knew of her desire to read more, and had often sent her historical fiction which he knew she would read. Her curiosity became more evident as she learnt about people who had shaped her world. He was equally proud of the way she inspired her sister to read with her.

For Lucy, life had changed now, as she woke hourly at night to feed her new companion. She would prepare the joey's feed every morning and Rufus would suck from a bottle until finished. Fortunately, Martha and her mother would share the responsibility when Lucy was at school.

Within weeks, Rufus was old enough to eat adult food as his teeth were beginning to appear. Jack and Uncle Rick both talked about the new home they would build for Rufus. They both spent hours building an enclosure at the back of the property. Lucy and her sister were excited. They were planning a great housewarming for their little brother.

Rufus had settled in well to his new abode. He was growing up and needed to have time out of the pen, so Jack made him a large enclosure so that he could hop around to survey his kingdom. It was not ideal, but it was certainly an improvement.

One afternoon, Jack made a grim discovery he would never forget. As he was passing the pen with his dogs in tow, he noticed that Rufus' quarters were in disarray. Moving closer, he discovered the flywire had been ripped from the tin that made up the side wall. At first sight, he knew what had happened. At least one fox had taken poor Rufus from his home. It did not take Jack long before he found the kangaroo lying between fallen branches. Rufus had been attacked for sport, this being a customary practice for foxes. Jack returned to the homestead to break the news to Lucy.

That evening, the Roddicks sat in quietness as they despaired over their loss. Lucy was not ready to repeat the experience by claiming another pet, but decided to concentrate on her studies instead.

Eliza, however, was very keen to replace Rufus and worked on her parents until they relented. It was not long before Jack came home with Mishka, a tabby kitten rescued from the Katherine Hotel.

"Oh, Daddy! She is beautiful!"

"Can I have a hold?" Eliza pleaded.

"Of course," he insisted. "Hold out your arms."

Within minutes, Eliza was nursing her new pet and singing lullabies to her. The family wondered if Mishka enjoyed the attention as she could not escape, however, in time, the two of them appeared to be incredibly happy together.

Like her sister, Lucy became overly excited at the prospect of feeding Mishka and sharing the responsibility. It was not long before the kitten became content within the home. At night she would run along the inside wall of the kitchen. One could hear her racing up the entire side of one wall, and then back again to retrace her steps. The Roddicks guessed she was following the bush rats inside the cavity of the walls. The vermin appeared at dusk, but the Roddicks, used to their scurrying, did not notice unless the lights were out, and all was quiet. One evening, Lucy and her family woke to shrieks in the lounge room. They all ran into the room to see what had happened. There, before them, stood Mishka with the dead vermin in her mouth. She took one look at the crowd above her and ran out of the door to place the dead animal outside. Jack turned to Eliza, smiling with satisfaction. To him, Mishka had earned her keep.

Summoned by their father, they sat at his feet and played with Mishka as he spoke.

"This homestead was built over a hundred and twenty years ago. Its stone walls flank all the corners of the building. These walls are solid, each stone having a circumference of 2.5 ft. Each of the rocks were carried by our ancestors from up in the hills. The early settlers helped William and Kathleen as they built the homestead, and then with the other buildings on the property. Mr William H. Roddick soon learnt to speak the native language and understood the importance the land held, for each of them. He learned, in time, to acknowledge them whenever he made changes to the homestead or station surroundings."

Jack made himself more comfortable, finding a cushion to place behind him as he continued.

"Like most cattlemen in the district, our animals need to work for us. Mishka has done that this evening, revealing that she too, can work for her keep." He laughed. "Now, girls, about your pocket money!" He laughed and the girls joined in.

The next morning, Lucy woke up to see sunflowers adorning the kitchen table. She enjoyed seeing the arrangement because she knew her mother had been gardening. This could also mean that later her mother would take her out into the bush to paint. Her uncle had caught his flight to Adelaide a week ago and Lucy was missing him dreadfully but knew that the outing with her mother would restore both to a better place.

Lucy collected her belongings from the painting table outside in the shed. She placed them in her basket at the front of her bike and pulled her boots over her feet.

"Make sure you wear your shoes, Lucy," warned her mother.

"Hookworms in the Territory can burrow up from the earth below and enter your feet. They then can travel throughout your body."

Shoes were difficult to come by, as her feet were growing fast and Mary had to replace them quite often from the southern stores.

"The shoes should also help to protect you if we encounter a snake," she added.

"Did you hang our paintings in the hall, Mum? I did not see them," Lucy cried out as they were assembling the painting tables.

"Yes, Lucy. If you look above the mantlepiece, you will notice both of them together in new frames, which your grandfather made recently," Mary answered.

Mary was familiar with the Territory and places to paint as she had travelled here with her family when she was younger. Her father, mother, and brother Rick, ventured with her from South Australia, north to Darwin in 1975. Her father then accepted a position in a Darwin bank and remained there for three years. The family returned to Adelaide via the coast road to stop briefly in Sydney, before returning to Adelaide. They often reflected about this adventure and believed that it was a learning experience that they would always treasure. Mary reflected upon her family's experiences as they rode into the red soil plains in search of a pleasing setting to paint.

After finding a cool location near a spring, the pair emptied their knapsacks and set up for an afternoon lesson in the outback. The two of them set about displaying the brushes, jars of water and paints, the charcoal and of course the canvases. Today would be special and the girls would be painting the view of the ranges on the horizon.

"You have a special gift, Lucy," applauded her mother.

"Your sense of perspective, tone, light, and shade gives your work a quality that I have not seen in a girl of your age. Well done, Lucy," she added. She complimented Lucy often as she knew that her gifts would come in handy when she was on her own, and there was always spare time in the evening.

"Your painting is good too, Mama. I love the colours you have chosen. You always manage to see so many of them," answered Lucy.

Mary was always pleased to instruct her daughter about perspective. The sun could be cruel in these parts and the glare from the ground could play unfair tricks when painting. The rippling effect from the moisture from the hot ground ahead, diverted their eyes from noteworthy features. It did not take long before both were pleased with their artwork, so they decided to return home. Their work would then adorn the walls within the homestead for all to admire.

When they both returned, Jack was busy installing the septic system inside the homestead and he appeared hot and bothered as he prepared the space in the bathroom. He was down on his knees as he reached sideways to replace the cistern in the corner of the room. Jack wore a cap to hold his hair back as the sweat poured down from his brow. His eyes were red, as he had been up the previous evening repairing the generator, the family's source of electricity. Without it, there would be no lights or water as the power provided water from the bore as well as the tank supply.

Jack grunted as he lifted the new fixture in place. He stood back to admire his handiwork. The girls entered as he was completing the clean-up and were overjoyed at the transformation. It had taken Jack years to contemplate the renovation, so Mary was particularly pleased.

An upgrade from a pan toilet to a septic one was something to behold! There were many humorous toilet stories in the family. It would often be confronting for Lucy, as it had been for everyone, when they were on the 'John', a term, meaning toilet. There were screams from that little room when a frog was caught looking up at them. They were noisy too, the drone could be deafening at night, as these slimy, but cute creatures sat in the water pipes nearby. They also often choked the water tanks, but fortunately, netting held them back.

The importance of rainwater could not be stressed enough,

her mother would tell her. When the tank supply was not available during drought time, bore water would be on tap for all to use. This was underground water, but at points in its navigation, appeared above ground. This water would be used by locals, including Lucy, as a swimming hole. It was for this reason that officials would sometimes condemn the supply as it had been contaminated. It was therefore recommended that bore water should be boiled before use, so that it would be more hygienic. Mary often complained that after boiling the underground water, it would still sometimes contain a stench, and appear discoloured so that washing in the copper turned pink. No matter how many times Mary boiled the sheets in the copper, they would still have a fine red hue to them.

During periods of drought, the family was keen to reuse whatever water they had. Water from the washing up, clothes and bath water, was used again in troughs for the animals or plants. Most plants, however, did not survive any drought season at the homestead, as cattle and the homesteaders were a priority.

Mary enjoyed being in the kitchen as she was a good cook. She had learned skills over the years, practising patience as she prepared lunch for all the stock hands. She prepared the vegetables from the garden; carrots, lettuces, cabbages, and peas, grown with expertise and manure from the cattle yards provided the compost. The fine green leaves of the lettuces and cabbages often went to seed in her earlier attempts, but persistence had allowed her to adopt creative gardening practices. Of course, Reg would assist with the vegetable garden, as Mary became distracted with work at the homestead. At one stage he erected a wire fence to prevent the animals from playfully pulling carrots out of the ground. Mary was amazed that she could spend so long nurturing the plants and then, in just an instant, they would be lying on the ground, broken and disfigured.

Mary had employed various cooks over the years as the constant grind of preparing food for the staff became too much for her to manage, so she made the meals only twice a week. This meant that Saturday nights and Sunday lunches were special for everyone, as she would make her special pies which everyone enjoyed. Her organic vegetables from the garden complemented the plate. She used the left-over chicken casserole or beef curry to fill the pastry on Saturdays, followed by the Sunday evening roast.

Rose was the first cook to grace Mary's kitchen. A theatrical setting suited Rose as she enjoyed the performance as she cooked. Her loud booming voice held the notes satisfactorily, as her large bosom assisted her diaphragm to belt out the words. She sang 'Carmen', 'Nessa Dorma' or 'Candide'. Her double-fronted apron was covered in safety pins, each one holding a piece of coloured linen. She used these pieces to label her cooking, each colour observing a different day of the week. That way, Rose would know what succulent pastry was fine to eat. She was English and hailed from the northern district, so her accent was inaudible at times. In her free time, she knitted for her nieces back home. Like most transient people in the territory, Rose moved on within a couple of months and left the position vacant for a time.

Magda replaced her, and did this with noticeable fanfare. She had been in Australia for a brief time, having come recently from Serbia. She had arrived with her husband and three children but had found work difficult to find. Her husband had decided that they should take work wherever they found it. He had found a truck-driving job south of Melbourne and would care for the children. She caught the Ghan and then hitched a ride on a road train north of Alice Springs. She was positive about everything; the kitchen rang out with her laughter and everybody's spirits became lifted since she arrived. She was no more than twenty-five years old, but her face indicated that life had not been easy. She missed her children and was often found crying over the stove as she stirred the pot. Nevertheless, Magda was a great cook and loved the girls. She read stories to them often and would recite folktales from her homeland. Her hair was dark, and she plaited it high upon her head, and wore a traditional apron which made her look out of place amongst the locals. Very often she cooked traditional delicacies, and the girls were keen to learn lessons from her. Jack would sometimes let Magda contact her family on the radio telephone. This was a special time for her as she could catch up with them. Eventually, the separation would prove too much for her as she left quite suddenly one Sunday morning.

Mary had difficulty replacing Magda, but in the end, she found Helmut who had been a top chef in a local Darwin hotel. He wanted to travel and thought that this experience would complete his diaries. Helmut surprised everyone in the kitchen at Mandalong, as he was often found asleep holding his schnapps close to his chest as he snored and chortled. There was always a reason to celebrate with Helmut, he would claim. He was generous as he poured his liquor into the glasses, and equally extravagant as he searched for another. The problem was, that he did not know when to stop, and this impacted upon his relationships at the station and his work there as the cook.

"Helmut!" Jack called.

"Yes, sir," Helmut slurred.

"My wife tells me the food is not ready and that you have been sitting here in the kitchen for hours, drinking. You know we have a policy here at the station. There is to be no drinking until knock-off time. Have I made myself understood?"

Helmut reached for another drink and slid quietly to the

floor. Jack got the help of two of the jackaroos from the yard to send him out and sober him up, before placing him onboard the next road train to town. So unfortunately, for all concerned, Helmut did not last long at Mandalong, as he was too unreliable. His drinking had claimed him this time as it had done too often in the past. Mary unhappily accepted the job of cook again at Mandalong, as it became too difficult to find dependable staff for the kitchen.

It had been two years since Mary had insisted upon having wooden floors laid within the walls of the homestead. The floors made a difference as they stayed clean and looked more appealing; the rugs, beaten until soft underfoot were strewn on the lounge room floor. Mary was pleased with her acquisition.

Martha would often have additional tasks running the homestead since she had to care for the medical needs of the girls. They had bouts of colds occasionally, but nothing could be worse than 'impetigo', a skin condition, or 'bung eye' which was rampant amongst the children. Bush flies could carry this infection, so a hat was an inevitable piece of clothing. Mary also encouraged Martha to address nits too, which were ever present in the Territory. Lucy and Eliza found the treatment worse than the condition, as the medication was so pungent that the air around them became quite toxic. Eliza would sit for hours as Martha tried to remove the eggs from her hair with a small-toothed comb. She was not patient at all, so it became quite a process for anyone who volunteered to assist. One had to reward Eliza for sitting still once it was over.

"Sit still, Eliza! Let Martha comb your hair. It will not treat itself, you know!" commanded her mother.

Eliza kicked the chairs in front of her, as if to openly protest about her dissatisfaction. A chair rolled over and made a loud noise. Lucy ran into the room to see what the commotion had been. She took off soon after, understanding that Eliza was just doing what Eliza does, and there was nothing that she could do to change that.

When Eliza was on her own, she could be quiet, doing puzzles or reading most days, but when she became anxious, she became unreasonable by demonstrating her feelings. Unlike her sister, she was not adventurous, but content to sit in a cool area of the homestead with a book. She read for hours, often taking herself off into a room on her own, to talk to her imaginary friend. When she was younger, Eliza's hair was a titian colour, falling below her hairline in small parcels of curls. Her hair was now turning light brown, and the curls were no longer visible. Her eyes never changed though, being the colour of ebony, and her skin was fair and translucent. Her fiery personality would not be as appealing though, as she would stamp her feet repeatedly while uttering noises and cries that were undefinable. During these periods, her face would go quite red, but the household would take no notice and Eliza would, in time, return to more appropriate behaviour. Her parents hoped she would grow out of these tantrums and adopt a more placid attitude, like her sister. In any case, it was apparent she was a creative individual who needed attention. Her sense of imagination grew as she got older while her outbursts tapered off as expected.

Chapter 7
The Metamorphosis

Martha had always been an important person in the children's lives; she saw them take their first steps, bathed, clothed, and fed them in infancy and childhood, told Dreamtime stories, taught them local law, gave advice, and understood them as they were growing up. Lucy learned about Martha's family, her clan system, beliefs, and customs. Martha was like a grandmother to them, and they were like the children she never had. She was patient and kind; she dealt with them in fairness and raised them to be respectful to their elders. She gave them unconditional love and did not expect anything in return. Lucy expected Martha to always be there. Unfortunately, not all things go to plan, and she was to learn that lesson one cold dark evening at the dinner table.

There was a knock at the door and Jack answered. In front of him stood Reg. He appeared most distraught and was punching the air as he spoke, an unusual mannerism not seen in him before. He moved into the kitchen, a place he rarely frequented and explained why he was upset. Martha had fallen in their home and was not responsive. Jack left quickly with Reg to inspect the scene. Lucy had to remain where she was until further notice. It became a long and tumultuous evening as she tried to sleep.

Sometime later, Lucy could hear a plane fly overhead and then leave within half an hour. Within minutes, Jack returned home, Reg in tow. He poured him a whiskey, and both sat down in front of the open fire to talk. Reg said nothing it would seem, but Jack believed he needed the company. Jack explained that Martha was in the hospital, and they believed all would be well.

Weeks later, Martha returned home, having had an operation that would help her move around without getting breathless. She had suffered a minor heart attack, but the medication would help to prevent a reoccurrence. Mary was to find another house-girl as the job was now too demanding for her.

Lucy missed Martha so much, but her mother reassured her that she would visit occasionally, and that her own home was the best place for her so that she could heal. Lucy reluctantly changed her expectations and considered that she was fortunate to have had Martha in her life at all. The reality was that everything was about to change. Mary decided upon Esther. She had formally been a cleaner at the school, so she was familiar with Mary's expectations. She was friendly and shared all her stories with everyone. Esther was married to an Elder from the Tanami community, Eddy. He was well respected and extremely proud of his missus as she had landed a coveted job; that of the house-girl to the boss. Jack had to routinely consult with Eddy regarding the residents and was pleased he could show his appreciation.

Esther began her work within the household the following week and became known to the family as a friendly girl. Everything appeared to fit into place and life went on as usual. Martha would occasionally step in and take over when Esther had an emergency with her children, being glad for the excuse to see the girls and do light duties. Each time Martha paid them a visit, the girls became excited.

Very often, Lucy lay awake in bed, conscious of the sounds coming from outside her bedroom window. The air seemed heavy, and the humidity foretold the rain that was yet to come. Cicadas bleated from the porch and orb spiders hung delicately from the window, noticeably spinning their web in the warm air. White geckos climbed the stone walls in search of a cooler domain. Their transparent bodies revealed their frail, but nimble skeleton. They moved spasmodically in search of insects and freedom. The louvred shutters sometimes allowed a small gust of warm air to move within the room but made no difference to the temperature. Lucy kicked back her sheets as they had been sticking to her small frame, restricting her ability to move. The day had claimed Lucy completely as she had spent it with their mother in the garden. As time wore on, she became frustrated at her inability to sleep.

The fan above circled with awkward carelessness. It occasionally jolted the dense air, whirring noisily before regaining its balance. Her father was at the 'watering hole' the name given to the local hotel. This venue was at the 'five-mile' where Territorians could use distance to remove themselves from the daily grind. They would use the venue to reminisce and make plans with friends. However, drinking could be a problem and life in the bush took its toll, removing, sometimes permanently, industrious men from their families and obligations. Lucy wished she could join him as sleep was further away from her grasp than ever. She lay there until the early morning. When the sun eventually came up, Lucy was at last fast asleep, leaving her sister to run to the kitchen to do errands.

Eliza ran quickly back to her room. Her mother wanted Lucy to wake up as they would be going on a trip to pick up their dad. He had not returned, and it was Mary's job to travel to him and haul him back home. This had happened a couple of times in the past, as there were chores and Mary was adamant, he needed to come home.

Upon entering the hotel, Mary climbed the great staircase.

Lucy and her sister followed. The stairs were steep and appeared deceivingly to lead heavenward. Lucy noticed that at the top, the whole floor was leaning to one side. With each step, the floor pretended to give way. *Maybe,* she thought to herself, *the way to heaven is not as direct as my mother imagined!*

"Mummy," Lucy called from the top of the stairs. "The whole floor seems to be falling," she shouted.

"Lucy, this floor has been like this forever! Hold on to the rail and do not look down. I need to concentrate on bringing your father home now. Just guard the door for me, would you please?"

Mary pulled Jack up from his bed and made him rest upon her small frame. She repeated what she had done countless times in the past, taking him below and outside into the Land Rover below. She started up the engine and began her long trip home. Jack snored loudly beside her as the girls sat upright in their seats in the back. The trip home was tense as Mary was not at all pleased with the situation.

At home, the air was still. Very few birds appeared on the limbs outside the homestead as the heat was so intense. Lucy often wondered where the wildlife would go when the weather was so uncomfortable. Occasionally, but not often, a magpie would appear, sing briefly, and then land on the chimney. It would appear to look beyond the wrought iron roof and beyond, and then leave, to find a cooler place to sit. An old, rusted aerial sat upright above the roof line of the homestead, but very often did not catch the broadcasts from the cities to the south. Lucy often listened to the home wireless, tuned to Radio Beijing as this transmission was stronger and clearer than the national servers. The family would then sit inside for hours under the noisy fans. On this occasion, Jack had regained his interest in the family and after a time resting, played a game of Monopoly with his girls.

Mary returned to the kitchen to prepare a late dinner.

The next morning was memorable as the family had slept well. The Roddick family knew that for now, at least, the weather would improve so they were busy preparing themselves for the day. Jack kissed his girls as he left and Lucy, Eliza and Mary made their way out to the driveway to set off in different directions. Mary would work in the garden shed and the girls would be going to school.

Hooded parrots swept in from the east with the hot wind that sand-blasted their faces. They squawked from up high, landing with great composure upon the high branches. The thick air was more noticeable now and the events of the week played with their minds as the birds scurried for cover. The noise was deafening as the rain belted onto the tin roof of the station house. The final screech announced a grand departure, as the flock of birds took off together in search of calmer skies. Then, the stillness before the storm. Torrents of rain pelted down, discharging from above and around them with tremendous force. It hit the soft red earth below their feet. The wall of water danced as it hit the ground, forming rivers on either side. The rains had come, and life would be more tolerable now as the humidity had eased.

It was Saturday, and the friends, Maggie, Winnie, Red, Jimmy and Lucy were off again on another adventure. With their bags packed, they headed out, this time to investigate the small gold diggings at the local gold mine site. Jimmy expected trouble as he had reported to his friends that the activity there had increased recently. Red prepared them briefly before they took off on their bikes. The ride would be long, so refreshments were essential. Lucy wore her hat as she negotiated the bends around the riverbank. The water in front of them held delights. The Chestnut quilled rock pigeon sat at the water's edge to gain perspective before retiring to take a rest from the morning sun. They kept riding and soon they were out into the open. They pushed hard against the wind. Lucy was pleased that the air was moving around her, as very often the stillness could be suffocating in the heat.

Mount Herbert was in sight and the friends continued their trek without any interruption. By the time they had reached the border of Mandalong, they pushed their bikes up into the shade. They sat down for a brief rest and to eat their corned beef and pickle sandwiches, made by Mary that morning. She enjoyed packing lunches for the children when they had their adventures. She trusted that they made sensible decisions and knew that Lucy was in good hands with Red and Jimmy, as they were gifted bushmen.

Wall-to-wall wildflowers spread before them, glorious colours carpeted the ground and into the horizon beyond. Lucy's eyes consumed the feast of blue, white, yellow, green, red, and pink. The girls fell to their knees and picked the wild blossoms from the ground. They scooped them up into their string bags to take the samples back home. The white paper daisy, the Sturt's desert pea, stork bill, sand drover, lily, mini daisy, bush tomato, the butterfly bush, and the Australian bluebell were all sprawled out in front of them. The black-backed fruit dove and the white-lined honey eater danced gracefully within the field of colour. Jimmy noticed the bees first as they hovered together, taking the sweet-smelling nectar to their hives in the paper bark trees above.

Once they had finished, they drank their barley water and collected their belongings. Placing their water bottles and lunch boxes back in their satchels, they continued the ride to the mine.

The landscape here was of red sand and cracked earth. The flat surface, pitted with small mineshafts looked uneven and planet-like. The larger gold mine site was a distance away, but the children had no intention of investigating it. The weather was extreme, the harsh sunlight noticeable as the harsh glare bounced from the barren landscape. The cacti and tumbleweeds, the dust devils, and crumbling rock were noticeable as they examined the interior of one of the shafts. The openings appeared as cylinders, sometimes being more than five metres in diameter. One could not estimate how deep the shaft was, however, Jimmy told them that one this size could be hundred to three thousand metres deep.

Jimmy and Red had brought a rope with them, and they used this to tie to a tree above the shaft. They then tied Jimmy to the other end and lowered him to the ground. At this point, Lucy realised that this adventure could be dangerous. Had Mary known that they were in this area, she would not have given them permission for the expedition. Lucy listened as Jimmy relayed what he saw beneath the surface. The ceiling supports were placed every four feet in the mine, he said, but the roof was low, and Jimmy needed to crawl to investigate further.

Then, rough rock walls began cutting his skin, but he continued bravely onwards. He was pleased that he was not a miner, and although this shaft was decades old, he thought that one must have been desperate to climb down each day to work within its walls. The thick cracked support beams every few metres down the shaft allowed him to see the crumbling rock and gold dust, together with the leaf debris that had blown in from outside. His torch assisted him as he viewed the old broken pick handles, bits of chain and rusted nails. At the next interval, Jimmy had to scream so that they could hear him. From here the roof was higher, and he could see the old rails and a rusted-out and broken handcart.

Jimmy believed that the entry to this shaft was dug out by hand using a pick or hammer, making the entire process very lengthy. This method was eventually replaced with fire, he told Lucy later, to clear tunnels and to reach greater depths at a faster rate. They would have achieved this by piling a heap of logs near the rock face and burning them. This would then weaken the rock and fracture it. Jimmy had noticed that there was more recent evidence of fire in the deeper reaches of the shaft, so he believed that area to be more recent.

Lucy's heart began to scream as she found the area at the opening, where she was standing, started to give way. She had been warned by Red that this surface was unstable and could cave in at any time. He added that falling in a shaft for even a short distance could cause serious injury or even death. Upon hearing that fact, Winnie let out a loud scream. Red continued to inform them, that any minor disturbances such as vibrations caused by walking or loud noises, could also cause a cave-in. Lucy and Winnie stood back and listened to Jimmy as his voice became less audible.

After some time, Jimmy peered out of the opening, and it was clear they were all relieved to see his face. He had red dust from one end of his body to the other, and he was coughing uncontrollably for some minutes. The children believed they would never try to seek their fortune again by gold mining. They all agreed that the miners deserved the gold they found, as it was a tough life for anyone.

After resting, the friends made their way to the Mandalong border to inspect the gold mine site, but there appeared to be no action at the time. They were pleased that for now at least, noisy prospectors were absent from this area. All five friends made their way home at last, believing that what they learnt that day was not just facts about gold mines, but also how reliant we all are on good fortune. Lucy decided not to tell her mother, Mary, where she had been that day, nor the trouble they encountered. Lucy was pleased at last, to be eventually back home and safe with her family.

When Lucy was not having adventures, she was at school with her friends. The community school was small by city standards, having three classrooms to house less than forty primary-aged children, and a playground, basketball court and outdoor garden. From the fence that encircled the classrooms, to the red plains on the horizon, each of the children certainly knew they were in outback country.

It was holiday time, and the children decided to approach the school building as they noticed a great number of people had gathered outside. The little schoolhouse was situated alongside the church on the western side of Mandalong. Built by the Roddicks and the Tanami community at the turn of the century, it featured a two-room cottage with a small open veranda.

A local was happy to share the story with the tourists who had congregated outside. Her topic was morbid as it related to the murder which had taken place early last century. Her acting was sincere, although, at times, one sensed she had paraphrased the details to match her deliberate actions and expressions.

"Documents attest to the murder which took place here in the early part of the twentieth Century. Little is known about the circumstances, but the resident teacher at the time, was jailed for murdering his daughter within the school residence. On this occasion, her brother had run from the house, calling out to his father in the schoolhouse. Rumour abounds that the daughter had a psychological condition which she had shared with her mother. This meant, that at times, she would be disturbed. The teacher ran to the residence whereupon, he caused grievous injury to his only daughter. After that, the details are sketchy, but prior records attest to an otherwise dedicated and caring teacher. It can be assumed that her father unwittingly became consumed by passion, as he carried out this heinous act of atrocity," she claimed. "Found within his residence after his sentence, were his possessions, the most notable being, a family piano which his daughter had played with great skill," she added. **(20)**

Lucy and her friends were oblivious to this history and the school had quite rightly kept them in the dark. In class, they had been separated in rooms grouped by age; kinder and infants in one, and primary in the other. In the early days, students became student helpers at times, and this worked well as it increased their self-esteem and sense of belonging. They would then have completed their formal training and be sent to teach elsewhere in the state.

There were fireplaces in each room as it had been known to get quite cold in the late afternoon. Older students would chop the wood each morning, providing enough for the schoolhouse and the residence. The bell was donated ceremoniously by the Mayor of Katherine fifty years before. The council there also restored the roof which had been blown away during fierce storms in the 1940s. The gardens were tended to by the children and included a vegetable plot and a variety of fruit trees.

Inside, there was a massive blackboard on each wall and rows of wooden seats with hooded desks lined up in rows. The teacher's desk was bare, except for a small hand-held bell and the school discipline book. The straight-backed teacher's chair stood before the desk, a formal representation of the overly zealous attitude of teachers in these parts. Brown paper blinds covered the windows. These would protect the class from the heat. Water tanks connected the rooms, and two outhouses were installed with a modern septic system. Children had been known to have run back into the classroom screaming after being surprised at seeing a red-back spider on their visit. These were venomous, as they inflicted a great deal of pain.

There was no play equipment, but the oval, although not revealing one blade of grass, was a popular place for the children during play. Books were donated by the libraries in the townships, and working bees were held to raise money to repair the buildings.

The local CWA in town would often allow the ladies from Mandalong, an opportunity to participate in cooking and craft competitions and would also approach their fundraising ventures with them in mind. There was even one time when these women were invited to the Royal Easter Show in Adelaide.

Attendance at the school was irregular in the main, as often children became distracted by the bush. There were a couple of students who, with Lucy and Eliza, would try to collect friends on their way to class. Although the teacher needed to divide his or her time between two classes, the days were full and eventful. Red was seldom in class with the girls, but Jimmy and the school rarely became acquainted. He believed he learnt more from the bush than in any classroom. Lucy occasionally agreed with him as he was brilliant at bushcraft and in knowing his native wildlife.

Red and Jimmy had always wanted to work for Lucy's father, Jack. For them, there was nothing better than being in the middle of the bush, having command over their horse and helping on the station. They could live in their saddle, and they often joked with their friends. They both knew that Jack recognised their talents and hoped that they could stay at Mandalong to grow into their ambition and work one day for him on the property. So,

Lucy realised that while Red may still attend school, it was no use trying to make Jimmy. Fortunately, although it was rare, Jimmy did attend school occasionally. If it had not been for his friends, Lucy doubted he would have come at all.

In the following years, Lucy and her sister left the little schoolhouse too, as they became tutored within the home. Mary had decided that home tuition was the best solution, as she did not want to send them away to boarding school. The first teacher began working at Mandalong when Lucy was eight years old. Her name was Elizabeth Janssen. Standing taller than most, her slim figure towered over those around her. She had straight black hair which was recently cut short above her shoulders. She had a pocket on her right, above her breast where she carried a lace handkerchief. Mary had her confidence, as she had shared her tragic background with her in her interview. Elizabeth's fiancé was 'lost at sea' years before, and his body was never found. It was believed that pirates were responsible, taking his vessel as he travelled in the southern oceans below America. His boat, months later, was found, with all hands missing. Ms Janssen found this event too hard to recover from and had spent months despairing over her change in circumstances.

Ms. Janssen rocked at times as she spoke, her stiff and proper appearance suggested detachment or disinterest. Her inability to laugh made it increasingly difficult to communicate with her. Her broken and inaudible conversation made the girls find their studies most challenging. They were pleased when Mary, their mother announced that someone else would replace her who had come highly recommended.

Margaretta Salvesen followed. Known as an adventurous woman, Margaretta had travelled the world with her husband for years. During that time, her recent exploits had provided great notoriety. Her handbag was made from crocodile skin and sewn together after hunting these animals abroad. The large scar across her abdomen, which she sometimes showed the girls, was a testament to her bullfighting days in Spain. Her curly red hair flowed over her shoulders as she reached into her handbag to find a lozenge to relieve herself of the symptoms of malaria. She would then hit a chair with a handkerchief, to dust it off, before seating herself at her desk. Margaretta spoke of her husband in glowing terms and credited him with having introduced Coca-Cola to the world. He had been based in New Guinea during the time the company patented their concoction, and had subsequently, shared in the financial reward soon after. As a widow, Margaretta was now happy to move on to untravelled parts of the country in search of new adventures.

Alison Rowe followed her. She had a large figure and entered the room with noticeable difficulty. She commanded attention as she took her strides with determination and purpose. Alison had come from the southern states to find a new life in the outback. She was in search of a new beginning as she had nursed her mother for years; a woman who had suffered major strokes this past decade. As a carer, she had been kind, but her resolve became broken as she entered the Roddick household. Lucy and her sister were diligent at their studies but found her to be formidable; the authority she emitted was made worse by her stance and her attitude. She stood, legs apart, her hands behind her back, remaining like this for hours as she waited for their assignments. Nervous breathing was heard from the other side of the room as the girls' tried to manage their daily tasks.

"Open your books, girls. As I said before, this work needs your attention now! You need to try harder!" she boomed from the entrance to the little schoolroom of their home. It was with great relief that the Roddicks learned that Alison had decided to leave the Territory for the former comforts of home.

A teacher from Western Australia, the daughter of a wealthy mining magnate followed. Marie Rothchild had travelled the distance in search of adventure and a husband. She was a petite woman, whose awkward frame resembled her personality. Her voice was frail and quivered as she spoke. Outward features alone should have somehow predicted an unsatisfactory experience for the children, but on the contrary, she rose to the occasion by instilling in the girls a great love of literature and history. She made the text come alive as she gave background to all their learning.

"Did you know that Marie Antoinette became a French queen, but was raised in a kingdom far more opulent than she experienced with Louis XV1?" Marie enquired.

"She had your name too!" remarked Eliza.

"Probably why I was always interested in her, Eliza!" she retorted.

Ms. Rothchild deliberated over philosophical questions, helping them to question and think deeply about their world and those who live in it. "Marie Antoinette was bored with life and ordered grand barns be built to house the cows she planned to milk," Ms Rothchild claimed. "She tried to balance her highly refined life with some peasant responsibility," Ms Rothchild explained that one needs to face the difficult tasks along with those that come naturally.

"The day came for Marie Antoinette to sit and milk the cows, but Marie could not make herself accept this challenge. She became repelled by the act of milking. In Marie's case, milking could have been her redeeming quality."

"To transform opposition into paradox," the children's

teacher explained, "is to allow both sides of an issue, both pairs of opposites, to exist in equal dignity and worth," she espoused.

"One wonders about the consequences to history, had Marie Antoinette accepted the task."

Both the girls began for the first time, to find themselves looking forward to the next lesson. Unfortunately, the lessons once again came to an abrupt halt when Marie left the station for a teaching position in Darwin. From that time forward, both the girls began to coordinate 'School of the Air' programs.

It was late June 1985. The early morning sun lay dormant on the horizon. The orange hue highlighted the openness of the land. Lucy leaned across to her window seat and scrutinized the undercarriage of the plane as the engine shuddered. Another glance, and she was examining the wings of the Cessna 210. The fractured light of the sunrise bounced across the metal struts and played tricks with her imagination. Her eyes then moved to the awakening sun. A purple hue sat beneath the horizon, and in the foreground on the plains before it, featured an illuminating light. It emitted a filtered glow as it fell upon the canopy of casuarina trees. The destination was set behind the picket fence which Lucy could make out between a grove of trees. This enclosure held her history and would now be the last resting place of her grandfather. The small vehicle touched down at last on the runway.

It was only days earlier when she learned of her grandfather's demise. She would remember the day forever, as it held for her, devastation and heartbreak. The dry leaves broke underfoot as she made her way down to the river. Her eyes had been stinging with the heat as she had made her way to the shaded screen of trees above the water's edge. She reached out to the base of a gum and fell quickly to her knees. She sat there slumped over her body for a time, opening her eyes carefully as the glare had scolded them.

Telegrams were rare in Australia, but for those who lived in remote areas, a telex or telegram was the quickest way to send a message. Daniel had been in the hospital for a week by then, and she felt nervous about the message, as she could see that it came from the Katherine Base Hospital. She remembered how she could feel Daniel's presence, so she dared not look up. Her hands felt restrained as she sat fast to the trunk of the tree. Her head was bent low, and her hair was hanging awkwardly about her. She read from the telex to discern its contents. The words of the text played with her heartstrings as the message was melancholic and brutal.

To the Roddick family,

It is with a heavy heart that we extend to you our greatest sympathy. Daniel Roddick did not wake up from his sleep Monday morning.
May he rest in peace.

Our prayers are with you and your family.
Katherine Base Hospital staff
November 3, 1985

That was days earlier, and now Lucy needed to focus on the present. She regained her composure as she left the plane. The convoy was there to greet them, and then take them by Land Rover to their destination. The air was suffocating as they left the craft. Lucy then stepped forward toward the pocket of trees, as the air should, she thought, be noticeably cooler. A gust of warm air hit them hard as it swept loose foliage around in circles at their feet. She then ambled quietly on her own between each of the graves. The memorials that lay at her feet became a testament to each successive generation.

The early morning rays shone with intensity and purpose; the text of the tombstones drawn into its light. The still sombre sky became noticeable as hanging branches created a dramatic backdrop. Then a mirrored dance from the surrounding foliage became reflected in the white alabaster at the centre of the enclosure. This memorial heralded the first owners of Mandalong. The giant monolith, inscribed with the words, *'Kathleen and Samuel Roddick. A life of Integrity, Industry and Virtue.'* In death, as in life, the matriarch and her husband were the centrepiece; the torch carried by Kathleen had inspired the wives of cattle owners henceforth. These forebears had adopted this land, working alongside and in harmony with their native brothers and sisters. Lucy knew that her purpose was to continue this robust history and endeavour to protect her heritage.

The open grave was there for all to see. The minister announced his blessing. Daniel had lived a memorable life, and the Reverend Wilson acknowledged him as the patriarch of his family.

"...Daniel, a much-loved father, and grandfather to the Roddick family," he announced, then paused quietly in reflection.

"He was a special human being with a great deal of love and patience. His humanity was evident in all that he did. The impact of his life was significant. He was the rock that kept his family together. May he rest in peace."

It had been until recently, that Daniel had assisted his son, Jack, in managing the station. It was only in the last few years that Lucy's father had taken over as he had experienced failing health. The small group then sang 'The King of Love my Shepherd is' to the tune 'Dominus regit me'. The Reverend's face appeared ashen as he lowered the casket to the ground. The group moved on, returning to the small Cessna to begin their journey home.

On the return flight, Lucy reflected on the special place she had for Daniel within her heart. She knew that she had remained inspired by his strong faith and unfailing spirit. He had left a blueprint for her to reflect upon, with her own life. She knew that his influence had a remarkable impact on her and that it would set her up for anything she faced in life. Her gentle tears trickled silently down her face. Her faith was unbroken, her hope was eternal. She smiled. Lucy now acknowledged that Mandalong, managed by one of the Territory's earliest pioneering families, had for successive generations, contributed significantly to the prosperity of all Roddicks, including herself.

Chapter 8
A Credible Inheritance

The local Indigenous Committee had negotiated plans for tourism of the 'sacred site' and gold mine with the Lands Council, **(8) (9)** so that by the summer of 1985, the operation became wholly operated by the local Indigenous people. Start-up financial assistance had been made available, and accommodation facilities, sewage, water services, and transport corridors were in progress, with training and mentoring in place to support the business, and access to government networks.

Mandalong had been a relatively peaceful part of the Tanami before the tourism operation became publicised. Some time had elapsed, but by February 1986, noticeable advancements were being made. The chief advantage of this tourism exercise, Lucy believed, was in providing work for the local youth in mentorship and training programs, that would be recognised throughout Australia.

"My only concern, however, is that the two cultural worlds could collide, meaning that the benefits would no longer outweigh the losses," Lucy declared.

Lucy, Red, Jimmy, Winnie and Maisie often followed these developments. They were excited at times, but a little apprehensive. They knew that their secret world of adventure within the bush would no longer be theirs alone. With tourism comes progress, and that means change. For these young adults, the potential was real; tourism could impact their land, and this change may not always be their friend.

The dust settled around the courtyard as Lucy and her friends ran out to the holding yard. There, beyond the outer perimeter fence line stood their horses, waiting patiently for a slow canter off into the bush. By the time the children had reached them, each of the friends had shared their fishing stories, becoming increasingly excited as they came closer to their horses. The friends loved to fish and today would be extra special. They had not gone to the bush lately, as the weather had been particularly windy. Blustery weather 'spooked' the horses, so they waited until it was calm. Each of them now acknowledged, that this day would be memorable, as it may be their last adventure together for some time.

Their satchels held fishing supplies, attached to the horses with long fishing poles, hung lengthways from head to foot. They then swung their bodies up and over their companions, leaning over briefly to whisper something calming into their ears. With their muzzles attached; they urged them forward with a quick nudge from the knees. Their horses cantered briefly, and then galloped when they could confidently view the valley below. The tall casuarinas enveloped them as they entered the bush. They were now approaching the valley walls. Knowing the following ride would be exhilarating but dangerous, they steered their horses carefully down the incline. Rocks tumbled below as their hooves slipped over the terrain. The friends held the reins, mouths opened as they concentrated on manoeuvring over the landscape.

Red arrived at the river first. Then the friends followed the stream beyond. The gum trees bowed down on either side of the waterway as if to closely watch the flow of the water on every bend. The children all knew that fish would be plentiful and that they would have full bellies by the end of the day. As the friends entered the river, they trod carefully, as walking was difficult on the polished rocks. Upon venturing upstream, the children discovered that the riverbed had altered, revealing undulating and deep pockets of sand. Jimmy informed his friends that for millennia, large rocks had been pommelled by the raging waters of wet seasons past. After some time, the children approached the northern end of the stream, their small feet now falling awkwardly within the wet cool sand.

The friends could see the creek up ahead. This was 'Ned's Beach' to locals as it featured white sands and was a favourite haunt. Here, the clear water settled into a billabong and after the rains, would feature a waterfall overhead. They casually dismounted and collected their belongings. After tying their horses loosely to a tree, they ran down to the water's edge. They raced into the jellybean-shaped pool with their rods, and from there, each chose a tall rock to climb upon. Respecting the first rule of fishing, they remained quiet for the duration, reflecting upon the day and how fortunate they were to be together again, enjoying another adventure. Each of them sat quietly for minutes, collecting their thoughts as they pulled in their first catch.

As midday approached, so did the intense heat. The friends now counted their fish and placed them in a foil carry bag. The catch was then hung from a branch under a tree until they were ready to cook them. Then, they raced each other back down to the water's edge and dived into the pond. When the water was deeper, they would often jump from a landing above the waterfall. They would also walk behind the falling water as there was a dark cave behind, and they all loved to sit there as it was the coolest place known to them. Ancestors had left carved arrows in the red dust, but they all knew they should respectfully leave them behind. The splashing and laughter rang out as these friends played freely together.

As the clouds rolled in, they all decided to make a fire, the fish would then be scaled and prepared for cooking. Jimmy and Red knew how to cook this white flesh, wrapping the fish in large leaves with paper bark to protect them. Then, they would place the fish amongst the coals. Fresh damper accompanied the meal, smothered in golden syrup. This would accompany a cup of tea, as it cooled the body down. The billy was an old sunshine milk can with a hook in the rim of the opening. The water boiled and Red threw the tea leaves in, and swung the tin around at shoulder height. The pot was then placed on a rock, and Red tapped twice with a stick against the pot, bringing the leaves to the bottom. The four of them, each poured their sugared tea into canisters and drank the sweet liquid, and then licked the golden syrup from the damper. They broke the fish into pieces and ate the soft flesh. This was good tucker, they remarked. In no time, their bellies were indeed full, and they reflected on how great it had been to have sunshine, cool water, and food which they had prepared.

"Look at that fish!" Jimmy shrieked with delight.

Below the river swam a grandfather fish that moved majestically through the water. This sea creature was in command of the entire waterways and held a captive audience. Jimmy had his spear that he had 'turned out' earlier on in the day, knowing the fish would swim in the cooler evenings to find warmer pathways. All was quiet as he leapt upon a rock and aimed carefully, holding back his weapon with great might. Balancing on one leg he threw the spear with great precision, the weapon leaving his hands and then hitting his target with one strike. Within seconds, the beast laid out between two massive rocks. Jimmy took the fish with both hands and removed it from his self-made weapon. He then held it high to reveal its massive size. The children all ran towards him, crying out in delight. They had again witnessed the skill of their friend, someone who they totally trusted and adored. He was an incredible bushman and although schooling was not a priority, they knew the bush to be his schoolroom and the animals, his friends. Jimmy kept the fish together with the leftovers from lunch in an old tin. He covered it in towelling and placed it in his satchel.

The friends resumed their fishing sometime later, swapping the pastime for swimming as the sun went down. The children dived between the rocks and fell from the cliffs above, making loud cries as they catapulted below into the clear water. They buried themselves between the leaves of the pandanus and the broad trees that encircled the water. They climbed the branches and stole the air, breathing deeply to fill their lungs with the eucalyptus and sandalwood-scented bush. The water bubbled as their faces exhaled, and then breathed again, the fragrant air.

As they rose, their bodies took on a new hue, appearing magically to have matured in a day. When they later recounted their experience, they turned to each other, holding out their hands, encircled in promise. It was then they pledged to always stay true, to continue their pact to stay close. Whenever the days became longer than they should, or friends were afar or forgotten, this promise brought them together. No matter how their lives changed, this promise was something that stayed in their hearts forevermore.

The breeze teased the clouds across the sky. They knew it was now time to finish the day with roasted marshmallows. Jimmy had bragged about them. He had stuffed them into his pocket earlier. "Eh, Lucy!" Jimmy called. "Look what I have 'ere!" Lucy peered into his hand. There, in front of her, was a mass of sticky, squashed and sad-looking mellows. She encouraged him to place them on a stick and cook them in the embers, and then all of them treated themselves with this gooey mess. It tasted sensational as it was hot against their tongue and a satisfying sensation. Each of them was apprehensive about the trip home as they realised that although they had promised to remain friends, changes were afoot and each of them did not know what that would entail. As they licked their fingers, they were surprised to find a fish carcass lying in the sand behind them, rotten from the sun's harsh rays. The ants, however, were not troubled by the aroma, and consumed the meat in record time.

They each gathered their possessions together and returned home to tell their families about their eventful day. They knew in their hearts that these times were special as they were 'coming of age', and would need to find work very soon to support themselves and their families. Today though, would be another special memory which she would keep in her heart and treasure.

It was the morning of the 3 April 1988, and Lucy was celebrating her eighteenth birthday. There had been much to do in the household as everyone had prepared a list of jobs before the long-awaited party. Lucy woke to a household bustling from within; the shuffling feet, trays of decorations, and furniture were carefully carried from the home into the large farm shed. The kitchen was full of people, preparing food and assembling dishes, pots, and pans. There was continuous laughter, along with scents and smells of various descriptions wafting down the corridor. Trays of food and delicacies were arranged on trestle tables with roses, wattle, kangaroo paw and bottle brushes arranged in large buckets. The flowers added another layer of fragrance and colour to the room.

Lucy spent the day swimming in the water hole with her

friends. They had all been looking forward to the evening as birthday parties were rare in these parts. Winnie, Jimmy, and Reg summoned up the courage to ask Lucy what they would be eating that night. They were so excited that they were jumping up and down as they spoke.

"Come on, Lucy! You must know what your mum is preparing for everyone. Please tell us, please," Winnie pleaded.

"Well, Winnie, I know you love midyim berries with finger lime pie, don't you?"

"Oh, Lucy! Really? Your mum is incredible! That is my absolute favourite!" Winnie replied.

"Red! My mama knew you loved the cottage pie she made for your birthday, so we decided to cook it again for mine," Lucy added.

"Co-o-l!" Jimmy and Red sang out loudly as they licked their lips. Lucy knew she had made the right decision.

"And Jimmy! We all know you love sweet things like honey and marshmallow. Mama thought we would make you toffee treats," added Lucy.

"Gee thanks, Lucy!" called out Jimmy, his body jumping with anticipation.

Lucy told them things she knew, but other details she left to their imagination. They would also be having garden greens with carrots from the homestead farm and Reg had collected the promised berries for this occasion. The Tanami community had been invited as her father believed their attendance would demonstrate to Lucy, the strong connection she had with them.

That evening, Lucy walked into the shed which had now become a magical arbour. Flowers intertwined with lights hung from the rafters, falling gracefully toward the trestle tables below. The seating was organised, as it displayed the guests by name and at the side of each setting lay a netted bag of sugared almonds, delicately held together with a shiny pale blue ribbon. Platters lay at the centre, containing various condiments and pastries. Lucy sat behind her name tag, grateful for a public show of affection and acceptance. She felt encouraged by the attendance and knew that all the participants felt bonded, and this gave her a great deal of satisfaction.

It did not take the locals long to arrive. Reg and Martha sat at the family table with Jimmy, Red, Maisie and Winnie. Her girlfriends from primary school, Janet and Cathy and their families, had flown from the southern states to be there, and now sat at the next table. There was the doctor who commanded the Flying Doctor Service who had flown in from Darwin and 'the crew' of course, who needed their own table as they would make the most noise. The patrons of the CWA from the townships attended, as did the local drivers for the road trains and of course, the Conair staff. The people from the church assisted, the women helped in making the birthday cake, and the men helped Jack assemble the trestle tables. The children from the school were sitting at the back with their parents who did not want to miss this night and had helped with the decorations. The Elders made a noticeable presence and had planned to speak briefly. Lucy felt uplifted as she felt proud that the locals had formally given their blessing to Lucy and her family.

Jack took to the platform above them. He briefly thanked the guests and then turned to Lucy. He requested her presence and without fanfare, preceded to announce publicly that her rightful place should be with him, at Mandalong. A surprised Lucy peered into her father's face, as tears welled up in her eyes. Her heart had stopped for a moment as she evaluated her new position.

"I would like to propose a toast to my beloved eldest daughter, Lucy, to whom I am indebted," Jack admitted. "She rightfully deserves a place on the team at Mandalong, and I am sure she is ready to pull up her stirrups and ride high with us in the stockyard. She has proved herself over and again out there, and she continues to impress all those who try to make Mandalong work. To Lucy!"

Lucy had grown quickly, her long legs highlighting her svelte body. She had grown into a beautiful young woman and the way she carried herself around the property, emphasised her style and grace. She was capable in the yards with the animals and gifted in her accounting skills. She was satisfied that she contributed well to Mandalong, and would never grow tired of living in the saddle. The crowd raised their glasses and drank to her health. Of course, most were drinking non-alcoholic cider, but the jackaroos were looking forward to less sobering drinks later in the afternoon. Jack then made his way to his table and joined the others in the celebration.

Lucy's life had indeed changed, but this event would certainly make the attachment she had with Mandalong, that much more important. One day, she thought to herself, she would be managing the station, and if that were the case, her ambitions would be realised. Jack stood up to pull Lucy's chair out and gave her a firm but loving kiss upon the forehead, and then proceeded to do the same to Eliza who sat beside him. Jack always treated his daughters with equal attention so that they would know he did not have favourites. It had, however, come to his attention that Eliza was not interested in the property and had recently discussed an interest in studying law and politics. She would often convey her desire to move to the city to further her studies, as she wished to be within the hustle and bustle of city life.

Preparations had been underway for her move, likely to take place the following year. She would briefly stay with her uncle in Adelaide, South Australia, before taking up residency at the university. Eliza was counting the days as she had spent her final years at school, working towards this goal.

That evening, there was laughter, dancing, speeches, and tears. The Roddick family shook hands at the door as the guests were farewelled and thanked their hosts for a memorable evening. Lucy and her family closed the door behind them to walk towards their homestead, delighted by the events that had played out, and grateful that everyone had reflected on this event as being one of the most memorable ever. This had been a special occasion for all, as it also became a celebration for both Red and Jimmy, since they were to begin as jackaroos at Mandalong the following month. Lucy slept well that evening as she looked forward to joining her team as a stockman the following day.

When Lucy was at work, she would often spend time up in the horse paddock half a kilometre from the compound. When she was younger, she would leave after school with the jackaroos from Yuendumu to watch a rodeo from a safe place outside the enclosure. The station hands loved to watch the champions of the ring, and sometimes entered the contests, but for them, the real game was played in the paddock, as they wrestled with the wild bulls at the station.

The jackaroos in this country were adept at moving stock across the Tanami. They would steer the cattle into the wind, and in later years they began to use a helicopter or motorbike. They would ride the plains which stretched southeast from them in Tanami country. Their task then, was to steer the cattle to the 12-mile camp and then load them on the cattle train, their destination being the Katherine abattoirs.

Both Clint and Baxter were the lead jackaroos. They were lean and rode 'like the wind'. Jack valued their expertise as they assisted him with the cattle in the yard. They were amongst the best horsemen in that part of the country, that was, until Lars rode bareback into the station late one summer evening. Lars had arrived at the camp in answer to a job advertisement, his entry noticeable as he rode as if he had been strapped to a horse his entire life.

Within months of arriving, Lars became familiar with the crew but chose to keep to himself as he worked the yards. On an evening, Lars chose not to sleep in the men's quarters, building himself a lean-to, to house his champion horse and himself at night. In time, Lars and Lucy developed a special friendship, as he was happy to assist her as she developed her skills in the saddle. Lars would often not talk, but would instruct through body language.

Lucy was always ready for a lesson with Lars. He took her to the backcountry to show her how he would collect the brumbies and lead them to the yard to be tamed. *They are majestic creatures*, she thought to herself. Lars rode with speed as he pointed westward to meet the brumbies from beyond the desert country. They came together in herds, each more beautiful than the last. When they had assembled, they grazed beyond the ranges and drank from the spring until their bellies were full. It would be here that young mares would calf and nurse their young. They were wild horses, born to the land and owning every part of it. The herd kept together, each connected and bound by blood. These were the wild horses of the territory. Men had tried to tame them, but their spirit would not yield; they were the *'Spirit Kings of the bush'*. Lars was the exception; what he did not know about these wild animals was not worth knowing.

Lucy stood captivated as Lars approached her. This time, however, the horses became spooked by her horse, and galloped away together, back into the bush. The horses, cattle, and mules immediately went crazy, stampeding dangerously. She left with Lars soon after, believing he would come back the following morning. He would conduct a muster when the horses were content, she told herself. The cattle below them would be kept in a holding paddock overnight, and could graze until moved. Each muster needed planning, but the bush horses to Lars would be his priority.

The next morning, they took off. The air above their hooves became clouded in dust as in packs, they mounted the steep ridges. Lars followed expectantly. He cracked his whip, projecting the high-pitched strike off into the distance, to then bounce against the steep cliffs on either side. The roar of their muster rattled the bush, fracturing the foliage as they passed in haste. Birds escaped the violent onslaught and flew off to calmer plains. Rocks fell and slid with the invaders, but the champions stayed upright until the end of the climb. Once above the steep divide, the herd grazed again on tufts of grass that sprouted above the ridge. From here, they would find a place to rest until morning, and then ride on again to claim new ground. The wild beast of the north was free on these open plains and controlled his kingdom it would seem, indefinitely.

Baxter and Lars would spend hours together each day managing the fence line surrounding the property; 137 hectares of cattle country. This land held 0.5 cattle per kilometre, so in these parts, land needed to be vast to make any noticeable gain. The helicopter musters were proving worthwhile. Once within the fold, the wild horses enjoyed the feed stock of sorghum, grown on the station. The riding partners were prepared to travel great distances to connect with these wild animals and bring them back to the station.

Jackaroos were plentiful as most local lads wanted to turn their hands to something they knew instinctively. Jack had employed local men, and they were of considerable value as they were familiar with the terrain and worked together very well. Lars had caught Jack's attention early in the piece. He had recently worked in the high country outside of Alice. He had spent time taming the brumbies that roamed the plains. Lars was one with the wild beasts that galloped beneath him. He spoke to them softly and broke their frenzy, but not their independence.

Not only could Lars ride these brumbies bareback but had trained them up for a long ride. Lars was a true equestrian; his skills were the talk of the land, as he was one of the top handlers in the district. His horses teamed up with him as he ventured out into the Tanami cattle country. Lars was quick, accurate and steady, becoming one with his horse as he claimed the rough, forgotten land as his own. When it was at last time for a dismount, Lars would tend to his horse as a father does to his offspring. The bond they claimed was as strong as any known to man.

Lars had come over from Germany in his early twenties and had become a jackaroo in the northern parts of the state. He was a competent equestrian, but also had an analytical mind. He had managed to solve delicate issues amongst 'the crew' and showed his skills at maintaining the property. Within a brief time, Lars had become comfortable working the station on his favourite stallion, Hector. The two would sleep under the stars with only an open roof to protect them from the elements.

Lars was a bold man, commanding others with a strong and definite tone, although the words that came from his lips were often indecipherable. His body, although majestic in contour, appeared stooped on one side so that when he walked, he pivoted up and down. He struggled to sit, as his leg gave way in mid-fall and the rest of his frame collapsed henceforth below him. His Nordic looks stood as a contrast to his dark companions, whose skin colour was a testament to their lives spent in the saddle under the northern skies.

Within months of his arrival, Lars had made an impression upon most of those who worked with him. Those who observed him noticed that he kept to himself, removing himself from all drinking bouts and conversations. The result was that, in time, others soon felt that Lars was different to them, and some believed he did not belong. As Lars became more isolated from the crew, Baxter and him became closer. They enjoyed spending time together and sometimes their colleagues noticed that very often, Baxter would not return to his bunker on evenings. It was clear that Baxter preferred the company of his new friend and confidante.

One morning in the cattle yards, a chance event determined the fate of the two friends for the foreseeable future. Baxter was sitting above the cattle vet cage, his legs propped up on the fence between the crush pen and the loading ramp. The cattle were anxious as the dust storm had appeared from the west, and visibility was low. To dispense with his normal procedure of securing the gates, Baxter hurriedly opened them too quickly and, in his haste, allowed two cattle through instead of the usual single entry.

"Whoa! Watch out below," called a voice from the yard.

Baxter turned to see two bulls dangerously stampeding towards him, advancing, with great speed, horns lowered.

"Great, heavens, what the…" Baxter yelled out at the top of

his lungs.

Lars began to fend the beasts off with a leap across the loading ramp. He advanced just in time, yelling, *"Hört auf, ihr Bastarde!"* As he fell to his knees, pulling at the gate behind him. The stampede had ended, and the two were seen struggling to accept what happened within minutes. They were hugging closely, which sent waves of dismissal amongst the crew, as they felt increasingly uncomfortable. There was another occasion when Lars and Baxter were found sitting against a tree outside the yard by two of the crew. The male couple acted awkward, and it was seemingly evident to the observers that these mates did not belong at the station.

It appeared to most of the crew that the relationship between Lars and Baxter was more significant than 'mates who worked together'. Jimmy and the other jackaroos ignored these notions and worked with both men. However, behind closed doors, the topic of conversation at night was about their relationship. 'The crew' from the townships eventually confronted Jack with their dissatisfaction. Being a reasonable man, Jack retired to his home again that evening, after offering his jackaroos an option to leave. He warned them strongly about stirring up trouble. After that, life resumed as it had done months earlier, and everyone got on with the job.

One afternoon in May of the same year, Baxter took Lars back to the compound in his Toyota utility. Baxter always took his old truck between jobs, and one could observe that it had covered vast distances, as it not only wore battle scars on every panel, but also held much of the red dust of the vast soil plains. The rattling noise from within the tray of the vehicle accompanied the barks, yells, and howls from the dogs as they journeyed southward towards home.

Later that evening, Jack strolled into the kitchen holding a bottle of beer. He was tired and had much to lament. Baxter and Lars had got into an altercation. According to Baxter, Lars had bragged about his mother country, Germany, and as it turns out, he admitted to being a Nazi sympathiser. With this, Baxter set upon him, punching him to the ground. Both had been in a punch-up for a time when Jack pulled them apart. Lars limped away at last, claiming that Jack could keep the pay cheque, because, for him, it was time to go. He mounted his thoroughbred, and without turning around, left as quickly as he entered. Jack had lost a great equestrian, but he claimed he had no time for any of his antics, and that if Lars felt that way about his 'motherland', then he should go back to where he came from. Baxter agreed and sat down with Jack to share a drink with him.

Lucy had completed her Higher School Certificate by accessing remote education through the School of the Air, a radio service for students which provided a dependable source of tuition. This radio program provided services from the cities to regional areas and communities with teachers who were based in Alice Springs. The conversations could be two-way or with a group of students, located throughout the regional areas of the Territory. This communication was important for them as remoteness prevented them from being together. Lucy had managed to achieve her academic results while assisting her father in the paddocks, but it was now time to appreciate a full-time commitment to her work at the station.

Lucy's school friends Maisie, and Winnie had recently found work in retail in the townships nearby, however, adventures were still possible, she thought, with Red or Jimmy, as they had followed their dream to become jackaroos at the station and were therefore close by. This dream, however, was short-lived as Jimmy and Red both became distracted by social engagements, making time less available for adventures outside of the station. It was not long before both Jimmy and Red had found girls from the town, and quickly settled down with families of their own.

The year was 1989, and Eliza was ready to begin a Law degree in the city, so she had moved down to live with Uncle Rick. He was looking forward to Eliza taking the spare bedroom in his house because his sons had married and moved away, and he was missing the company they always shared. His wife was a great cook so she too, would enjoy the feedback on every dish.

The most surprising event for Lucy was in receiving a letter from the National Broadcasting Group. They had requested that they wished to do a story on her station with her family and the local Indigenous community.

Lucy knew that the documentary would feature the compelling story of the discovery of the Indigenous rock paintings at Mandalong in 1977. The experienced journalists had researched the story and were very keen to have an interview with the Indigenous Elders, but Lucy felt that the leaders would need to make this decision alone. Consultation with the Tanami community would need to take place before proceeding was essential.

The following week, the Council meeting was conducted with the Elders and her father, Jack. The negotiations were brief, the committee finding unanimously in favour of going ahead with the television program.

In late July, the broadcasters, editors, and journalists, arrived with the dust from half the Tanami. They approached the driveway with speed, eventually stopping near the front door in a single-line procession. They were noisy as they slammed the doors of their vehicles and removed their swags from the back of each of the four-wheeled drives. They would be sleeping in tents, set up in rows at the back of the homestead.

After a considerable amount of time, each of the crew had erected their accommodation and made their way to the lounge. It was here that the planning would take place. Logistical operations managed personnel, supplies, technicians, and ground staff. Several generators were brought in as a back-up for the additional population now housed within Mandalong. The weather could not of course be pre-arranged so road trains would bring tarpaulins to shelter the crew.

After a period of five days, the crew were ready to stage a rehearsal. This would mean that the director would walk the cast through the proceedings, so that they could prepare the final take. Within the homestead, a common room had been set up for interviews with those who shared this adventure. Legal advice was central to all communication made, as it was necessary that they did not lose sight of their objective. Lucy was task-oriented, following the direction of her team of minders at every stage. The days were long, and it was difficult for Lucy to balance her work on the station and commit to the demanding work expected from the ABC crew. At night, Lucy would play pool with them, and these evenings lasted well into the night. She made lifelong friends from this visit, as she learned to trust them, understanding that they were honest and hardworking; two characteristics she admired in others.

The day started routinely at six a.m. when Mary and Kraus, her assistant, would cook a hearty breakfast. Most of the crew preferred a coffee or a bowl of cereal, but some had a larger appetite. The meal consisted of two fried eggs, tomatoes, hash browns, mushrooms, and toast. For lunch, the cooks would set up a long trestle table. Platters consisting of buttered rolls, salad, a selection of meats and a fine choice of cheeses, fruit, and cold drinks were placed in the centre.

The National Broadcasting Group had gone to a great deal of trouble. A trailer with a generator held a refrigerator. The crew appreciated this as cold drinks were always available. There was also a tent which provided cover to lounge chairs, desks and electronic services which proved to be valuable to all. These services made the days more bearable, but everyone enjoyed the cold shower of an evening, as their bodies needed to cool down. For Lucy, her relief came at her favourite spot by the spring.

One afternoon, Lucy was especially tired and longed for a swim before retiring to her room. The day had been exhausting as filming had been time-consuming. She rode the distance while in thought. Lucy then jumped down from her mare and surveyed the scene. The water was cool, and her feet were enjoying the relief it gave. After a brief swim, she climbed the rocks above, as she had always done as a small child.

Lucy looked beyond, and for a minute, she remembered the boat trip she had with Millie and Luke all those years ago. She thought about how close they all were to capsizing that day. Lucy was reminded about the tragedy that occurred on Boxing Day in 1893, when a group of picnickers perished during a boat ride at Minnamurra in NSW. Captain Thomas Honey and Miss Charlotte Pike drowned as they had accompanied the Wood family for the day, and it is believed they lost their lives trying to save them from certain death. George Wood and three of his children also tragically drowned that day, the eldest son Henry, and the captain never being recovered. Elizabeth Wood, the captain's wife was the only survivor. Lucy realised that the long clothing must have pulled them down below the water. Those who were found, now lie in Kiama cemetery as a reminder to others to be careful on the water. Fortunately for Lucy, she was reminded that nowadays, children learn to swim and family drownings such as these are rare. **(19)**

It was at this point in her life that Lucy realised that everything had fallen into place. The land she shared with her Indigenous neighbours was rich in history, in mineral wealth and beauty. It offered itself up for those who honoured it, sharing itself so that all could live abundantly. The ancestors had blessed this land; it was from them that all these good gifts had come, and Lucy felt truly blessed. She knew that her path had been set from the time she first placed her feet on the ground. The director called 'cut' and the crew packed up their possessions for another day. Lucy retired with them for another evening under the setting sun.

The period of filming at last ended, and Lucy returned to her menial tasks at the property. The production team had left in a cloud of dust, and the popular program aired on television for weeks that year and closed for the Christmas holidays. The public responded positively to the broadcast and great interest resulted from the airing. The locals felt the impact of the resurgence of funds, and made preparations to spend this money wisely.

A council meeting had become a more regular practice now, as it was necessary to address this new investment. Construction and renovations would begin on the hospital, airstrip, the schoolhouse and the surrounding sporting locations. There were even plans for a pool and gymnasium sometime in the future. Conair now supplied regular flights and there was talk at one stage about a competitive airline, supplying regional services to the area. Plans included an upgrade to the airstrip, with a service centre attached.

Mandalong and its Indigenous community could now function independently. Managing the planning of personnel and supplies had become, at times, a nightmare, but Lucy was pleased that these were no longer her responsibilities. For the next few months, Lucy was busy travelling and organising opportunities for increased beef export to the Middle East. This could potentially place the station in the best position it had known. She left Jack to manage the station while she negotiated contracts.

Janet and Cathy were childhood friends of Lucy. They had grown up together, having shared their lives at the local school. Each of their fathers had worked locally, Cathy's father as an electrician, and Janet's as a plumber. Since leaving the station in year seven, they had tried to get together every couple of years to have a holiday and reminisce. This time was an exception. Upon hearing about Lucy's demanding workload at the station, the two friends decided to surprise their friend with a visit from beyond. Lucy was naturally ecstatic upon hearing the news. The girls did not leave her side as Lucy continued her workload and prepared 'the crew' to take over for a couple of days. The administration would have to wait, she told herself, as she would spend the next few days with them.

The girls had a surprise to share with Lucy. Each of them had recently found jobs working at the station, and this meant that they would have hours to share together every week. Until recently, Janet had been teaching in Adelaide. Her new appointment was for a two-year stay, so her husband and two children packed their belongings and left the remaining items in storage. Janet was pleased as Dean, her husband, was to work at the local cooperative store. Janet had become a dependable friend to Lucy. She had blonde wavy hair, which was wiry and full of curls. Lucy had once thought that if Janet removed her elastics, her hair would hit her in the face. She was exceedingly tall, but very striking.

Cathy was also a friend who now worked as a nurse at the local two-roomed hospital. The friends spent time together, often as they loved sharing stories and laughing. Cathy was hilarious, and her stories would make them all laugh for days. Lucy would often catch herself laughing at something Cathy had told her days earlier. In these parts, it was important that there was humour, as it helped one move forward.

A memorable time they shared and often talked about, was in late May 1988, when the three were stuck together in one room of the school after a bush fire threat. The girls were on a holiday with their friend, and on this occasion had been minding the children in the school as the teacher had left briefly to do a chore. The students remained playing at the other end of the room, while the girls all decided they were hungry.

There was nothing to eat and being ravenous, decided they would open what looked like an incredibly old jar of olives they had found in the cupboards of the old kitchen. The three girls did not like olives but decided to eat them anyway. It was an exceptionally large three litre jar and by the end of the day, and when they were at last called upon to leave, they had eaten all of them. From that day on, the girls always made sure that with their glass of wine, the olives would be a priority. They replaced the jar often in that schoolhouse and enjoyed sharing them as they talked and laughed for years to come.

It was now 1992 and the friends became settled into their new roles on the station. These quiet times with her friends were special, because Lucy could focus on herself rather than her work. She and the girls would laugh together, share, and reminisce for hours under a tree in the open, before curling up in the shade and falling asleep under a large wattle tree out the back. When awake, they would often make themselves a big pot of pasta and eat it, with a fresh loaf of bread and a glass of red wine from the kitchen. They would giggle as they planned their next escape to town and arrange to meet up with friends to see exotic places far away. The girls had planned a trip to Darwin the following month, and they were thrilled at the opportunity as all three had managed to take the required amount of leave to make it all possible.

These times were special too, as they shared memories of past adventures. There was none so poignant as one they shared when they were much younger. The girls were in their early teens, and happily walking along a path in the undergrowth surrounding the old schoolhouse. They were intent on finding cover for a game of 'hide and seek' which they still played with great enthusiasm. Lucy ran forward to find cover, but as she did, knocked herself against something that was hidden amongst tall grasses. As she moved, she felt her pendant fall from her neck to the ground below. She swept her arms casually in front of her, in search of her jewellery. This piece had been given to her by Daniel years earlier, and had belonged to his great-grandmother, Katherine. Lucy would often wear it, to remember him, but kept it hidden under the folds of her collared shirt.

As Lucy swept the long grass ahead of her, her arms hit metal, and a surprising discovery unfolded, she thought. She lifted the tufts of grass to one side, and to her surprise found a wrought iron fence, marked by rust and decay. The white enamel had worn away, leaving broken shaved pieces of iron in its place. The fence was like she had seen in the family cemetery alongside the church. She wondered why this plot was outside the burial ground. Lucy called to her friends who ran quickly to be by her side. They sensed a matter of urgency in her call and briefed each other as to the reason the grave would be here.

Lucy then noticed a glint on the ground in front of the wrought iron fence. She leaned over to pick up the locket, holding it tightly in her hand, for fear of losing it again. The girls moved the tall grass back over the grave, so to respectfully replace the natural growth that protected the site. The breeze had come up from the north, and Lucy was aware that they may not get home ahead of the storm.

As the storm arrived, the girls stood together searching for a place to hide. They ran with speed along the path they had come upon earlier and climbed up the steps toward the schoolhouse. They had not been there for years but were happy to find the door unlocked. They swung the door ajar. There, sitting in the corner of the room sat an old gentleman at the piano. He was playing softly on the keys. The tune was familiar, 'Greensleeves', being the song, their class would often sing together most Friday mornings. Lucy loved its wafting melody. It enchanted her because it sent her into a dream state. That was a pleasurable sensation, as it removed her from the present and helped her to dream.

Each of them waited a time and when the old man had finished playing, they looked up from where they were sitting on the wooden boards below. Lucy asked the elderly gentleman if he had been to the schoolhouse before because schoolchildren always sang the tune that he was playing. He answered without turning his body. His rough hands were now hiding in his lap, and his head stared off into the distance. He said yes and confirmed that he had played this tune before in this very place, but it was a long time ago, before any of them were born. Lucy looked over her shoulder at her friends, who were now standing up preparing to leave as the storm had eased, and the sun was shining.

The old man too raised himself out of his chair and took what Lucy noticed, were wildflowers knotted together with twine from the top of the piano. He pushed his chair aside as he walked behind her friends, excused himself briefly to turn, raised his hat to them and left the building to walk back down the path. They eagerly followed, as they knew him to not be a resident. As quickly as he could, he moved towards the grave and, pushing the grasses aside, as Lucy had done before him, placed the posey of flowers inside the fence. It was here that he bowed his head and muttered something unfamiliar. The sun shone dramatically as he lifted his head. Lucy noticed his features; they were dramatic, and she sensed him to have had striking looks at one stage of his life. His bone structure was noticeable, but the years must have altered his looks, and she wondered what may have happened to this man to make him so serene. As he turned to leave, Lucy ran home with the wind behind her. She turned to look back, but the vision of the old man was no longer evident.

Days later, Lucy and her friends heard the story of a young, troubled girl who came to teach so far from her home. After hearing her fiancé was missing in action after the First World War, she left her home in Western Australia to escape her demons and come to teach here at Mandalong. It would be years after her death that a young man came to visit the schoolhouse in search of his betrothed. He had been missing, not killed in action, but awaiting their reunion. He learned of her sudden death soon after returning to Australia. She had never recovered from hearing about this plight, and willed an eternal solitude upon herself. As soon as the soldier heard of her death, he returned to the battlefront, his body later being interred at Normandy. Some say that at the same time each year, two ethereal figures appear on the horizon outside the schoolhouse, hand in hand. She would be wearing her wedding dress that she had made herself, so long ago for an occasion that was never to be, and he, in army attire, his broad-brimmed slouch hat set to one side with his gaze only for his love.

Lucy and her friends remained conflicted. Who had been the man they saw playing at the piano and could he have been her betrothed? If so, he had long since been dead, so was he? A spirit? What was her name, and why was she buried so far from the cemetery? Why was there no plaque, cross or gravestone and why had no one mentioned her name? Like so many before her, a grave outside the hallowed ground meant 'not consecrated'. The 'Greensleeves' tune was a song she played often to her pupils and would remain a melody that was popular at the schoolhouse for years to come. Lucy would catch herself humming the tune into the future, often recollecting the sad, but romantic tale of 'Greensleeves' and the hero who came back for his bride. She knew that they would have found each other at last, and that they would be together forever.

Lucy had been assisting her father full-time for months now and her connection to the land was more noticeable than ever. She had become manager of the station and Jack would only assist his daughter on the rare occasion. He had found a position on the Local Council in Katherine and that meant that both Jack and Mary, her mother, now resided in town, and would commute every few weeks to oversee the station administration.

Since moving with Jack to town, Mary had become interested in continuing her teaching career which had abruptly stopped, when she had married Jack. She was excited about this opportunity as she still had a passion for teaching. She found purpose when seeing the students' young faces smile up at her.

"I love engaging with them, Lu," she would say. "To help them to realise their potential as they continue to grow in skill and confidence."

"Besides," she would continue, "I miss my girls, and this is the only way I can get back some of that time."

Mary's aspiration in life remained the same: to age with dignity, and practice kindness and humility in all her dealings.

"That does not mean I realised any of these traits, but I can sure begin to try!" she would remind everyone.

Mary had always been a keen observer of human behaviour. She enjoyed inspiring young minds to reach out and think in a different mindset, to occupy their time thinking positively about themselves and in helping others.

Her mind settled upon the lengthy line of teachers the girls had shared during their years at the station. Mary tried to remind herself that she should not feel guilty about not having been able to teach her own children, as she understood that those early times were challenging. She did not have the time or the inclination to teach Lucy and Eliza then, as her work was demanding and took priority. However, she was proud that both had grown into upstanding young ladies.

Since moving to the township, life for both Mary and Jack had changed considerably. Mary promised herself that she would aim to live in the moment by making the best of each day. Apart from finding work at the local council, Jack also found himself assisting small businesses, by giving advice to managers and company directors on managing production. Sometimes, this would take him interstate, leaving Mary to herself. Time did not stand still for either of them, as they made every moment count.

Mary had been in two minds about fulfilling her obligation to herself and beginning to teach so late in life. Jack told her that he was proud of her because she was very capable, talented, and resourceful. Jack also felt content as he did not feel the pressure that he had at Mandalong. He looked and felt more relaxed, and he enjoyed taking his wife to work and picking her up each day. They would often go out at night and enjoy a bottle of wine together and a meal, something that they could not do back at the station.

As time went on, Mary and Jack became very comfortable in their new abode and positive about their move. Mary was always confident in her own skin, particularly now, because she was getting so much support from her colleagues and parents of children. This feedback had a positive effect on her approach to her life and her relationship with Jack. The two of them spent many hours together, talking about the past, and planning the future. They took holidays to Europe and around Australia and for Mary, cultural venues in the cities were the top of her list. She also enjoyed seeing the Botanical Gardens in various states, the theatre, and dances at the Opera House in Sydney. The two of them relaxed on these occasions, and Mary would enjoy the massages, pedicures, and beauty salons that were not available to her in her younger years.

The season had been milder, and Lucy had spent time establishing the privet hedge and magnolia grove at the entrance to the property. Poplar trees had also been planted and lined the drive for the three kilometres to the first gate. These trees were served by a very ornate irrigation system which Baxter had set up for her. The trees would be able to shade the courtyard and provide the privacy that Lucy wanted. Beyond this enclosure, there were two cattle grids, which prevented the stock from absconding and entering the homestead area. From the road beyond, postal drums lined the entrance. These provided the station with a postal service which had become an essential link to the outside world.

Life remained busy for Lucy, as there were always manual tasks that needed attention. Her companions, the stockmen and jackeroos supported her tirelessly as she had known them for years, and they were always on hand. Her day consisted of an early morning start around four a.m., a light breakfast and then a ride out of the compound, and into the vast wilderness. Very often, she took a short break. That might be to rest by the lagoon, take a quick swim, or a hike above the cliffs of Mount Herbert.

It had been sometime since Lucy had lost her grandfather, and to mark the occasion she decided to visit his grave for some soul-searching. After a breakfast which consisted of muesli and freshly squeezed orange juice, her staple, she decided to make a long ride on her horse to the cemetery on the outskirts of the property. Here she would sit quietly to recollect her thoughts, and plan for the upcoming week, and, if possible, further into the future. After a brief time, Lucy became impatient, as she had become distracted by the problems at the station. She stood erect and casually brushed the pine needles from her hair and then wandered down to the marked gravestones that stood in front of her.

The epitaphs reminded Lucy of the family story Daniel had often recounted. In front of her lay Kathleen Roddick, who arrived with her husband, William, and two children, James, and Anne from Northern Scotland in 1854. They were to have three more children who would support their father with the demands of station life. The land had taken its toll on the free settler family. At first, there was little to offer, as stocks and supplies were sourced from an area that was over three hundred and thirty-five miles from their settlement. This journey would take more than fourteen days, as stock horses regularly stopped to recover from the long trip. Wagons were loaded up with the necessities at the township, which included goats, sheep, flour, salt, and a variety of seeds. The Roddick family would spend their time tending to the animals and fencing the property, until, in 1872, the property was handed over to Samuel Alfred upon his marriage to Brigitte Anne Walker.

Samuel and his wife had twelve children, seven dying before reaching adulthood. In 1905, Samuel did not return from clearing the back paddocks, a two-day ride from the homestead. A tree had fallen on him and this was not evident until the jackaroos discovered his body days after. His wife Brigitte, then tried to run the property, but found it necessary to rely on Aboriginal stockmen to assist with all the chores. Edith, aged eighteen, had displayed skills on horseback from a youthful age and had taken on the responsible task of a stockman. She continued until her death in November 1908, when she drowned as she crossed a flooded creek northeast of the one-mile boundary fence. Kendrick Fenn was twenty when he became the leading stockman at Mandalong. Born in 1885, he managed the station to then marry Rebekah Roddick in 1912. Tragedy took hold again when Albert, much younger brother to Rebekah, and then aged twenty-one, enlisted for World War I, but died at Gallipoli in early March 1914. Kendrick continued to manage Mandalong for thirty years with his three sons, Raymond, Abraham, and James. Abraham found work elsewhere, but his brothers prospered well and would go on to make the station one of the most prestigious in the Territory, a beef cattle property of repute, and one of the fastest-growing exporting properties in the region. Raymond survived his brother and went on to build the property further until his death in 1952 from Tuberculosis.

Daniel had acquired his cattleman skills from his father, Raymond. At the age of seventeen, he brought his new wife, Gladys, to Mandalong in 1955. He had written to her constantly after meeting her at the cattle auction the previous year. She was visiting Australia from England with her father and had become desperately attracted to him as he was known for his charm and sense of humour. Jack was the only child born to Daniel and Gladys Roddick in 1956. Apart from two years studying at Kings Grammar for his final years at school, Jack spent his youth learning from Raymond. Jack then married Lucy's mother, Mary in the summer of 1968, and in 1970 she was born. The couple would later extend their family with another daughter in 1972, her sister, Eliza May Roddick. Daniel and Jack worked together managing the responsibilities of the station until 1985, when Daniel became ill with pneumonia and never recovered. His death marked a new chapter in the history of the Roddick family.

Lucy had grown up with the memories of his ancestors' past. Those stories had been handed over in good faith, and Lucy knew she would share this family history with successive generations. Before her lay smaller headstones, marking the lives of children taken too soon from their loved ones. Amelia 'Maddy', thirteen years old went out riding one day in 1884, but fell from her horse when it became spooked, allowing her long skirt and petticoat to then become caught up in the stirrups. Maddy was dragged a distance before a stockman was able to retrieve her from the mulga beyond, she died from her injuries, days later.

Beatrice, 'Bunty' died at three years of age, from burns, in 1875. Samuel had once told her how a candle had accidentally fallen from its cradle, and she died from an infection caused by her burns. For a moment, she felt extreme discomfort at seeing Bunty's name before her. Her heart skipped a beat and Lucy looked beyond into the skies. For a moment, a vision appeared before her, a young figure dressed in white skipping amongst the low foliage.

She continued to look at the remaining headstones. Thomas died a hero, at the age of nine in 1887, when he tried to save his little brother from a runaway horse-drawn carriage. He pushed his younger sibling aside to take the full impact of the vehicle. Then there were those young children who died in infancy from fevers and ailments, the stillborn, and infirmed. With little access to doctors or medications, hardship for these young families was inevitable.

Lucy had become momentarily distracted by the sound of wind within the gated lot. Ahead of her lay the central monolith; the epitaph to her forbears who came from Scotland. This shrine became bathed in a veil of light. Above her, Lucy could see the Desert Star to which her grandfather had often referred. It directed her gaze to its source, and momentarily blinded her. It was a star like no other; it stood poised above and in command of everything beneath it.

The Desert Star moved slowly, and Lucy obediently followed as it led her across the barren plains and over to the other side of the boundary fence. It was here that gold, mined by 'men with tin hats', as her father once claimed, worked at this site. Lucy led her horse toward the boundary fence. It was here that she could view the machinery on the leasehold beyond. Open-cut trenches now formed a line diagonally within her property, and she was certain that preparations to excavate were beginning inside the boundary fence at Mandalong. She feared that this contusion could impact upon the sacred site at Mount

Herbert. **(18)** This site was also close to a watering hole, frequented by varieties of fowl, facing extinction. With a final glance, as she mounted her mare, Lucy began her ride home, her heart in her mouth as she realised the impact of this discovery. She knew that she would indeed face brute force when dealing with this matter and was not looking forward to making any further legal deliberations.

When Lucy returned home that evening, she shared her concern with her father. As Jack sat with his daughter at the table, he expressed his concern about the gold mine. The mining corporation had taken liberties, by extending the area in which they were able to mine. He felt that as the site brought such good yields, it may, in fact, end up in a high court. He promised to check it out to see if the activity had increased. After another pot of tea, Jack gave his daughter a final kiss and stretched upward before removing himself outside the door and beyond the car. It did not take him long to leave as he knew Mary to be waiting eagerly with supper on the table back at home.

Lucy tried to keep a distance between herself and the outside world. It was now 1993, and she had become significantly concerned about security. She had learned while she was young, that intruders take what they can, coveting what is not theirs, and sometimes, expecting instant gain at someone else's expense. She had learned that a few employees she had hired from the township lacked industry, skill, or commitment and this could prove to be an extremely dangerous cocktail. Fortunately, Jimmy and Red were dependable cattlemen, and it was now more than ever that she relied on their skill and their loyalty. Her father's pledge assisted a little, but she felt at times very alone and vulnerable.

Lucy settled into her evening program of administration at

the kitchen table. Her papers and book were stacked beside her as she worked under the table lamp. She considered the amount of work that lay ahead of her and rested her head within her cupped hands. Within minutes, a cloud of dust swept over the compound, followed by the sound of screeching tyres. Lucy looked out of the window, her eyes, temporarily blinded by the lights shining into the bedroom window. A shudder, then an engine ceased, and a car door slammed. Chains clanged as they bounced from the metal bars. Lucy could not see their faces, but she sensed trouble as these noisy intruders claimed the night. Lucy believed that since the activity had increased on the boundary fence, so had the trespassing. These guests were not welcome, and she now feared for her safety.

Lucy heard another noise off in the distance, so she decided to investigate. Hoping that one of the intruders had not broken in, she ran all the way to the front door and then down the hallway and as she approached her bedroom, ran inside. Breathless, and gasping for air, she reached for the handle of the door and closed it softly. She carefully looked for the papers which Jack kept in the safe. These were legal ownership papers for Mandalong. She opened the safe and grabbed them quickly, holding onto them tightly in her arms. She glanced at her feet below, as she hid behind a screen and waited, listening carefully for footsteps. She had frozen into this position for a time, but she was not ready to take a chance. Her instincts told her that there was too much at stake, and she should remain locked in this position until she felt secure.

Time passed, and Lucy was about to break her cover. Then, at about a quarter to midnight there seemed to be an almighty commotion at the front of the house. She held on tightly to the parcel and hurled herself toward the door, and down again through the hallway. She broke through the back door leading to the shed and ran as fast as her legs could carry her.

Her body pumped; her head was screaming; her heart was racing. Then, without fuss or any explanation, Jack appeared in front of her. With his arms outstretched, he stopped her in her tracks. Leaning down, he reassured her. She was safe and he would protect her from whatever she feared. Jack had turned his vehicle around, when, on investigating an uproar a kilometre down the road, he decided to turn around and check to see his daughter was safe. He was not wrong, these hoodlums meant to stir up trouble, one of them with a hoodie breaking into the house. After clearing the property, Jack had reassured her that Mandalong would not succumb to the pressure placed on them by mining companies. That also included, he added, any hicks who thought they could bully their way into the property. Their station had been in their family for generations and the papers she held onto tightly, justified her legitimate claim to ownership. The urgency she felt was impacting upon her, and her father understood her sense of hopelessness. Little did she know, however, that he had everything under control. The two walked together quietly as her father assured her that everything was in place to protect his family and the people of the Tanami.

Lucy had lived here all her life and understood the country, the people, and the customs more than anyone. This was the Tanami desert. It was the Warlpiri country. It consisted of desert plains, arid wetlands, ancient riverbeds, and sandstone outcrops. Since the mid-nineteenth century, various groups of people had mined the land in search of a better life. As prospectors, these individuals braved the conditions of the Tanami. The most notable expedition had been made by Alan Davidson, who arrived in the area in 1898 and continued prospecting for gold until 1901. **(7)** He took the name 'Tanami' for the region from local Aboriginal people who visited his camp. Lucy liked to imagine that both Samuel and Luke may have met Alan Davidson. She wondered what their relationship may have been like.

At various dates in the history of this area, certain individuals continued to have an interest in fossicking for gold in the Tanami. There had been no suitable agreement to protect the rights of these Indigenous landowners in the past, but Jack felt it to be a priority now. He instructed his daughter that he had handed over the concern into the hands of the authorities. For now, at least, they had to bide their time and wait patiently for a decision.

Lucy would focus now on managing the cattle. As a twenty-one-year-old, Lucy would continue to concentrate on managing her responsibilities. She knew that she had a great support network, however, maintaining the administration of the settlement, together with the physical demands had taken its toll over the last few months.

Lucy craved adventure and it was Baxter who had suggested she find something that would 'awaken her soul'. He promised to assist, by managing the station for the day and prompted her to go to Katherine to take a skydive, a sport she wanted to undertake, but had never taken seriously. Later that morning, she was on the trip of a lifetime. She knew this adrenaline burst would help her prepare for the months ahead at Mandalong, especially with the unwanted experiences of late. She knew in her heart, it would help her conquer her fears.

The sky was vast, the engine throbbing as the wind blasted her face so far up in the air. She was experiencing her first parachuting adventure after a morning collaborating with her team, and folding parachutes for the afternoon's flight. The object of the exercise was simple; stand alongside each other in a circle and step forward with two sides of the parachute. Before long, all corners were squeezed into a tiny package and placed within a woven bag. The chord would detach the parachute and then release the folded silk into the air.

The pilot was a little apprehensive as the wind made it a difficult climb. The problem with the jump, he reminded them, was that the wind could prevent them from landing on target. They were nervous as each of them had to return to Katherine by sunset. It was only six months earlier, that a friend from the group had a jump organised for a competition in Darwin. The group temporally disbanded following her death as her main parachute and reserve had failed to open.

By the time the group climbed on board, the weather had improved, and Darin radioed into the traffic controller. He arranged flight plans and waited for clearance. At that stage, one would not have known how difficult the day would get.

All eight of them sat in the cabin, waiting for a response. Then, after an anxious couple of minutes, approval was granted, and they began taxiing across into the eastbound lane on the airstrip. After waiting a further couple of minutes, they anxiously began to ascend. The chilly air pinched her face as the door was open for the action that would take place soon.

They finally reached the altitude and levelled out to wait for the first respondent. Lucy approached her seat and moved to the back of the plane as she would be the last to descend. Then the second, third, and fourth skydiver jumped. At this stage everything was normal, but suddenly a wind shift approached the plane from beneath and the divers became rattled, their chords choked together, making it impossible for a free fall. The fifth and sixth player then quickly fell from the plane, to unravel the mess below. With much difficulty, the removal of the twist became at last, possible. Left in the plane alone with the pilot, Lucy wished not to add to the confusion and kept quiet. Once they had landed, the band of troupers hugged one another, glad to have made it without any injury.

After this experience, it was obvious to Lucy that she must try to jump again with improved results. She shared a couple of drinks with the crew, before planning to join them the following week. Lucy left Katherine for her ride home. She was eager to continue back to Mandalong, as the mustering season was about to begin again soon.

The parachuting was a way to separate her anxiety about performing well at the station. It was a release that eased her pain and gave her the confidence she needed to continue her work. The fact was, that without a release, Lucy would spend the entire night tossing and turning in bed, worrying about concerns she had for the property. Adventures were an important part of her regimen, and they also helped her to become more focused on important things. Another contributing factor was that it offered her an occasional break from the station.

The following week, Lucy collected her bundle from the back of the plane and strapped herself in. This was her parachute, and she would need to rely on it to take her to the ground safely. Lucy stood at the edge of the open door, knowing that at any moment she would be in the air. A dizzying confusion overtook her, as the wind hit her body. With her hands clenched in apprehension, Lucy made her way closer to the edge. It would all be over soon. She wondered how she could have placed herself in such a predicament. She jumped! The sound of the chute opening was deafening. It ballooned open above her, jerking her forward and upward, while the harness cut into her skin.

They had been flying at four thousand feet, and now she was floating in a veil of white silk. Lucy sensed the smoothness of the fall and now felt that it was not as fast as she had expected. She could look around her and appreciate the scenery. She landed, feet first, with her body then caving in on top of her. She picked herself up and made her way to her team. Lucy believed that this jump was important as it symbolised her growth as a person; she believed she now had the resilience, to combat her enemies in whatever form they came. Lucy felt that she did not need to prove herself again.

The rain had fallen, leaving the sweet, stale scent from the cow pads to linger. As she ambled through the herd, crop in hand, she told herself that she would prepare for an extensive visit south of the border. She would ask her father to take over temporarily so that she might try to find solace away from work and the constant demands of Mandalong.

Lucy bent over briefly to retrieve her saddle. She stood upright again after unlatching the gate and prepared her horse for the ride home. She anticipated a joyful time ahead as the decision to take leave was quite spontaneous and unexpected. It would be a working holiday, she told herself as there were consignments; both legal and financial concerns to be finalised. She waved to Red as he prepared the stockhorses for the night. His presence became appreciated as he often slept in the barn alongside the homestead.

No matter how she tried to stop her mind from wandering, it did what it liked, and she found herself remembering the conversation she had with her grandfather, years earlier. He warned her that the deeds to Mandalong would need to be safe and that the gold mine would increase the interest of people who had ill intent. This meant that the challenge to keep the title was even greater than before, as itinerant contractors continually moved to the area to mine before moving back to the cities. It was these tradespeople, her grandfather claimed, to be the most questionable of characters. They were often running away from someone or something, he told her, or had done a stint in the 'lock-up'. He had told her to take care, and to always be 'on the lookout'. Lucy had held on to the moment, remembering the times she would share with him. She missed him being there for her. She imagined for a moment him being there beside her.

The rain now beat heavily upon Lucy as she recollected her day. It had been intense, and she had become so exhausted that sleep was too far from her to catch it. Instead, her mind played tricks upon her; making her feel vulnerable. For the first time, Lucy heard the night noise; it fell as a backdrop to her inaudible screams. She shuddered, as she realised how isolated this homestead had now become.

The wind rose as the temperature fell, causing the shutters to bang against the walls of the homestead. Shales fell from the roof above and night owls hooted as they tried to find peace. That evening, each noise kept her a slave to her bed. Then, without a moment to lose, Lucy sprang to her feet and crept bare-footed to the door. The violent wind pushed harder, moving in every direction and with increased intensity. The thunder and lightning flashed noticeably across the sky.

Lucy knew that Baxter was in town, so she was not expecting company until morning. She fought back her fear as she moved quietly along the corridor. The door to the second bedroom was open. The safe was within this room. Opening the door slightly, she observed a shadow out in the hallway. Her heart jumped violently, as she pulled her body towards the bedroom. She moved behind the open doorway to observe that the curtain was blowing, and a dark figure was now entering the room. He had a hood over his head, so Lucy believed it was the same intruder who now had returned to double his chances. What designs did he have on her, or on the property?

Lucy felt a hand on her shoulder. She knew her grandfather was protecting her. Her breathing was laboured while her heart stopped briefly. Feeling faint, she now slid sideways across the darkened room. As her eyes adjusted, she became startled. Then, out of nowhere, a torchlight shone into her eyes. Temporarily blinded, she reached outward toward the assailant, knocking a rife from the wall above to the bed below. Her eyes re-adjusted, and there, standing over her in the dark, were the eyes of the intruder. The stale and acrid smell of cigarettes and alcohol was noticeable as he breathed heavily down upon her. He grunted noisily, grabbing her by the arm and then pushing her toward the bed. He fell upon her as if possessed. His body was heavy, and she laboured to move from under it. Lucy moved awkwardly from beneath the assailant and tried to reach for the rifle that lay alongside them. She pushed herself to the side and used her arms to move above him. Lucy stretched herself upward with all her might as the intruder tore the clothes from her body. The intruder then propped himself up as he stood over her. Her eyes had adjusted to the darkened room, and she could see his face clearly. His dark eyes looked into hers and left her spellbound; he seemed evil, and she knew that she had to do something quickly.

Within seconds, everything changed and the air around her became heavy. The bullet fired into the shoulder of the assailant. The sound barrier instantaneously broke from around her, as red-pitted images hit the walls. She could see his image falling in front of her. The red blood turned black as it hit the walls, and the odorous smell claimed the room briefly. Stunned and bloodied, the large open wound noticeable, as the bullet had hit at close range. She dropped the gun to the floor and held her face in her hands.

By this time, Red had come over to investigate the commotion. Lights and noises had alerted him to trouble and then, of course, the gunshot. The police arrived hours later. The intruder was now taken from his hold in the shed, where he had been hand and foot tied, a little more securely than expected. Jack and Mary soon returned to the station in a convoy of trucks, with locals gathering from the district to support Lucy in her hour of need. This had been the second home invasion within a matter of days, so Lucy now kept the deeds to Mandalong at the bank. At times like this, Lucy noticed how her father had continued to provide the security she needed.

The months following the invasion were onerous. It was not until the local Indigenous Council meeting took place in November 1992, that Jack and his daughter began to feel more comfortable. With the authorities on the side, the protection of the Tanami community at Mandalong became assured.

The Council mapped out the events to date, signifying the contribution the Council had played in establishing sustained growth and productivity through mining agreements. The financial burden of the past was now lifted, and the transfer of land would be won back to the Indigenous peoples. Legal services advised the Council that the intervention of the government had provided recognition and approval. **(5)**

The committee believed that mining in this region was of great significance because of the mutually beneficial relationship it afforded to both parties. The mining companies benefitted from the extraction of gold on Indigenous terms, and the Tanami people benefitted through royalty payments. **(6)** Tourism featured as the mining company was keen to reveal the now 'clean' program they had put into practice. **(10) (11)** This brought additional funds to the traditional owners.

The wind howled and the sheets flapped loudly on the clothesline. Magpies squawked in packs above, and the birds flew off noisily, searching for cover. The gust of hot dusty air grabbed the windows and shook them fiercely, the gates clanged together outside, and the roll call bell seemed to clang indefinitely. Coughs of air burst out into the open quad in front of the home to carry with it the leaf litter and dead twigs of the sweltering summer. Lucy walked home to prepare her evening meal.

"Introspection often occurs when momentous events have been delivered simultaneously and in rapid succession," Lucy read that night when feigning sleep.

For Lucy, there had been disruptions over the past months, and these had caused her severe anxiety. Her response was to spend an increased amount of time thinking about work rather than removing herself from it. Her work had increased and there seemed to be minimal time to complete tasks. At night, she would experience times when she would overthink her problems. Lucy wished she could share her time with someone, but that had become impossible. She had to think of a solution. She had previously dreamed of a holiday, but her parents were unable to take over until later that year.

One night, she removed herself from the bedclothes. She had not slept, so decided to sit in the open air. She made her way to the garden and lay down on the wicker armchair. Her body was stressed, her muscles were sore, and her head was too tired to think. She closed her eyes and enjoyed the quiet. The clouds dispersed across the darkened sky. They shielded the stars as if to protect her from their light. Her eyes were heavy, so she closed them softly. She imagined lying on a chair, but beneath her was a deck with a rolling ocean. She felt the symbiotic movement of the waves. She lay there for a time until her eyes opened at last. Lucy returned to her feet, feeling refreshed. She returned to her bed and enjoyed a deep sleep like that she had never experienced.

Sometimes we experience awakenings instantaneously, and at other times they appear in stages. This time, Lucy was confronted in her sleep with a tapestry of visions from her past. She remembered the painting, the one she had shown her uncle when he came to visit in 1983. Then she remembered the boxes that lay beneath the ground near the river. The two visions were connected, as the painting depicted these containers Abigail had collected and then stored away. The puzzle began to fit, and it became clear to her, that Millie had been trying to send her a message.

Lucy ran out of the gate to ride to the river to investigate further. Surely, Millie had something to show her, she must look again amongst her collection. The humidity was intense as it was now midday, and her lips felt sore as they were parched and broken. She pulled her kerchief up to her face and placed it over her nose to avoid the sunlight from doing any further damage. She also thought it may assist in helping her to avoid the dust when breathing. Her mind was swimming as she felt Millie with her. How could she have missed this message which was given to her so long ago?

Lucy became airborne as her horse jumped over a huge log which was obstructing her path. She continued until she reached her destination. Lucy held onto her mare as she led her to the river to drink. She then began to dig under the tree, discovering that the cloth which had been used to wrap the items was threadbare and unrecognisable. In front of her lay the tins, poorly held together, and rusted at the seams. It was then, that she knew which box to open. Fortunately, it was the least decayed and held another tin box within. Her eyes were drawn at once to what she had now in her hand, a brooch of significance. Luke had once told her that this piece of jewellery had been made from the gold at Mandalong. It had been beaten out to resemble a flower and William had arranged for it to be custom-made in Victoria, from several gold nuggets he had found on the property. William presented it to Kathleen, shortly after their fifth wedding anniversary. While it may not be worth a fortune, the brooch symbolised the love shared between the couple and the life they would begin to share with their extended family. For Lucy, this brooch was significant, as she believed it to be a cherished heirloom within her family.

The days were long and the heat intense, as Lucy completed the mustering. The cattle auction signalled a new season at Mandalong. Alternate activities would then resume to make ready for the breeding season which was drawing closer. Red and Jimmy now had their own partners, but they enjoyed special times with their friends while they were working. Red no longer slept in the shed alongside the homestead, but Baxter accepted residence in Daniel's room at the back. Lucy felt far more secure, as he in his quiet way, had supported her and given her the company she had, for so long craved. Although he appeared distant at times, he shared the cooking with her which meant friends could come over. She had endured a challenging time recently but had come out of that period understanding herself more and appreciating those around her. Lucy agreed with Roosevelt, *'A smooth sea does not make a skilled sailor.'* Her set of experiences, she thought, had taught her invaluable lessons. Lucy valued her abilities and had become more positive about her journey throughout life. Her demeanour was more approachable, and she now anticipated a bright and productive future.

As evening hit, the air became cold, dry, and motionless. Lucy lay in her bed as she turned her attention to the window. The blackened skies would have appeared more ominous, had it not been for the stars, as they appeared brighter than any sun. *They envelope you*, she thought, *they seem magnetic, pulling you towards them, as if holding you in a conversation.* Lucy pulled the rug closer to her body as she looked into the eyes of the sky. She felt comforted by the peace she saw before her, and quickly dozed off to sleep.

Her mind drifted off to sleep thinking of Philip, so it was not surprising that she was thinking of him when she woke. Lucy had only met him occasionally, but he had left his mark on her, and she was rightfully impressed.

Lucy often reflected upon her chance meeting one month ago, with Philip, a captain from Conair P/L. She remembered the morning she stood on the tarmac, waiting for supplies. It must have been last October. It was now September 1992. After the plane touched down, this tall, dark, and striking young man in uniform caught her eye. He communicated to airport staff and assembled packages in the cargo hold with authority. She noticed he had an angular face with a determined chin. Her mother had sometimes commented that a strong jawline meant resilience and commitment. It may have been an 'old wives' tale', but for now, it suited her that she recalled the comment. Lucy found she was drawn to him, and very shortly the two exchanged a brief conversation. They had much in common, she thought. The attraction became stronger as she spoke to him. After he returned to the cabin to make his departure, she believed in her heart she would see more of him. She quietly promised herself to try to meet him again.

Lucy was exhausted, as life at Mandalong was demanding and she had for years, fallen asleep too late and woken far too early. Her private life was non-existent. Every day was a challenge, so the problems were hers alone to face and conquer. The station was now exporting top-quality merchandise; the beef was highly sought after in top restaurants throughout Australia and overseas. Lucy now had the opportunity to travel nationally to promote her product. She could escape from the pressure of managing the station but continue her administrative role from a distance.

It was on one such occasion that Lucy stumbled upon Philip, quite by accident in the waiting lounge at Sydney airport. She was about to place her orders for stock feed and supplies that afternoon and planned to resume her return trip to Mandalong via Katherine that evening. All that was about to change. Upon seeing Lucy, Philip walked over to catch her attention and sit down with her briefly. She looked up from her laptop and turned to see him approaching. He was again in uniform and looked extremely smart. After a brief hug, they began to relax in each other's company.

"So, Lu!" Philip enquired. "It just occurred to me that, if you're not doing anything special today, you might like to accompany me to the city."

"I have places to show to you, 'haunts' if you like, that I enjoy visiting when I have the time," he added.

Lucy tried not to reveal the excitement she felt as she gazed at him. They both set off for what would be a memorable adventure together. They learned about each other as the day progressed. Philip had lived within the vicinity of the city, completing his education at a GPS school and then at Sydney University. He had studied engineering, but had decided eventually to follow his passion, which was flying and so became a commercial pilot, working in remote communities of the Northern Territory. He had one relationship in his early twenties, but it had not lasted, due to distance problems as he was based in Darwin. Like Lucy, he had become busy completing major contracts. This had brought him considerable notoriety within the air transport industry.

Born in 1967, Philip was an only child, born to Italian parents who had migrated after the war and moved from the western suburbs of Sydney, shortly after immigrating from northern Italy. Philip spoke well, having led the debating team at university and in various amateur productions in his local theatre. Philip was enthusiastic about the environment, often engaging in debates at the university on liberal economic policies. He had recently supported his local government for a position in council in the electorate of Darwin. He had told her that he had been taught to cook Italian food by his mother, and he liked to practice his cooking by sharing great dinner parties with his friends. His parents were comfortable, as they enjoyed dabbling in the share market and money was not a problem.

Philip was gregarious and enjoyed the company of others. His sense of humour was noticeable as he could turn the conversation over to laughter very often. His greatest charm was in his ability to make others feel important. Philip was confident that Lucy would not be an exception. Lucy was equally delighted to find that within a short space of time, Philip had shown that he shared her interest in the property at Mandalong and volunteered his services in mustering the stock by air.

The days that followed were memorable. This time away, allowed her to understand the man who had captured her heart. Philip had told her that since moving to the Northern Territory, he had always tried to visit his parents whenever he was in Sydney. Anna and David lived on the Northern Beaches, a home that looked out over the harbour. Anna had made Lucy feel comfortable. She explained that since moving into the neighbourhood thirty years ago, the area had changed considerably. Lucy found Anna very gracious, realising from the outset that each of them enjoyed the other's company.

Lucy had learned things about her future mother-in-law and her life's history was contrary to any she had heard at Mandalong. Born Anna Blankenstein, she was one of two daughters born to Kurt and Elke, who had escaped Italy in 1939 as their country joined forces with Nazi Germany. This period had been difficult for Anna's parents. Lucy would understand later, that, as a Jew, Anna had experienced hardship and segregation, and it was for this reason, that she remained 'tight-lipped' about her childhood. It would be Anna's sister who would tell Lucy about the difficulties of that period. She reminded Lucy how much it meant to her parents to have the freedom here that they had lost in their homeland so long ago. The family would experience a menial existence after leaving Germany, living in France for a time, before eventually migrating to Australia in 1946. Anna met David soon after she arrived and within months they were married. David worked two jobs to support his family in Canley Vale, and eventually became mayor, this being memorable as he would later have a street named after him. Shortly after, he moved with his family to the Northern Suburbs, where he built himself the home they now shared with Philip.

Philip and Lucy explored the North Shore one morning, walking the promenade of Manly Beach before removing their shoes to dig their feet well into the sand. They held hands, as they bounded up to the waves. Philip took a sideways glance at Lucy before diving into the surf, the waves pushing his body through to the crest. Then he surged forward, the force of the waves pushing him closer towards the beach. With his energy renewed, he shook the water from his body and mounted the beach, his hair swept back behind his brow. Philip felt at home here, as it was the beach to which he frequented as a teenager. He enjoyed it as it offered him the surf that Balmoral Beach lacked.

Philip and Lucy realised that they had a short amount of time to organise themselves before making a home at Mandalong. This meant that they would have to make a trip to town to organise paperwork; meetings with accountants, and trading partners who organised the export of their product at Mandalong. The day came at last. It was long, and Lucy finally decided to meet up with Philip sometime later. She would catch the train to find an outfit for the impending engagement party. They had lunch together at Centrepoint Tower and then went their separate ways, promising to meet up in a couple of hours. Lucy caught the 1.35 p.m. train to Strathfield, to travel the remaining distance by bus to Leichhardt. She remembered how fondly her grandfather felt about trains, and how he would often talk about them.

"It's not always about timetables, Lucy," he would say. "Without the engineering, the 'points and shunting', the trains would not carry us around as they do today," he would remind her.

"It is a necessary feature of this travel, as trains cannot turn around," he added. His face would become animated as he spoke about them, of course expecting that she too, would be as enthusiastic to hear about these details as he. It was shortly after she remembered these details, that everything changed for Lucy, a change that would affect her life forever.

It came upon her suddenly. A vision of petticoats ran before her. The image captivated her as it brought back memories. It reminded her of someone, but she could not tell who. Was her mind playing tricks on her? Who was this girl and where had she met her? Almost immediately, Lucy became lost in her thoughts as her mind passed over the events, she had experienced so many years before. She found herself entranced by this apparition. She was looking at Millie, but she was no longer a young girl, but her teenage self. Then Lucy's mind became clearer. As the fog lifted, Lucy found herself remembering the young cousin she loved so fondly, and the memories began to flow.

The young girl passed Lucy, papers flying in the air as she stumbled down the platform staircase. Millie then dashed forward, falling heavily onto the platform seat. Lucy took her train ticket from the window and returned her gaze to Millie. She knew there was a considerable time difference, but what if Millie had defied time too?

Millie's face looked up at Abigail. Lucy fell into the deep ebony eyes looking kindly up towards her. Millie's hair was dark and sat in bunches at either side of her face, with blue ribbons that extolled her good looks. She smiled broadly, bursting out with an occasional cheeky laugh, as she played with her 'cat's whiskers', a game she played by turning wool. Millie was swinging her legs uncomfortably before her, just as she had done in the past. She had always swung her legs beneath her when she sat at the dinner table. It made Abigail wonder how she could concentrate on eating and swinging her legs at the same time. Millie wore a laced-front, starched cotton blouse with puffy sleeves, and a dark blue pinafore which reached below her knees. Her stockinged feet were covered in laced-up boots, but Lucy knew that Millie would take every opportunity to remove these when she could. She much preferred running bare-footed across the ground.

Lucy remembered her friend and cousin from all those years gone by. Was it possible then, that as she herself had stepped into the past so long ago, Millie too, had joined her friend into the future?

Lucy could not stop recollecting the special times they enjoyed. She loved it when Millie shared secrets; she would move in close to Abigail with her hand upon her face and whisper softly into her ear. Her soft curls fell around her face of an evening when she ran to the hot bath in the kitchen. She would then get into her nightdress which sat around her, appearing to be far too large for her lithe body. Millie would then gather her attire up and run down the corridor, jumping into bed by falling heavily upon it, and then, lifting the feathered eiderdown above and over her head. She would then magically coerce Abby to join her, and each would be laughing together for a time before they fell asleep.

Lucy walked up to Millie and sat down beside her friend. No words were possible as she felt stunned by the events that had transpired that day. Lucy sat there in thought for a moment, but the grey noise around her was making it too difficult to think.

Then, between her forefinger and thumb, Lucy noticed that Millie had been rolling a marble, white and blue in colour. She held it firmly for a time, before placing it away in her pinafore pocket. Lucy vaguely recollected the marble, as she remembered her rolling it between her fingers.

Lucy found herself in between the earth and this lighter place. She could not explain it, but she knew there was something special about the connection she had with the earth and those who lived on it. She knew she had a gift and that it was special. Then, before she could open her mouth and speak to Millie, a whistle, a screech, and a yell came from the conductor in front of her. Millie rushed forward with her case full of papers and the door opened, the train then leapt forward, noisily left the platform, and was then out of sight. Lucy sat for a time contemplating her lack of action. Had she been dreaming? Did this mean that what happened to her all those years ago could happen again? And yes, the experience was not a dream. It really did happen!

The bench was bare, as Millie had disappeared and there was no evidence that she had ever arrived. Lucy moved desperately forward to examine any piece of evidence that might prove that this was not a vision. There, before her, lay upon the bench, to the left of where Millie had been sitting, a small key, the sort that would wind a music box. Lucy picked it up swiftly and placed it in her purse. It would remain there, she thought to herself, until she was home at Mandalong. She would keep it to remember Millie, Samuel and all their family. She believed she would be close to them forever.

As Lucy alighted from the train on the way back home, she reminded herself that things should go back to normal, but in her heart, she carried with her, the spirit of Millie, and used her energy to go forward. She returned to Philip, and they made their way to the Northern suburbs that evening. She felt that it was important to stay tight-lipped about her encounter as she feared that Philip might think she was crazy, should she tell him.

Lucy and Philip did not waste time, and within weeks they were celebrating a brief engagement party with friends from the aviation industry. Every day was eventful, as they prepared for their new life at the station. They would return the following month to be married, and then, they would enjoy their lives together at Mandalong as Mr and Mrs Stanford.

Back at Mandalong, Lucy ignored the work for one morning as her focus was on finding a home for the key she had found. Her curiosity became aroused after she thought she heard the clock on the mantlepiece chime. The only reasonable explanation was that the key might fit the clock which had been handed down through the family. She looked up above the fireplace to the mantlepiece. The clock was brought out from Scotland by William and Kathleen. She carefully pulled the large clock from its place above her and placed it on the dining room table. The encasement within had stood the test of time until now.

Lucy was clenching the key between her fingers, then without delay, opened her hands to reveal its contents. The glass window revealed the workings of this intricately carved mahogany clock. Lucy viewed the lock on the door and placed the key inside. To her delight, it fitted. She turned the key around in the lock and the door opened. She would now adjust the time and then turn the mechanism from behind with the barrel. As she reached within, she felt something at the bottom of the encasement. It was a piece of paper. Lucy was apprehensive as she pulled out a chair from the dining table and sat down to read.

Dear Abby,

I am this morning, writing to tell you that I have missed being with you. Your friendship has always meant so much to me.

It has been years since we have been together, and my heart is constantly pining as I wish to see you again, sweet Abby. You are missed by all of us here, but my loss is greater, since you are a sister to me.

My father, Samuel told me you have a special place in our family and that you will never leave us. I look for you every day and hope you are well.

Ruby often reflects on your good humour and patience and awaits the day that she can introduce her new family to you. She was married on her eighteenth birthday to her sweetheart Ernest, and they have a small, but thriving family of five. She has been actively involved with the Emancipation of Women and travelled to the city of Melbourne in 1884 to protest. She considers herself a Suffragette with a cause.

My mother, Brigitte, has told me that my grandmother was from the local Indigenous tribe, and that her parents had known Samuel, my father, since he was a small boy. Did you know that makes us both Blackfella? **(14) (15)** *Now I know why the spirit dancers often visit you.*

Abigail, if you are reading this, then you have found my letter. I know where you are, but I have found it difficult to reach you. Quite by accident, I have visited you often in that other world, but you have only once recognised me. I saw you once at the railway station, but I could not talk to you. You look so much older, and all grown. In my hands, I carried the letters of your cousins, but I was not able to hand them over to you once we met. Instead, I placed mine in the carriage clock, and if you are reading this letter now, I am pleased that you have found it.

I have not been able to communicate with you, as our worlds would not let us. I fear it is not to be, and therefore, sweet Abby, I look forward to seeing my sister 'Bunty', **(16) (17)** *in heaven with all the angels.*

I am to be married to William 'Billy' Child next spring, and will call my first daughter Abigail, after you.

Your loving cousin and friend,
Millicent Roddick
17th August 1885

Lucy felt as if a weight had been lifted. She felt breathless as she knew that the adrenaline in her body had climbed significantly. She sat down to compose herself. Not only had she been in touch with her dear Millie, but the letter had placed her within the Roddick ancestral fold once again. Lucy missed them more than ever. Millie had not only confirmed the family's great love for her, but she had reaffirmed the ancestral ties Lucy had with the traditional owners of Mandalong. This news validated her. The future looked bright for all who were invested in this great land.

Lucy placed the grand clock back onto the mantelpiece after setting the time carefully, however, her mind was not on the clock, it was on Millie. She was, for a brief time, distracted as she saw a blue and white marble inside the encasement of the carriage. Tears came to her eyes, as she picked it up carefully and held it in her hand. Lucy became determined to find out what had happened to Millie. The search was not in vain, as at the bottom of the tall wooden bookcase, sat the Child's family bible. She pulled it carefully from the shelf and carried it to the table. Lucy opened its pages to find the family tree. Manuscript handwriting revealed the names and dates that were so familiar to her. Then the name that she saw at last made her temporarily stop breathing. Millicent Roddick died in 1926. She had three children, the eldest named Abigail. Inside the bible was a family photograph. Claude, her eldest child was not present as he had left Mandalong to work in Sydney. Lucy considered Millie to have had a pleasing life but would have liked to have seen her again. She sat down to reflect on the girl she knew as Millie and the impact she had made on her life. Lucy would never forget the sweet girl who made her laugh.

There would always be a mystery surrounding the life of her dear friend, but Lucy felt that since this precious timepiece was now operational, she could wind the clock regularly and have something in the house, that reminded her of Samuel and his family. It also served as a reminder that she had been transported to that special place with her ancestors.

Life for the couple had become insanely busy, and the two of them rarely saw each other as their jobs got in the way. Philip was absent rather than in attendance, as his work carried him to all parts of the state. He would do a surveillance of the property from the air, as jackaroos would manage the musters from below. The couple cherished time away together, so they hatched a plan which made it possible for Philip to retain his position flying planes for Conair, while still enjoying himself in Lucy's company.

One Thursday morning in January, Philip taxied into the runway at Mandalong. He had recently organised its service for the day and was confident it was ready for the long trip ahead.

His responsibility lay with the communities to the far north of the Territory, in particular. His travel plans to Katherine would be to pick up laboratory samples for pathology, before flying out to Maningrida to deliver much-needed supplies. This settlement depended upon barge links with Darwin, but when the weather made the voyage difficult, the people became isolated and, needed to be serviced by air transport. Philip had suggested Lucy come with him as the time together would be assured and they could stay over if she wished. This would mean that the flight might be rough due to the inclement weather, but the trade-off would make it worth it. Lucy would have Philip by her side.

The morning was clear, and take-off went to plan. Lucy had brought her overnight bag together with delicacies to share mid-flight. Their trip was smooth for the next couple of hours, until landing in Katherine. Before take-off, Philip became informed about the perilous skies above. He was not fazed and persevered with his flight plan. Philip manoeuvred his plane so that he would avoid the heavier clouds, and in time was able to recover lost flight time. After a couple of hours, he landed for the first stop-over for the day. With provisions loaded again, they took off along the runway without incident. The trip only showed signs of problems as they approached the outer reaches of Mataranka as gusts of air were shooting forth from under the aircraft and carrying it forward, before dropping it heavily metres below. These thermal pockets, together with great gusts of wind, brought sporadic rain, making the trip uncomfortable, and at times dangerous. It was now that Lucy realised the expertise Philip demonstrated when flying. He comforted her at times as he knew the trip was a difficult one and he reassured her at all stages.

The landing was difficult. If it had not been for the load on board, the touchdown could have been riskier. In weather such as this, the weight on board is essential as, if correctly balanced, it prevents the wind from lifting the craft and flipping it over.

Philip walked to Lucy's side of the plane and escorted her to the hangar nearby. *So, this is Maningrida,* she thought to herself. She had been impressed with the white sand and turquoise water she viewed from the air but paid little attention to it while on board. Lucy knew there was a crabbing industry here run by the locals. Operating as a department-run Aboriginal settlement, the residents worked here as export demanded. This industry turned over a recognisable income for the locals. This money went back into the community, so it was a viable option for all.

Philip took Lucy's hand to walk past the terminal and venture towards the water. He had spent the afternoon unloading the cabin of the Cessna and now he was taking his fiancé to visit the beach. They would be staying that evening at the Superintendent's residence which had recently become vacant. They left their bags inside the gate, and walked down the sandy path that led to the water. The day had been hot, and they both welcomed this relaxing outing. Lucy dipped her swollen feet in the water and the waves washed them with the cool salty liquid. Philip took her hand again and they strolled the length of the beach in search of shells. They managed to collect a couple, but Lucy later replaced them by the water's edge. She felt guilty taking these pearls from the sea. Instead, they walked to the co-op and bought crabs. They later ate the tasty soft flesh with the bread and butter that Lucy had brought with her from home.

The pair sat and drank wine with their meal. Sprawled on the throw, they later laid back to take in the setting. The water birds were present, returning from the islands in the distance to feast on the diet the oceans served here.

"Philip. I have these small pastries I learned how to make

with your mum. She said they are your favourite?" Lucy enquired.

"Not the 'crow's feet'?" he asked in good humour. He laughed intermittently as he grabbed one, and scoffed it down with hot coffee. "They are croissants, Philip! How long have you been calling them 'crow's feet'?" She laughed.

"Always called them that, Lu!" he exclaimed with a mouthful of pastry. "Thanks, haven't had these for years!"

For a while, both dozed off as the air was more comfortable. When they woke to the soft breeze blowing from offshore, they realised that since they had landed, the weather had been more kind. They appreciated this gift as it set them up for a special day. The residence was small in comparison to their home, but it was cute, and they looked forward to an intimate time together.

Early the next morning, Philip and Lucy took off to collect the mail from Katherine. The flight in the Cessna was uneventful, so the couple relaxed as they sped off in a southerly direction. The day was bright and clear, and Philip knew Lucy would love the adventure he had organised. A taxi took them down to the river, where they alighted and began walking towards an open boat. It held at least twenty passengers, and they made their way to the back.

Lucy was so grateful that they could share this trip together. They travelled along the extent of the river, finishing eventually at the Gorge. Lucy had never seen anything more beautiful. She and Philip gazed into each other's eyes and became moved by the experience. They knew this would be one of these memories that would last forever. On the return trip, Lucy and Philip exchanged loving thoughts with one another. They believed that this time would be special, and looked forward to their impending marriage in September.

The wedding took place in a small ceremony at Saint Clement's Mossman Church on the fourth of September 1995, followed by a small gathering at Philip's home on the North Shore. The latter affair was composed of a closed group of family and friends: Anna, David, Mary and Jack, Uncle Rick, Sandra, Eliza and Robyn, Janet, and Cathy and then of course, Max Cameron, the legal representative for Mandalong Inc. Sitting at the top of the guest list had been Jimmy, Winnie, Maisie, and Red. They had turned out in new outfits, all looking very noticeable as their colourful attire became a conversation piece amongst all the guests. Jimmy and Red had their hair slicked down smooth against their scalp and Lucy wondered about the quantity of hair tonic Red would have needed, to make his curls comply with the comb.

"You look amazing!" exclaimed Lucy to Jimmy and Red. "Thanks for coming all this way. It means so much to Philip and me," she added.

The four of them were overly excited, although they did understand that they would not be able to spend time with Lucy, their friend. That did not phase her friends though, as they knew they could explore the city later and find novel places to interest them.

Lucy placed her friends at a table with Janet and Cathy as their families would not be accompanying them. They all knew each other, and it did not take long for the friends to be sharing laughs and enjoying the entertainment.

Flowers adorned the lounge and the back area, and the meal was catered for by a local Italian restaurant. Men in black suits served cocktails and trays of appetisers. The three-course meal followed outside in a pavilioned area, while a small orchestra played in the background. Philip and Lucy would return to

Mandalong the following day, looking forward to a life together as husband and wife.

Turbulence followed them for the flight home. The pockets of wind held the aircraft up with its mighty hands, and then, dropped it below to hit the clouds. Lucy imagined for one moment that these unforeseen weather events could be prophetic and that she should take care moving forward. She held Philip's hands carefully and sank into his body. He played with her hair as they sat together laughing, and Lucy quickly left her fear behind.

That night, the cicadas throttled outside the bedroom window, as they spoke in hushed tones and shared secrets. He was a good fit because he believed in her and comforted her when she needed love. He listened and offered advice when she asked for it. She in turn provided the safe place for him. She hoped that with Philip by her side, life at Mandalong would be less challenging, and together they would carve out a new life together.

It was Sunday, in the middle of March, and exceedingly humid. The sky was an intense blue and the rains had filled the water tanks to the brim, the excess spilling over the sides and into the garden below. Reg was busy raking the needles on the dirt paths surrounding the homestead, something he had done for decades. His tired old body was slower now, but he was determined to complete his project as usual. Martha, his wife had been to visit the Roddicks, but these outings were inconsistent now, as she was experiencing failing health. This time, Lucy would complete her day by visiting Martha and reading to her as she had done so often in the past.

Lucy approached Martha's bedside and reached out to hold her hand. She was in bed and struggling to breathe.

"I am here for you now, Martha. Now, it is my turn. Hold my hand and I will not leave you," she whispered. Lucy then knelt beside her and held her closely.

The time was soon approaching when Martha would be with her Maker, but she did not fear, as she had a solid faith and was prepared to meet him. Martha took one last deep breath, before looking up into Lucy's eyes. Martha then tried to sing to her, as she had done when Lucy was a young girl. The words were still unfamiliar, but this time, Lucy recognised that the rhythm of her heart was beating in time with the music. Lucy then read to Martha and kissed her. Martha let out a contented sigh as she squeezed Lucy's hand tightly, closed her eyes softly, and fell into a deep sleep.

Lucy learned the following morning that Martha never woke from her eternal sleep that evening. She felt relieved that her comforter and friend would now be free from pain. Lucy felt an extreme sense of loss, as Martha had treated her as her very own and this love was incredibly special.

Lucy now sensed the impact of women within her life and knew that they had all made a difference. There was Kathleen, who bravely accompanied her husband out to Australia as a pioneer; Ruby who stood bravely for the rights of the 'fairer sex'; and Millie, whose 'love of life' inspired all who knew her. Then there was her mother Mary, and Martha, who supported her as she set out to make a life for herself, and of course, Rebekah, who discovered the healing power of transformation. These women served others and never lost hope as they journeyed forward. Lucy now knew, her transition from childhood was complete. 'Like footsteps in the sand.' Mrs Lucinda Stanford-Roddick would now, like them, leave a lasting impression, hopefully fulfilling the plan that had been written for her all those years ago.

PART II

Chapter 9
Reflections

The rain washed down the entire wall of the sterile hospital windows, the light still showing forth within. Lucy looked up from her bedclothes. She lay third in line from the door to the corridor. She had a prize view of the world outside.

I moved towards her slowly, carrying the books that I had promised. Lucy looked pale as she struggled to sit upright. Her eyes were on me as she turned to find a chair. We exchanged small talk at first, but then the conversation turned. Lucy asked me if I had been to Mandalong. I paused and examined my words carefully as I stole a sentence from my head. I had been to Mandalong, but I thought it's best not to mention that Philip was in hospital with her, and not at home as she expected.

What Lucy did not know would not hurt her, at least for today. Philip and Lucy had crash-landed his helicopter at the five-mile intersection. There had not been time to call the air ambulance and wait, so those who attended the crash had decided to take them by road to Katherine. Philip was critical and the trip delayed his healing as he needed intensive medical procedures. He had no memory of the accident, nor it would seem of the last few months, and it became clear that his road to recovery would be an extensive wait. For Lucy, the journey would be less radical medically, but psychologically more intricate. For now, at least, nothing had changed on the station but her loved ones there were waiting patiently for her return.

My instincts were that Lucy would want to know the truth about her predicament, but it was not the right time to tell her, as her place was in her hospital bed where she could receive the best counselling. Days turned into weeks, and Philip had left the intensive care ward and could travel for short visits elsewhere. He would soon be visiting Lucy who needed his reassurance.

Shortly after lunch, one Sunday morning, Lucy woke up to see Philip's face in front of her own. She opened her arms out to him. It was then that she realised, that he was in a wheelchair and then it hit her. He had not stayed at Mandalong to manage the station; he had been physically unwell for a time. She turned to me as she watched helplessly. Philip held my hand as I told Lucy why we had kept his pain a secret. We felt it was important that both felt protected, for in revealing the truth, each of them could become vulnerable. Lucy understood, and so both of us followed the discussion with a group hug.

"Anna?" Lucy called out as I was leaving the room. "Would you mind taking Philip home with you when he leaves the hospital tomorrow?"

"Of course," I called back to her. "I do not need to be asked to have my son with me for a few days before he returns to Mandalong."

"Well, it is settled then," Lucy remarked. "I will continue concentrating on getting better, and then we can both go home."

"Not without me!" I called out from the other side of the room. "You will need me to help you get around."

"Thank you, Anna," Lucy added. "I don't know what I would have done without you."

Lucy kept her mind active, keeping abreast with the ledgers from Mandalong and occasionally reading the novels she had never had a chance to read when she was younger. Her mind would naturally catch up with the events that had preceded this accident, and she would find herself questioning her motivation to move forward. Then, she would look back at her life and remember the good times, the feeling she had when her two sons were born, the special ties she had with her community, her love of the bush, and of course Mandalong. She appreciated Philip and the amount of effort he was taking to restore her health and well-being. He often brought her flowers and would sit alongside her bed and read letters to her. Friends too, would often write and encourage her to get well. Then there were the times she played her life back to herself. Philip had retrieved her diaries, and she read these with anticipation.

January 1995

As a young girl in the outback, there were seldom opportunities to dress up and look like a lady, as the daily attire warranted comfortable clothing for a day in the saddle. Distant were the days, when my mother would sew my special dresses and I constantly looked forward to ordering a party dress to mark an important occasion.

I now believe, that there should not be a reason to dress up; that a girl should dress as she felt, and this could be something different each day of the week. It was for this reason I embarked upon getting not one dress, but a couple. I smile as I write, because I remember one dress that caught my attention when I was fourteen. It was presented to me on the window of St. Kilda dress shop; it was bright, having horizontal and vertical red and white stripes. The boldness of the outfit demonstrated how I was feeling about myself and life in general.

Lucy Stanford Roddick

September 1996

Lying back in the warm bath, I recollected the past months as I prepared for my baby. As I moved my arms up from the warm water and onto my swollen belly, I smiled. Just then, I saw from the corner of my eye, a large dark eagle fly above me. My spirit animal had surfaced to send me a message. I gained an inner strength at these times, as these peacemakers were never far away. My journey had become a testament to the faith of my forebears; the sojourn into unfamiliar territory had not yet concluded.

Then the heavens opened and moved the spirit dancers over to welcome the ancestors of old. Songs of Thanksgiving showered from the sky. The clouds opened to one last burst of light, appearing with a final and glorious array of iridescent colour that rippled within, then darkness, total and deafening.

Lucy Stanford Roddick

October 1999

Angus and Edmund are growing up quickly. Angus has an enquiring nature and keeps us on our toes as he is always having little adventures. We have often had someone deliver him back to us, after he has had a long walk in the bush. Fortunately, the folk here are always on the alert, ready to assist in any emergency. While Edmund is much smaller, he too, can get himself into all sorts of trouble. One morning, we found him on the floor of the kitchen with an opened milo tin in front of him. He was spooning it out in heaped spoonfuls and there was chocolate flavouring from one end of the room to the other, where he had crawled and left a trail. All this, and it was only three a.m. in the morning.

Lucy Stanford Roddick

Lucy looked up from her diary. She laughed as she read, remembering each time as if it were yesterday. Lucy was thankful that she had recounted these events at each stage of her life.

Life had been simple in the early years, but since the near-fatal accident which nearly claimed the lives of both their parents, Angus and Edmund discovered a new independence from within, and this had consequences for all of us. Lucy and Philip eventually returned to Mandalong and life for them became familiar as they resolved the daily problems of station life.

Lucy, although busy, knew she was blessed, as her young family were her inspiration. The independence that she experienced when she was younger had now evolved into a life of dedication and commitment. She was no longer autonomous but had to ascertain whether her decisions were always appropriate for her family. Their lives were the centre of her universe; every decision was solely about them.

Angus and Edmund loved to run out and play each day as Lucy completed the household chores. Her house-girl would then take over, so she could join Philip in the paddock. She enjoyed these times because it felt like business as usual, and she was always ready for a ride. Recently, she had been grieving the loss of her special companion, Ned, her gelding of thirteen years. He had been her constant source of strength as she battled alone to manage the property with her father. She confided in Ned often in those quiet, lonely days. He had been there as she fought with the intruders and gave chase to the dingoes and wild boars that overstepped the boundary.

It was fortunate that at this time, she had Angus and Edmund, as they were the ones she would care for and protect. She often wondered how she might manage not having them around when she was older. She had heard how some mothers feel a great sense of loss after their children leave home. Lucy hoped that would never eventuate, and that she would be prepared for the natural progression of life, when both stepped out on their own into a new world. She knew she would be happy for them.

Lucy folded the washing from the laundry basket and sat down at the kitchen table to drink her coffee. She could hear her children playing outside. It would not be long before they would be attending the local school, and that day was fast approaching.

The family had recently flown down to be with the grandparents in Sydney, and this offered, both Philip and Lucy, the time to escape to their favourite 'haunts'. When they were not off doing quiet things as a couple, they took their sons to the beach. Here, they would play in the tidal pools, and catch small crabs that darted between the rocks. Other times, Angus and Edmund would watch their father surfing the waves, followed by a walk on the boulevard to have an ice cream. This had been a special holiday and contrasted briefly to their strict regimen of work back at home.

Angus had his bags packed weeks before he started school, and Edmund joined him at the preschool. This meant, that Lucy was free to decide her priorities. For now, at least, she would help Philip with the chores on the station and help with the work-life balance that went hand in hand with being a parent.

It was pleasing then, to see her boys leave home each morning when they finally began their education. They were accompanied by Ben, their new border collie puppy, who would jump up at their feet as they walked. Ben had been in a litter of dogs from Dan, the jackaroo. The children instantly attached themselves to Ben and were a team from the onset. Ben pulled at their laces as they walked to school, jumping erratically until they reached their destination, and finally landing on their shoes when they had stopped. Ben was always busy pulling, pushing, leaping, circling, and falling. His energy was in stereo performance, as he had both Angus and Edmund to impress. His fluffy black and white coat was soft to the touch, so he was always receiving a cuddle. His busy pink tongue would then hang from his mouth, as he would close his eyes and pant.

Each morning, Dan would collect Ben from the school to start him on patrol in the stockyard. From there, Ben would learn to muster and recognise his master's call. Ben would remain in the yards until sun up and then Philip would bring him home to Angus and Edmund.

Angus and Edmund enjoyed the routine of school, and it was not long before they boasted many friends and acquaintances. As they grew, they enjoyed hanging out with their mates at the water hole, just as Lucy had done before them. Angus was the sportsman and brought home the ribbons from the Athletics Carnivals, but Edmund kept himself occupied with quieter projects at home.

Ben had grown during the summer. He kept active at the station, but his performance was controlled as he followed the lead from Dan. He spent the evening quietly settled by the feet of the family and on the colder evenings, would sit in front of the fire with his head between his legs. Angus would play ball with Ben at times, but he was discouraged by Dan and Philip, as familiarity could, they warned, encourage playfulness and abandonment in the 'worker dog'. Angus and Edmund were fortunate to at last have their way as they in unison, expressed a concern at Ben being settled at night outdoors. Philip knew he may be risking Ben's obedience on the field, but relented, as he knew his boys found his removal from them to be challenging.

It was time to leave Mandalong for a long drive to Katherine and Lucy accompanied her sons, as they marched with their school in the Anzac Parade. Each of the students from the regional schools looked immaculate in their uniforms. Angus would be eleven at the end of the year, and Lucy knew she needed to start planning for the next part of their schooling.

Lucy read from her diaries again in earnest, smiling broadly as she remembered some of the details.

February 2004

Philip and I were attracted to each other as we held fast to similar morals and values. We understood that this was important to both of us, as we were constantly busy at the station, and it reassured us about our future.

During our marriage, we have grown together, and it has helped us to understand each other more. That relationship assisted our sons as they grew into adulthood. They both felt protected, nurtured, and valued. Our vision for Mandalong included our children, and this resolve, helped us to stay connected during difficult times. The challenges were testing to all of us; the seasons had been difficult, and stocks suffered noticeably. The impact of this stress on our lives was at times insurmountable, as we worked a twenty-four-hour timetable in these times of drought.

Recovering from pestilence was similarly fraught with difficulty. Fortunately, Angus and Edmund revealed their strength by assisting their father as he reinforced supplies, travelling at times long distances.

Both Angus and Edmund are growing fast and have taken to studies seriously. I have recently assisted the teacher and enjoy this work. This experience has also helped me to view my children mixing with their friends. I have also noticed that the classroom has certainly changed since I was young.

Lucy Stanford Roddick

April 2005

It is Easter, and I have just finished decorating the eggs with Angus and Edmund. They enjoyed painting the eggs, as it was a customary tradition in our home, as the decorations then go on display. A short morning at church completed the plans for the day, and then our family sat outside at the cedar table and ate the fish Philip and I had prepared for them.

We were all pleased with our salad garden, as it has provided so many refreshing greens for our meals. I can now competently grow produce and am determined to keep this interest, as I find it rewarding.

After our meal, we walked up to the holding yard, as we had seen something in the distance that caught our attention. To our right, there were kangaroos, with joeys, eating from the tufts of grass below. They seemed content. This was their home; they knew no other.

Lucy Stanford Roddick

Education was a priority, and for that reason, a boarding school had become a necessity. Of course, this meant Lucy and Philip would miss their sons during term time, but homeschooling was too difficult to manage. It was for this reason, that Philip asked me to put things in motion; to provide the details for a suitable school.

It was not long before the Scott's School in Sydney was selected. It not only provided lodging but was also a suitable distance for me to visit. The necessary preparations were made and by the end of the school holidays, Angus and Edmund had packed up and sent to their new lodgings. The following months moved slowly for them as there was an amount of adjustment necessary, but with time, they found the regimented timetable helpful, made friends, and experienced noticeable advances in their studies. They were also becoming leading athletes, representing their school in both rowing and fencing.

During holidays, I would arrange the complicated travel arrangements for Angus and Edmund to visit Mandalong after a small stay at our Mossman home. For Jack and Mary, their new home, while it was small, was adequate when their grandsons were visiting as each of them slept in a small, but comfortable lean-to at the back of the property. Occasionally, Jack and Mary would pack their own bags and visit Lucy, Philip, Angus, and Edmund, particularly during the holidays. They would then take Angus and Edmund on many adventures around the Northern Territory.

David, my husband, would often take Angus and Edmund sailing. The slip was moored at the spit, and they would take a picnic lunch with them. They would sail often until it was time to leave us for Mandalong. We would watch them take off from Mascot airport.

As time progressed, Lucy became aware that her energy levels were diminishing. It had been years since the accident, but her body had never recovered sufficiently. Her doctor blamed it on age, suggesting that the impact of life working in the cattle yards had possibly come to an end. The impact of balancing motherhood with the constant pressure of station life had taken its toll and Lucy now felt it was time to step back for lighter duties. Philip had taken on more responsibility, coordinating the profile of the business, which meant, he was away from home more often. This meant Lucy had more time to herself, as she had given the station hands much of her work.

Lucy often enjoyed relaxing at home. She would look out the large windows of her bedroom or sit in the shade of a tree. She would read with interest, catching up on the novels she had not read from her vast collection.

Days rolled into weeks, and the Stanford family had life taken on a different pace; one that was less demanding, and more centred around each other.

It was at this point that Lucy realised, that she was a very different person to the one who had grown up in the homestead all those years ago. She confided in Philip one evening.

"The time has drifted past me, Philip, and it seems that I spend longer reflecting on my memories than I would like," she mused.

"I now realise, that the first part of my life has been devoted to a cultural process of gaining my skills; the second, devoted to restoring my wholeness of life," she admitted.

Lucy was content within herself and believed her gift to view the past had helped her to understand herself more clearly, and to view those around her with perspective. Lucy placed her diaries beside her bed and turned over. She fluffed the pillows and sank into them. Her dreams could take her into the past. This was the healing she needed. She took a deep breath and drifted off to sleep.

It was February 2008, and it was the hottest time of the year. Philip had been working for weeks now at Mandalong, but it became increasingly difficult, so Eliza decided to join him at the station. Eliza arrived at the property with her companion, Robyn. They had been in a relationship now for three months, and they appeared to be serious. Robyn was a musician and spent her days working in a music store when she was not composing or recording. As she loved working in the kitchen, Robyn spent her days trying out new recipes for the crew. They all loved her food, and she was exceedingly popular, especially among the jackaroos, as she loved making them pocket pastries to eat on the run.

"Half the pastry is filled with savoury, and the other, with jam," observed Baxter. He opened the contents to destroy them as he ate.

"This is an old recipe from Wales. It was made by the miners' wives, so they could eat as they worked down under the ground. It provided a meal of meat and sweet biscuit all in one," advised Eliza. "…And all packaged in one, and tied in a handkerchief! For us, alfoil should suffice!"

"Then, where is my handkerchief?" enquired Red. They all laughed.

'The crew' did not want Robyn to leave because they said, they had enjoyed being this well-fed at work. Eliza too, was valuable, since she could very often keep up with the jackaroos at night, drinking beers as she would join them each evening to play snooker. Eliza was good at playing the game, and they felt comfortable sharing conversations with her as they spoke of their exploits and misgivings.

    Friday nights were important to the station hands as they used this time to reflect upon their week. Steak was on the menu, as it was naturally in good supply, and 'the crew' ate nothing much else, but Lucy and Eliza would insist upon an ample amount of healthy salad to accompany the plates. The beer was flowing, and the pool table became less popular as the night wore on. It would not be surprising for Lucy or Philip to find a body or two, stretched out in the yard the following morning. Their heads would very often be hidden beneath their broad-brimmed hat to shade them from the rising sun.

    Eliza was not as tall as her sister. Her dark hair was cropped short, and at work, she wore her suits with confidence, as she performed her legal duties in the city. She was a determined individual with a plan for life. She was confident, capable, and highly intelligent. Lucy was proud of her sister, considering her advice whenever she needed it. Since travelling south to complete her university degree, Eliza had achieved so much. She was now living in a self-contained unit in Newtown with Robyn. During the last few years, she had become a capable spokesperson, working tirelessly in the Legal Aid sector, and assisting those who needed her services.

    Eliza had travelled the world extensively and had conquered her fears, particularly the fear of the unknown. This, she felt, had an enormous impact on how she managed herself in court. She enjoyed taking on challenges, and problem-solving was never a task too difficult. Everyone knew Eliza to be an independent, self-made woman. She enjoyed having a purpose and accepting responsibility for the things she thought she could change. Her free time was often spent doing charity runs or in freelance work in Redfern. She had many friends and enjoyed meeting them on a Friday night at the local pub. Here, she would share her thoughts in discussions over topical issues.

Lucy felt extremely proud of her sister Eliza. She knew that her parents had been particularly impressed with the way she gave her time to others. She came face to face daily with those who experienced hardships; they were the marginalised few who had nowhere to turn. Take for instance, her first meeting with Irene. She had lived in a remote township and was married with three daughters. Her husband regularly displayed emotional abuse as he would often leave her without money or access to food. Then there was Katy, who had a philandering and often absent partner, that she would not receive his constant physical abuse any longer but was then violently attacked in front of her children. Since taking up practice in Redfern, Eliza also had clients who had their lives turned around. Robyn would often go down to the office and assist, as she was impressed by the work her partner was doing. She worked tirelessly for justice for women, but by far, her chief work was for those who suffered domestic violence from their partner or occasionally, offspring.

"Violence continues to give the power to the perpetrator," Eliza would remind us.

"It leaves the victim powerless and desperate. Gay partners are included in these statistics," she would insist, "and they remain highly represented in both male and female partnerships."

"The impact on these individuals is onerous," she claimed. "In some cases, the victims remain tight-lipped about their experience for decades. Once they confide openly, the mask can be removed and from there, healing is possible," she admitted.

Eliza was passionate about the issue of domestic violence, having seen evidence of the 'fallout upon these victims' within the court system. She was committed to her calling, as she felt there were too many who needed her support and guidance. Having a partnership herself that was strong, helped her as she wrestled with the intensity of each situation. Her resolve remained consistent. She reassured them in their hour of need that they were not alone.

Another concerning matter for her was the impact of assimilation policies, such as the 'Stolen Generation' upon Indigenous families.

"These children were forcefully removed from their families, the trauma playing out onto forthcoming generations," she claimed.

"This process of removal is still practised today, whereby the recipients frequently experience unnecessarily harsh conditions, limited education opportunities and, more importantly, removal from their cultural identity." Eliza would allege.

Philip had recently invested in a Cessna, a two-door plane to transport staff from the property when their weekly shifts were complete. Mandalong had also acquired a fixed livestock carrier to transport stock to the cattle yards. The business was progressing well, his agent was no longer needed. Philip's vision was to equip the station with its very own abattoir, but for now, spending more was out of the question.

Venturing back to the Territory to help at the station was exciting for Eliza. It was Philip who managed the aerial work, but Eliza would often tag him across the paddocks. Eliza had learnt to fly years before, and it was important that there was a coordinated approach when rounding the cattle. When Angus and Edmund were on a holiday, they would help Aunt Eliza with the groundwork, riding below her, to support the work she was doing. Once the stock became contained, Eliza would close the gate from behind and then attempt to locate any strays that may have missed the initial catch.

Mandalong was now on the share market, and shares were increasing annually and the export market demands kept the stock managers busy. Philip regularly attended the cattle auctions and at times, supervised cross-breeding practices to increase the quality of his stock. The vision for Mandalong had now become realised, as the stock had grown in number, and beef production was expanding. Lucy and Philip believed it was time to increase the stockmen at the station to support the extensive trading and market demands.

Lucy had lost weight in the last months and the flying doctor who visited, suggested she take regular strolls to keep her muscles in good condition. She was also handed a strict diet and Philip would supervise her as she consumed her porridge for breakfast each morning. It was on such a day after Philip had left for work, that Lucy decided to take her morning walk.

She adjourned quietly into the bedroom to complete her preparations for the day. She decided on a sleeveless summer frock, sensible walking shoes, and a broad-brimmed hat. She would take a small backpack with a book, a pair of reading glasses, an apple, and a water bottle.

Before long, Lucy was on her way. The day was cooler than was normal for this time of the year, she thought to herself. Her feet had not carried her this far for a time, but here she was, taking great strides out in the bush. She felt quite content and proud of herself. For once this summer, she was trying to step out of her comfort zone and continue forward. She believed that before too long, she would be back leading 'the crew' again in a station muster. For now, however, she had to concentrate on her exercise, as she believed for the first time in months that this was indeed possible. More now than ever, Lucy sensed the pull of the bush. As she walked, she felt that familiar tug she experienced so long ago.

Lucy was so happy. She had spent most of the day walking around the property when, all at once, her eyes looked up in wonder. The earth and the planets that held her in its orbit, paused briefly to shine upon her with love. The spirit dancers returned, and Lucy's heart beat a little faster. Coloured lights appeared out into the sky behind the clouds; softened hues of indigo, green and blue moved in circles up in the sky, before her. The breeze, now getting stronger, picked up the leaves and branches underfoot. Then, Lucy could see the waves of colour move with grace as they swept the horizon. As they touched the land, they spread out like wild creatures from above, prancing between the wind-swept clouds and the horizon. Chants, softly at first, then humming, and with time, becoming louder. Lyrical and melodic, the song of the bush and the stories of long ago. Then her eyes opened slightly, to reveal the dusk on the wind-swept open plain. The mulga bushes lay rolled out like thorny carpets in front of her.

At last, she approached the outer perimeter of the homestead. The wind howled as the water birds squawked in packs above. The gust of dusty air grabbed the boughs above her and shook them fiercely, the gates clanged together, and the cow bell rolled indefinitely. Coughs of now cooler air burst out into the open quad in front of the home and carried with it, the leaf litter and dead twigs from the sizzling summer. As evening hit, the sudden outburst became forgotten, as the air became dry and motionless.

That evening, Lucy looked out at the blackened skies that held stars brighter than the sun. They seemed magnetic as they pulled and held her transfixed as if in conversation. Lucy pulled the rug closer to her that night. She looked into the lit skies and her body felt light and carefree.

Philip was castrating and branding the cattle in the yards. These procedures would protect the stock from overbreeding. It was strenuous work, having to hold the animals down and stretch their back legs, before completing the task. Unlike her partner, Lucy redirected her energy to land care, believing that regeneration would provide a more sustainable living for her family and prevent the degradation of Mandalong. Her first plan was to supplement the income at the station, by nurturing the native flora and fauna, by growing Indigenous plants to be sent to local restaurants. She became committed to this work and began to employ staff to start producing the kunzia, bush pepper, native violet, pepper berries, and small-leafed pig face to be farmed as produce.

Everything was going according to plan and Lucy had contacts in Darwin who were interested in her produce. Her homemade pepper berry ice cream was a success and the kunzia plant was used in making Indigenous dishes of wild kangaroo and crocodile. Quandong, sandalwood and macadamia trees were grown on the property for the nuts, and these would, it was hoped, become a great source of export. It was believed that they would do well as pine nuts, a competitor, were imported from Asia and took up to ten years to grow. Before long, Lucy realised that she had created something special, but her limited skills in this area were holding back production. Eventually, Lucy sold the business to move on to new projects.

When Phillip had returned from being away, they would plan a trip somewhere. They were free to go abroad, so they invited me to take their place at the station. They saw many places across Europe and the States, and eventually wound up in Western Europe. Lucy felt completely free as she travelled, the destination not important, as she knew the journey itself to be rewarding.

It became apparent to Lucy that her strong relationship with Daniel, Jack, and Uncle Rick had prepared her for life on the station. They had each been her confidantes and had understood her from a very young age. She had a deep relationship with each of them, and now Philip had taken their place.

Daniel was always special to Lucy, and after his death, she tried to remember some of the special times. Her grandfather tended to her like a gardener tends to his plants; so that every time Lucy blossomed; Daniel would praise her.

The closest memory she had of him was when she was small. She would run to his room when she was afraid of the night. He would tell her stories; great tales that she would always remember. Sometimes they would be Indigenous Dreamtime stories, and other times, they would be fanciful, and these would make her laugh. Lucy would lay on his arm and turn towards him as he spoke. He had a prickly face she liked to touch, and his eyes looked gently into hers as he spoke. Daniel would sometimes casually ask, why her head was not relaxed on his arm, and she remembered vividly, how she placed her head softly upon it, so she would not hurt him. She remembered these times fondly, and at times, she often pretended that her head was still resting on his arm, but this time relaxed, with him, bearing all the weight himself.

As Lucy had hours to devote to memory, she poured through the files of Mandalong, the primary and secondary sources that were kept under lock and key. Folded within the safe were the photograph albums belonging to her family. At the bottom of the drawer below, wrapped in stale tissue paper, was the Roddick tartan that she knew so well. Its vibrant colours were noticeable, and she imagined Samuel dressed in it as he spoke so often to his family. The Coat of Arms was also there in an enamelled box. Lucy collected the items from the safe, folding her arms carefully around them as she walked to the dining room. She placed them on the table and sat down, to go through them one by one. The photographs appealed to her first, but most of them were post 1925. There were Raymond and Leonora on their wedding day, and photographs of Daniel as a baby.

Lucy was happy to know that she did not have to rely on the photograph album, as there were portraits that adorned the lounge walls. There was Kathleen, who was always known for her beauty, and it was easy to understand how William fell in love with her, as she had a striking presence, which the artist had managed to capture. Her dark hair and eyes enchanted the viewer. Beside her, in an image far more regal, sat Samuel, his white hair flowing carelessly in front of him. In contrast to his appearance, Samuel's life became ordered and fixed; he kept accurate records and enjoyed communicating with the household so that life would be predictable and abundant. Maddy was also noticeable in her riding outfit; the loose-fitting skirt was holding her small waist so tightly. The long blond, curly hair hung softly as her riding hat and crop were held tightly in her hands. Some claimed she was the image of her grandmother, but she did not live long enough to prove any of them to be correct.

It was now time to investigate the big metal chest that had sat for decades in the corner of the room. It had a bent lid which disguised the initials carved into the side, *'Amy Roddick'*. This belonged to William's mother, and had remained in the attic in his home until the couple decided to take their belongings with them to Australia. Now it contained the mementos of Kathleen and her descendants.

Lucy opened the box to retrieve a bundle of items. The first were two photo frames which housed paintings of innocent looking cherubs who had feathery wings attached to their rounded naked torsos. There were camphor boxes in which there were folded lace tablecloths and napkins, nightdresses, and babies' booties, first edition books including poems of John Donne, novels, and picture books. Lucy was excited to find the 'Secret Garden' and 'Enid Blyton', both of which had been read to her by Daniel when she was a small child. Then, right at the bottom of the chest, was a box with a velvet-covered lid and a metal lock. The key was attached so Lucy could open it. There were legal papers, wills, birth, and death certificates. Her parent's marriage certificate lay there too and looked older than she expected. One of the most surprising finds was a gold-leafed book which housed pressed flowers from Mandalong. These belonged to Leonora, Daniel's mother. Lucy loved picking the bush flowers too, so she realised she had more in common with Daniel's mother than she first thought. Lucy then discovered gold bullion and with it, a jewellery box covered in gold leaf. She opened the pin that held it together.

There, before her was a locket belonging to Kathleen. Inside the case, behind the glass, was her great-great-grandmother's braided hair. The braid was held together with cotton, which was used to tie things together, as elastic was not yet invented. A receipt certified its authenticity as it was gifted by William to the eldest son, shortly before Kathleen's death in 1869. Legend has it, that the piece of jewellery had been given, upon the couple's engagement in 1849. This was by far, the most valuable possession Lucy had, as it provided her with a link to her ancestry and bloodline. She was proud of her inheritance and this small piece was tangible evidence of her connection.

The mist lifted and her mind wandered in and out of

memory. She had become fixated on a conversation she had with Samuel all those years ago. It centred upon the origins of Mandalong. Her forebearers had lived below the Scottish Highlands at the Roddick Estate. The Castle sat between two high mountain ranges, but the moors that lay on either side were terrifying and unpredictable. There were some who, in trying to navigate their way through the terrain, had become lost in the wind and the pelting rain, forgotten amidst the virgin rock and moorland. The wind howled tunes and happily stole innocent visitors before they had a chance to enter the doors of the castle. Last century, a daughter of the Earl of Cavendish ran out into the night. The cold wind tore at her bones until she could not move. She lay in the moors until the following morning but had fallen into a deadly sleep before she was discovered. Her betrothed, it was claimed never recovered and 'self-murdered', the term used to refer to suicide in the day.

The Roddick Castle in Scotland was a sprawling seventeenth century set of buildings and it was claimed to be one of the most majestic homes in the district. By the late 1840s, the extended clan lived in its many quarters and were supported by a large staff, however, all that changed by the end of the decade, as Captain Angus Roddick and his wife Roberta cut the extended family from their inheritance, leaving the children behind, and in the care of a governess.

Captain Roddick and his wife rarely appeared, apart from when the couple held balls and dinners for society's elite. It was therefore up to the children to entertain themselves and they did so with pleasure. They spent many hours running barefoot on the moors and climbing trees in the orchard. When the weather was ominous, they would bunker down in the playroom, and climb the furniture to peer out of the windows. They played many games as their noise could not be heard below the attic and their secret life was treasured by each of them. The playroom was in the left wing and had large central windows which looked over the manicured gardens below. When the wind blew between the rafters, it was claimed that the ghosts of Roddick Castle came to visit. The children were oblivious to claims such as these, as they spent their days being tutored and then played in the attic space when they had completed their studies.

The two brothers, Douglas and William, were sons of Captain Angus Roddick. Arthur was the third and only living son of James David Roddick, the late Earl of the Manor. They played daily after lessons and would be accompanied by Kathleen, daughter to the local farrier and coachman. Kathleen's father, known as Manning, was in favour of Angus and his wife and decided on his attendance while they travelled. It was then determined that Kathleen was an imposed orphan at the castle.

As children, Kathleen, Douglas, William, and Arthur enjoyed their time together and were inseparable. Captain Roddick was happy to have the governess instruct all the children, as he felt he was too incumbent with duties to be otherwise involved. It was therefore not surprising that Kathleen became quite close to the Roddick children. As teens, they would watch from their perch above the grand staircase when the Roddicks hosted their large parties. Then everything changed when, Captain Roddick, his brother, wife and attendee, Kathleen's father, were 'lost at sea' during the winter of 1852. Balls, dances, and secret trysts would now not be a feature of the home, as it now was to be handed over to the next of kin.

Everything appeared to be running smoothly until Douglas, the eldest son, contracted consumption and passed away. His presence was missed as his energy had always inspired others.

His good looks were painted by his mother shortly before her death, some years before. As Douglas was the eldest son, William had now become second in line to inherit the Roddick Castle. William shortly after renounced his claim to his birthright, as a formal attachment had been made with Kathleen, and she by birth was found to be unsuitable to hold a position as Lady of the Manor. Arthur (Arty) would now claim the inheritance as he was next in line. This opportunity was a surprise to all as Arty had no interest in marriage, having demonstrated a cavalier lifestyle, living the high life as a bachelor with almost no responsibility.

Shortly after the handover, William left the Scottish moorlands for a new life with his wife and two children in Australia. Unfortunately, the outcome for Roddick Castle would then become dire. William would hear that within the decade, shortly after Arthur's death, the castle would become abandoned and, left in ruins.

Kathleen was not born into the house of Roddick, so she was bound to be excluded from the castle once grown. She soon realised that her strength of character would define her in her adult years. William was not persuaded by wealth and married Kathleen. Her spirited character compelled her as, with her new husband, she turned her back on the Scottish moors to brave the seas and make Australia a new home. It was this will and determination that carried them forward.

The subsequent voyage was perilous, as the parents of two young children managed sickness and adversity to begin an uncertain future in the middle of a foreign and unfriendly environment. Kathleen had raised her small children in the Roddick castle in Scotland for some years, with her husband as head of the house, but soon realised that the life he saw before him was a pre-determined one, and as such, decided to map his own way in the world. Without Kathleen by his side, he may not have felt the challenge. The hardship that followed began on entering the wild seas, as disease and malnutrition forced many of the crew and passengers to suffer a wretched death. For most of the free settlers who did make the trip alive, their fortune lay in their ability to apply their skills once they had landed. For Kathleen and her husband, their future was already determined as they made their way to the ends of the earth in search of good fortune.

Once in Sydney town, the Roddick family found accommodation at some quarters in The Rocks, Sydney, and then made their way south to find suitable horses and a carriage. They walked down Penny Lane, a cobblestone alleyway where locals would sell their wares and beggars would plead for food in front of doorways. Kathleen had seen these things before in England. She was particularly disturbed at the number of children used to plead for money, as she realised that education here was not foremost in the eyes of the establishment. There were squabbles and fights, boxing and wrestling and the unsightly scenes of prostitution distressed her significantly. The roadside gutter contained rotting food scraps, and wastewater was thrown at irregular intervals from rooms above. The pavement was continually subjected to mud, as the carriages would rattle past the pedestrians.

The family left Penny Lane to turn from Playfair Street into George Street. They hurried along Circular Quay, which appeared as busy as some ports in England, but was dirty, and the family kept close as they negotiated the vehicles and calls of the vendors. Kathleen had learned since arriving, that prostitution was rife as a proportion of the young women, after having lost their husbands, found it necessary to work to feed their families. It was common that many new farmers lost their lives after felling trees or drowning while crossing the rivers on horseback. As they turned the corner into King Street, they realised that pick pockets were in abundance. William had his money hidden within his garments as he had done when traveling the high seas.

The young Roddick children had toughened up somewhat after the trip from Scotland, and Sydney town continued to throw surprises. They all realised that this would probably be their last opportunity to see the city, for some years at least. The family tried to remain positive, but they were a little apprehensive as they had heard stories about the English colonies and the harsh living standards that settlers had experienced. Added to that, stories about the American Indigenous tribes abounded, with stories about death by decapitation. Some naturally believed the native Indigenous tribes in Australia may do the same.

Little is known about how the Roddick family made their way to the Tanami desert, but it can be assumed that the journey must have taken months. The trip overland possibly began at Port Augusta, following the track which was named the North-South Road to Darwin, later to become the Stuart Highway. It can be assumed that the Roddick family would have stopped at Katherine and made their way westward to the Tanami. There would have been various stops along the way, the roadhouses offering an overnight stay and a place to feed their horses and replenish stocks. Upon their arrival in the Tanami, they would have provided themselves with adequate shelter, as they built the Mandalong homestead. The Roddick family were pioneers, as few people ventured so far across Australia at this time. For this reason, they should be admired for their stamina and commitment. For them, the choice was simple, continue their journey and their chance at a better life or turn back to an uncertain future.

William became proud of his Australian inheritance, and one could say that the separation between the English aristocracy and this free settler were distinctive. He believed in the resilience of the members of his family, as they had separated from a relatively easy life to begin anew, in a country which was foreign to them and at times as dangerous as it was mysterious.

From the moment the Roddick family stepped onto Australian soil, they became aware of the significant lifestyle change that confronted them. Their saving grace was a very early introduction to the Warlpiri tribe. Fortunately for William and Kathleen, the family were not perceived by the tribe as a threat. The relationship between the Tanami people and the new Mandalong tenants remained optimistic as they learned to work together. From that time on, each respected the other, as shared custodians of their land.

Lucy removed the certificates from their pouch. Documents were there, but earlier records were found on the family tree within the bible. Fortunately, Samuel, and then Daniel, had recorded these primary sources meticulously. Lucy made her own record as she was interested in ancestral archives, knowing that these details may one day be observed by future members of the family. She hoped that they may indeed acknowledge the contribution she had made as every detail would be of merit.

Within the records, Lucy was surprised to find another piece of jewellery, a pendant with *'Millie, 1905'* that needed explanation. It was Uncle Rick who helped Lucy piece together the story. William 'Billy' Child married Millicent in 1886, but had altercations with Albert Roddick, which soon became acrimonious. Millie tried to appease the two, but the misunderstanding brought bitterness to the one-time peaceful community. There were many who could not understand the separation that brought the two men to blows. The upset continued until Billy learned of Albert's sickness. The two resolved their long-time dispute, much to the relief of Millie who had tried to bring peace between the two for many months. After the death of Albert, Billy bought his wife a pendant in the shape of a mandola; an almond-shaped segment, with two circles that partly overlapped. It was described as the intersection between heaven and earth, representing reconciliation.

Lucy replaced the family bible and returned to the kitchen to make dinner for her family. She knew that life for her was far easier than it had been for her ancestors, and relished thinking about what she would make to show her appreciation to the important family members who now depended on her.

Chapter 10
A New Generation

The staff at the Tourism Centre at Mandalong had grown as the work had now become more intensive. It was now 2009, and advertisements had been sent to the states around Australia to manage administration and logistical operations. Indigenous personnel filled positions from all over the Territory. There would be cultural guides, dancers, and artists of all descriptions, needed for the centre. Craftsmen from Yuendumu and beyond, then sent their work to be sold and dancers were found locally, with Red and Jimmy volunteering their services for night-time displays.

Wyatt, a local school friend of Angus and Edmund, had been taught how to make didgeridoos by his uncles and was known throughout the land for his skill in painting them. The didgeridoos were made from hardwood, often eucalyptus, hollowed out by termites. Wyatt would walk in the bush each evening and tap trunks of trees and branches to find a hollow piece. He was notably efficient at this task as he had seen his uncle's play regularly after painting them in traditional colours and emblems. Wyatt keenly observed his kin playing these instruments and was pleased to be paid for making something that he loved to do. He decided he would join Red and Jimmy to play the didgeridoo on these evenings to the tourists.

The Community Progress Association building housed the artefacts for the Indigenous community at Mandalong. It was

Maisie and Winnie who coordinated the craft and later Josie and Wyatt joined them as the orders increased. Josie was Wyatt's sister, and while much younger than her sibling, was a capable artist, so was happy to assist the girls in making the popular craft. The tourists were particularly interested in the baskets, and these would be woven from the grasses the girls found around the local watering holes, and then dyed before being woven together.

The Progress Association was made up of a variety of members who represented the community at Mandalong, and with little exception, provided the necessary support to keep the tourism sector viable. The local hall was shared with the association and the local CWA and the local Council. It was for this reason that the building needed a storeroom to house the necessary artefacts and wares for the group. A kitchen workspace provided the necessary area to provide refreshments to the members, although for Maisie, Winnie, Wyatt and Josie, a preferred area outside was often claimed, as they could make a fire and cook their damper within the coals when they were hungry. The building had been erected during Jack's time at the station. He also conscripted 'the crew' to help him erect the sheds that would eventually house the Tourism staff at the airport and gold mine. They were simple structures, weatherboard construction with a tin roof, and plain pine board flooring. They each had a tank for a water supply and a little house for daily ablutions.

The chief Mandalong Tourism Centre was located at Mt. Herbert, a sacred site and the open-cut mine continued to supply a steady stream of mineral deposits, including gold. Wilbur and Henry, local lads, had been cultural guides here for some time. They had local families who were proud of their efforts and whose children wished to follow in their footsteps. Wilbur and

Henry would instruct the visitors on the cultural aspects of the site, and would also facilitate understanding of the mining environmental practices to date.

Rhonda was chosen by a panel of members during the early days. It would be she, who was the first successful applicant from outside of the area. From the onset, Rhonda had a plan. She was tough and her manner made onlookers step aside to make way for her. She was a muscley, able-bodied woman of Welsh stock who knew how to take care of herself. Her formative years were spent under trucks, her father instructing her in mechanics. She was comfortable with men, and could not abide those who depended on others. Her job was simple; Rhonda would travel with the guests and take them to the site to meet up with Wilbur and Henry, who would lecture them on the cultural significance of the area. Rhonda wore her sturdy hiking boots as she set the procession of visitors in motion.

The Progress Association had for months, now been interviewing applicants to work in the business at the centre. Angela Josephine Wheatley was also chosen by the board. It did not take her long to adjust to the demands of the Territory nor to the peculiar terms of her contract in Katherine, this being the second centre for the tourism business. This building was leased from the Katherine Council as a connection point between the centre at Mandalong and the Regional terminal at Katherine Airport. Not long after, Angela had become familiar with the lifestyle and settled into life at Mandalong.

'Angie', spent her formidable years in Ulladulla, NSW assisting in a general store as a bookkeeper and salesgirl. Her husband, Peter, ran away with a local girl, and left her to fend for herself and her three young children. When the children had left home, Angie looked for work. She did not have friends as her work and family had kept her active and she had no interest in forming attachments as they invariably became a distraction. One morning she had searched the Northern Territory Gazette, and she came upon an advertisement to work at the Tourism Centre at Mandalong station.

This could be an opportunity for me, she thought to herself. *I have nothing to tie me down any longer.*

Angela assembled her belongings together, which consisted of little more than a small collection of household items. She then took herself to the Tanami with her small bag and savings and embarked on her pilgrimage into the unknown. Her brief was simple; earn enough money to set herself up to retire and then happily travel back to be near her children. Angie would never again consider moving from Mandalong as the client base and crew with whom she worked, made her feel joyful, and she celebrated her freedom regularly with her new-made friends.

Shortly after, Albion, as he was to be known at the Centre, was chosen by the members to coordinate the third location at the airport. His responsibility was to maintain the administration for those who were entering, and then departing from the site. He would oversee the public as they were flown in by private plane from Katherine, and then bused out to the ranges for the expedition.

Albion Everett Worthington was the son and only heir to the late Major General Everett Worthington of Port Arthur. Albion held a degree in Tourism and Management from Monash University and had applied for the position at Mandalong for experience in the field as his qualifications had not found him a position elsewhere. Albion was short in stature and his broken, stained teeth were a testament to his poor health in childhood. His looks were not assisted by his unfortunate humped back which prevented him from standing erect. Albion spoke in a small and startled fashion, as he had endured years of neglect from his insufferable father. It was at his hands, that he experienced weekly floggings and verbal abuse. One could say that Albion was not confident amongst his colleagues. Most days he would remain by himself and apply himself to his work. On occasion, he would look up from his desk and gaze into the eyes of Rhonda. This would bring on a stuttering, that made his body shake awkwardly; his memory reliving the days of his beatings. Albion would then begin to involuntarily dribble and clutch at his large handkerchief to wipe away the unwanted spittle.

Rhonda was satisfied with her position here as it served her well. She had handed over multiple numbers of tourists to the guides and was pleased that the position did not require her to say too much. Rhonda did, however, hold one reservation; which was, being paired with Albion. His type had always irritated her. She believed everyone should be able to speak up for themselves. With Albion, this was not so. She found him to be weak and less than equal to the rest of the crew at the centre. There was often a barbeque or party at the complex, but Rhonda made it her job not to tell him.

Albion was very particular with his work, displaying a recognisable affection for order. This was noted by the chief superintendent, Douglas Mulvaney, whose job it was to visit the Indigenous Tourism Centres throughout the Territory. He had noted that Albion had revealed his strength in administration and asked him to join him in visiting some of the other centres. Albion was unusually pleased with this offer as he was not used to displays of appreciation. A temporary replacement was organised. Jill had been working at the station as a jackaroo. She was a striking girl, with an affable personality to match. Rhonda liked her and tried hard to win the girl's affection, but Jill was not impressed. Jill was not abiding by her antics, as she was not comfortable with the stand-over mannerisms that she had placed on others in the past. This was a temporary position, she told herself, and Rhonda should be assisting her with the baffling bookkeeping. Albion would be back soon, and she could resume her rightful place back in the saddle at the station. Unfortunately, that was not going to stop Rhonda. She had set her eyes on Jill, and she was not going to let her get away.

Rhonda had made her presence known to Jill, and it was becoming noticeable to all that for Jill, at least, life was uncomfortable. Lucy heard about her predicament and arranged for Jill to join her back at Mandalong, promptly returning Albion to his desk at the airport.

Albion had, for a time now, been receiving prompt and regular feedback and returned with a much-improved attitude to his work and performance. Upon his return, Rhonda approached him at his desk. Albion looked up to her face-to-face. He did not appear nervous or distracted and this challenged Rhonda. Albion had changed, she concluded. Little did she know, that he was shaking uncontrollably within. He answered her questions curtly, and then went on to examine his books which, he had noted, were more recently absent in detail. It then became apparent to Albion, that the arrogant and highly proud Rhonda was not the suitable manager she pretended to be. Rhonda soon became aware that Albion had noted this shortfall and avoided contact with him whenever possible. It was not long before Rhonda was moved from the airport centre to the post at Mt. Herbert. From that time on, Albion and his inspector friend would be seen regularly chatting together over pots of tea. Albion enjoyed his time at the airport Tourism Centre and continued to astound the inspector with his skill, until, with great applause from his colleagues, he was transferred to the Central District Centre at Katherine.

It would be at this location that Angela quickly became known to Albion, who was quite taken with his intelligent friend. They both quickly formed an attachment, and within months of their meeting, Angela and Albion were married in the local church, and then quietly became noticeable fixtures within the community. Rhonda continued to inflict disparaging insults upon the employees at the centre, until one day, she, like so many of her contemporaries, left without notice.

Lucy had been told many years earlier that the Territory drew a certain group to its vicinity. There were those, who believed they could try their luck and take advantage of the opportunities it offered, then quickly return to the southern states; those who were running away from the law, or a responsibility they felt they no longer needed; there were also those who were simply looking for adventure, shunning the consequences; and some who felt they had a 'calling' to convert; and then the very few who longed for a fresh start, somewhere removed from their place of origin. Lucy was hoping that the new candidates would be from the latter category.

Rhonda had not been a 'good fit', so Doug, the inspector, joined the team to find the best replacement. Harrison had a resonating voice, and his noticeable presence could not be avoided. He had served in the armed services with combat experience in Iraq and Afghanistan. He appealed to the panel as his knowledge about logistics was impressive. His former experience in the military had been in maintaining transport operations within the combat zone. It would be a unanimous decision that would see Harrison chosen to coordinate the services between the station points, the timetabling of the crews, and to manage employee salaries. He would work with Douglas the inspector, to maintain efficiency at each of the locations.

The following week, Ike Andersen, known to most as Izzy, came to work for the station, replacing Baxter who was retiring down to the Central Coast of New South Wales. Upon his departure, Baxter disclosed that he was returning to his family who he had left some two decades earlier. His three children had grown into adulthood and their mother was no longer living. He was hoping for a reconciliation with his offsprings, and believed that the money he had saved would persuade them to take him back.

The station hands, and Lucy and Philip, were particularly upset with Baxter's departure, as he had such a strong affiliation with the property. For Lucy, he would be missed, as he had supported her at critical times in her life.

Izzy had spent his entire working life playing in bands and travelling around Australia, but he was now forty-two, and felt it was time to settle down, with a steady income and a predictable future.

Izzy's hair stood up on one end. His crown was dreadlocked, red in colour, and tied up into a bun, save small curls that encircled his long, rugged face. His shirt, unbuttoned to his waist, revealed his bony, hairless chest. Izzy loved to trade his less comfortable riding gear for his coloured board shorts upon retiring for the day. One tended to wonder if Izzy had lost his compass bearings, and had turned left, instead of right, when trying to find the surf beaches of Australia. Izzy would spend the evenings strumming his guitar and singing to 'the crew'. He quickly won the hearts of the men as he loved music and would spend most evenings playing around the campfire. Some of the melodies were familiar to the audience, and some he claimed, were his own.

Harrison and Izzy liked nothing more than to venture off to Darwin to spend a weekend or two after a payday. Lucy and Jack often commented to each other that they thought 'the crew' had spent all their money to date, on wild living, but understood that for most of the time, they were hard workers and deserved some rest and relaxation.

One night, two police officers came knocking at the homestead door. Philip got up and stretched his tired body, before moving to the entrance. He formally asked them to step inside to then be told that both men, Harrison, and Izzy, were in the Darwin lock-up and that they had requested their employer arrange bail. Philip was not understanding, and needed some coaxing from Lucy. After some deliberation, Philip decided to fly up the following morning to retrieve these jackaroos and bring them home.

This pattern of behaviour became more evident as time went on, and Philip was forced to give them a final warning. This came, with an ultimatum; that should they request his attention one more time, he would not only not come, but their jobs would not be waiting for them upon their return. Harrison accompanied Izzy back to Mandalong soon after. It was apparent that both had received several war wounds, and Philip hoped that they had, at last, learnt their lesson. Months later, Harrison took up residence with a local girl but was forcefully removed by the police, as his behaviour became unseemly, due to alcohol intoxication. He was removed from the station and instructed not to return until his court hearing had resumed in Darwin. They heard nothing from him from that day on. Izzy continued working for Philip and became good friends with Red as they shared similar interests. He was no doubt, dependable, and Philip shortly, thereafter, gave him an added responsibility. He was promoted from station hand to assistant manager.

It was now 2010, and Lucy appreciated me stepping in to take Angus and Edmund. It pained Lucy that because of distance, our children saw less of Philip and herself; but this was the sacrifice of living so far away. Their grandparents on her side were no longer living, and this was difficult for Lucy, as both Jack and Mary had shared so much time with Angus and Edmund when they were young. Both her parents had semi-retired in the late 1990s, but by 2005, Mary contracted a terminal illness and died in 2007. Then in 2009, Jack had a fatal accident south of Uluru. He had been travelling north on the Stuart Highway from Adelaide, when he hit a massive storm. His car and caravan rolled. The air ambulance had taken Jack to hospital, but he died shortly after. Lucy believed that if her mother had been alive, he would have been more careful.

The void left with their absence was noticeable, but Lucy tried to focus on what had been handed to her, rather than what was missing. It was up to me, as her mother-in-law, to be the rock that she needed. Lucy knew that to dwell on these events would destroy her; she must be strong for each of her children. Time stood still for years after that. She missed her parents, and the pain becoming more noticeable with her sons' absence. She felt this loss constantly, however, Lucy was strong, and her resilience was only just becoming evident to her.

Lucy fell into her usual habits of attending church on a Sunday. The congregation was small, but enthusiastic. Local Elders and their families attended, and a handful of workers from the station, including those who had been baptised in the church as small children. They had remained committed by receiving holy communion every week. Sunday School was a special event for the children, as they were able to do craft and crosswords, and sing aloud. Mrs Spence played the piano, and Mr Hall gave the lesson. The teenage children from the congregation would then sit at trestle tables with the young and help them with their activities.

Tea and cordial were served for morning tea, with Arnott's biscuits displayed in ample supply. The week's events were then discussed and measured against expectations and compared meticulously against previous years. Such deliberations were important, as the potential for improvement was now possible due to the program set up by the Central Lands Commission. Most of the women wore hats to church and Lucy was no exception. Her hat had bows on either side. It was black and trimmed around the brim with netting. She was proud of her outfit and wore it most weeks as it was her best frock. The men would wear suits if they owned one, and the children would have clean and bright outfits, to mark a special occasion.

One Sunday, Lucy sat in the church pew to hear the pastor convey his thoughts about redemption.

"Indigenous tradition places the 'bogey man' **(20) (21)** in high regard. Just as in India, the Indigenous community believe him to take the evil deeds and as such, is revered and powerful," he claimed.

"The teaching of the church acknowledges that the Lord offers himself as an atonement for sin. The 'bogey man' and the Christian belief gives us access to the dual nature of redemption. You, as his faithful servants, are thus guaranteed that deliverance," he theorised.

David and I were also content. Life had been good to us, and we enjoyed the bonds we shared with family. Lucy had completed her recovery, and for now, most things were normal again. As the only surviving Grandmother, I tried to be present for my grandsons. I understood how essential it was to be there for them, so I often took them home on weekends. That became easier for them, than traveling the long-distance to Mandalong.

Each holiday break, our Angus and Edmund would look forward to spending time with their family. Angus was a natural around the station, and performed, as his grandfather had before him. He loved the bush and knew that, although he appreciated boarding school, his heart ruled when it came to where he wanted to be. His father was proud of him, because he learnt skills quickly, and assisted him with many of the tasks around the yards. His interest in learning to fly was also impressive. Angus spent hours in his room, learning aviation, so that he could assist on the station one day in the future. After a period of study, he was instructed by his father in the air, and looked forward to sitting for his qualifications the following March. The two sat together every evening and shared their stories. They both found it easy to talk to each other, as their interests were similar. Angus wanted nothing more than to take over from his father. He knew that if he worked hard, and demonstrated his fitness for the job, his parents would have no alternative, but in time, hand Mandalong over to him.

Edmund preferred city life, and his favourite activity was spending time with his grandfather, David on his small sailing boat. Most weekends, they would sail for the day and then buy fish and chips to take home and share. Holidays at Mandalong were a different story. Although Edmund loved being with his family, his affection was not for Mandalong. Instead of joining his father and brother, Edmund preferred his own company during the day. He would read, write, and study, and later join the family for dinner.

There was one hobby that both Edmund and his father shared. Edmund enjoyed chess and his father would often join him in a game. He also enjoyed mind games and problem-solving as his skills in logic were noticeable. Before retiring, Philip would request a game, as he was aware he had spent all day with Angus.

"Feel like a game of chess, son?" Philip would ask.

"Sure!" Edmund would answer. The rest of the evening was quiet, as they mumbled quietly to themselves and occasionally deliberated about position and rules.

After a day in the saddle, there was nothing that Lucy enjoyed more than making her sons their favourite meals during the holidays because she wanted them to enjoy their time away from school. During the day, they would help her reclaim the gardens as she remembered them to be when she was growing up.

When Angus and Edmund were home, they would often catch up with their friends from their childhood. The brothers would sit with them and be taken by the jackaroos for a 'spin' in the utility. The crew were happy to do this, as it reminded them of earlier times when they would join Lucy and go for a ride in Jack's Land Rover. Those days were in the past now, as they had married local girls and Billy already boasted a family.

'Friends forever!' Lucy remembered the promise; *'Whenever the days become longer than they should, or friends are afar or forgotten, we shall stay true'.* This promise always brought them together. No matter how their lives changed, this promise was something that stayed in their hearts. It had been years since Lucy and her friends had been together, and yet they promised each other they would not become idle and forget. Red had reminded Lucy some months before, that the girls, Maisie, and Winnie, were eager to come back to Mandalong to meet again and exchange gifts. They had made artefacts to share with their good friends, he told her, so they were both looking forward to reconnecting. Their baskets and paintings were in high demand, Red had assured Lucy, and would now be sold on the station to tourists.

Jimmy collected the girls from Katherine the following morning. After many good laughs and hugs, they shared a good lunch of barramundi, salad, quandong tarts, muntrie (known as emu apples) and ice cream. They ate quickly as they were excited about being together again. Jimmy was pleased to tell the girls that his tribal dancing was enjoyed by tourists, and the income supplemented his wage at the station.

Lucy took a photo of the girls, but Jimmy and Red did not approve, as they believed the camera to hold bad spirits, so they laughed in the background. Many hours passed, and Lucy knew, soon it would be time for Jimmy to return the girls to Katherine. This visit encouraged Lucy. There was a special bond between all of them.

In December 2010, Edmund and Angus accompanied David and I to Italy. I wanted them to see some Roman ruins, and to understand the culture, language, and passion of the Italians, as it was their birthright. The country would help them understand the country's rich history and how it had enabled Italy to be one of the most successful countries in Europe. Angus and Edmund learnt to make pasta from Italian chefs and enjoyed eating Italian delicacies, including pizza, pasta, and gelato. They travelled to the Amalfi coast and ate fresh fish, which they collected from the trawler each morning. At night, David and I would take them to experience operettas in Italian. This experience helped them to learn Italian.

Angus and Edmund began to learn how important food is in the Italian culture as our meals were always a delight. Breakfast consisted of a hard roll, butter, strong coffee, and fruit or juice. Traditionally, there would be a large lunch. Pasta was served, along with soup, bread, and perhaps meat or fish. Dinner nearly always consisted of leftovers. Angus and Edmund became familiar with Saint Joseph's bread, Easter bread with hard-boiled eggs, Saint Lucy's 'eyes' for the feast day, and the Feast of the Seven Fishes for New Year's Eve. Our family travelled to Lombardy, on the Po River, and to Milan, the chief commercial, industrial, and financial centre. I enjoyed shopping there as textiles and clothing are in ample supply. They are also known for their iron, steel, machinery, motor vehicles, chemicals, furniture, and wine.

We then all journeyed back home on a cruise. We allowed the boys 'free rein' on board, and they enjoyed the independence. When they returned from their trip, there was little time left to spend at Mandalong. They knew the visit was important to us, and the holiday would always be memorable, so they did not complain about not seeing their parents.

Philip had always believed that times were changing, and, as landowners, his colleagues were turning their backs to life on land and finding work elsewhere. For too long, the economy had not supported these farmers. The day was fast approaching when large corporations would manage highly refined industrial machines, coordinated remotely, redefining work on the station. Multinational companies and interest groups would be the way of the future, he believed. He would regularly get into a heated discussion about the way forward. His one wish was that Angus would become a politician, and do what he could to save the nation, however, Angus eventually ignored his father's pleas to remain at school and continue his education. He returned to Mandalong by Christmas with the intent of staying indefinitely. He showed his father that he could help him move production forward.

Mandalong was now in competition with the larger stations to the north, and had lost its rightful place in export sales. Philip understood there was a certain difficulty in trying to get Angus to see reason, as the boy was headstrong and determined, so in time, Philip relented. It was for this reason that for now, he thought he would welcome Angus back to the property, at least until he had resumed the quota of expected sales.

Boarding school was an institution, removed from the love and acknowledgement that home provided. For Angus, life away from home had been rewarding as he was an academic, a scholar; he had formally held clear aspirations to be an orator or statesman. He was popular, deliberated on debating teams, was well respected and enjoyed team sports, his colleagues often promoted him to represent them in most away games.

Edmund did not fare as well, in fact, his personality did not suit the GPS school to which he was sent. He did not enjoy life away from his parents. Each day was a trial. Edmund rarely saw his brother at school, dormitory life was exceptionally hard as he was bullied and rebuked often by his peers. His best friend, Paul, was the only person who kept him stable the entire school year. There were consolations though. Edmund did enjoy learning and at the boarding school, and was given ample time to study in the library.

For those children like Edmund, who enjoyed their own company, boarding school was not a satisfactory experience. The dormitories were loud and the area between the beds within the rooms were small and lacked privacy. There was one redeeming feature, Mr Mac (short for McPherson), taught Latin and History. Edmund found both these subjects interesting, and obediently observed his homework time to prepare himself for the week's tuition. Mr Mac would make the subjects come alive, and for those who believed Latin was dead, his teacher had other ideas. Edmund was a highly creative boy, and he could imagine the Roman Emperor and his conspirators easily as he learned about betrayal in the government of the day. Edmund, gifted at archery, pretended to be King Richard when he slayed the enemy at Bosworth. Of course, the outcome for the king was sobering, but Edmund believed, that Richard stood his ground in battle, and bravely fought on.

Mr Mac was tall; his thin wiry body gave him a distinctive look as he wore his suit well and carried himself with confidence. Edmund often spoke of him. Mr Mac was always in the habit of carrying books under his arm and marching promptly to his destination. He was a graduate of Harvard, they said, but there was no accent to indicate he had ever been abroad. What was known about him was little, other than his life was very much centred around the school. He remained at Blaxland House as Master during the term and holiday break, and one wondered if he had any family at all. To him, his family were the students he tutored, but Edmund believed that could not be possible, as so many of them were disinterested in his lessons or company. On the contrary, Edmund found Mr Mac to be exciting. His knowledge about so many topics was exceptional, and he always showed remarkable patience, as he listened to his endless questions.

One morning in June 2014, when Edmund had returned from his school holidays at Mandalong, he learned of the sudden death of his tutor and friend. Edmund was now seventeen, and his dependency on his teacher had become noticeable. The school displayed noticeable attention, as they sat him down in the foyer when he came in for morning prayer. They then began to break the news gently before he entered the chapel. Apparently, Mr Mac had suffered a massive heart attack and had been discovered the following morning in the library.

The establishment was in shock, as Mr Mac had been 'part of the furniture' for many years and his absence was indeed noticeable. Edmund was quite distraught. The funeral was taken that Thursday in the school chapel, and a memorial plaque was mounted on the wall of the library entrance, to remind others of his contribution and faithful service. Edmund was heartbroken. He feared he would never find a substitute for Mr Mac and did not know how he could ever enjoy his studies quite the same.

I was looking forward to a family reunion to mark thirty years of marriage. David and I would have the opportunity to celebrate with our loved ones. I had welcomed our grandsons into our home nearly every weekend since they had arrived at Scott's, but this time would be special, as Lucy and Philip would be joining them. I had also invited Eliza and Robyn who would bring Uncle Rick and Sandra. I carried the decorations out to the long trestle table that David and I had set up in the garden earlier that morning. The setting was pleasing. The grapevine hung above and around the alcove of wooden arches, above the outdoor setting. The water fountain was set to the side of a garden of roses that David and I had both tended to regularly. The scent of the flowers wafted through the air as I brought platters of anti-pesto, smoked fish, and warm homemade bread. My spaghetti marinara would arrive sometime later, after the guests had relaxed with their Italian wine and sparkling mineral water.

I welcomed our guests briefly, as I took them to the special place we had prepared for them out at the back. The day was pleasant, as a breeze was blowing in from the harbour foreshore, removing any humidity from the air. I looked around, and noticed that everyone looked content, relaxed, and happy. Angus and Edmund were the exception. I could tell they tried to look interested, but I knew they were more excited about the party they would be attending that evening. Often referred to as a 'gathering', I knew these occasions to be troubling, as parents often did not know many details. It seemed now that the older our grandsons became, the less we knew about them or their plans. I was sure that these circumstances were normal, as we had experienced them when Philip was growing up. I knew that it was not wise to confront them; one just had to go along with the arrangements, and hope that nothing unforeseen occurred. Angus and Edmund were responsible, I thought, and their friends seemed to be respectable. It was important that both understood that we trusted them and hopefully that would be sufficient.

Angus and Edmund had been on their iPhones as they sat down, awkwardly remaining distant as they scrolled through their texts. Everyone else was absorbed in the conversation, laughing intermittently. It was Philip who reminded Angus and Edmund later about their manners, so they quickly removed their phones for a later time, and broke bread with their family.

As usual, the family was impressed, as I brought out the spaghetti marinara. I had learned to cook this recipe when I was last in Italy, as I believed the Italians to have the most favourable seafood recipes; this one being a favourite. After a relaxed afternoon of discussion and music, the family excused themselves to leave until the next special event.

That evening, I briefly looked down upon the opera glasses and program that lay beside my evening clutch bag. I hoped that I might be able to attend another session before the season had reached its conclusion. Until then, I would carry out my promise to Lucy; to care for our grandsons. They would be home from the 'gathering' soon, and I would then be less concerned. Till then, I remained seated as I completed my crossword under the night light. Later that evening, Angus and Edmund returned home. I then knew that my trust was not ill-founded, as they had decided to return promptly home.

During breakfast the following morning, I peered across the table at our boys. Angus had stubble on his chin which needed attention and I reminded myself to buy him shaving gear, so he could begin to groom himself before he returned to Mandalong. Then I looked at Edmund. He needed the next size in trousers, as he was showing more leg than he should when he sat down. They would visit the Department Store in town upon their return trip the next day.

Edmund was growing tall, and his maturity grew as he accessed more regular trips up north. The frequency of these visits helped Lucy too, as she could invest more time with both her children more often.

In time, Edmund was to sit for his last exam before leaving school. He had always wished to enter the legal profession like his aunt Eliza, but she had tried to deflect this ambition, as she felt, the profession would be more than he could stand. Instead of encouraging him, in his own interest, she tried to steer him toward engineering. He listened to her and believed he could work hard and show her he was up to the task.

Edmund managed to apply himself solidly, as he was now

determined more than ever to complete his time at boarding school and make his way into the wide world on his own. He would not yet be 18 when he walked out of the main doors of the school for good, but he believed the memories of the place would remain fresh for some time to come. His friend Paul accompanied him to university, and Edmund took up residency temporarily with his grandparents, rather than lodging at the university dormitory. When Edmund had completed his studies, he worked briefly for an engineering company in the North Shore until he felt that he had gained the faith of his employers. With a string of credits to his name, Edmund was promoted and the success that followed gave him the added confidence to lead others in his team.

Edmund's family were proud of his accomplishments as they understood him to be a capable engineer with gifts in leadership. All that was about to change on an evening in September 2018. Edmund left work one afternoon with a debilitating headache. He was hospitalised for observation. Nine weeks later, he was heading home with little explanation, doctors had described his condition as being a severe case of depression and insomnia.

For both David and I, the shock was noticeable. We had only recently received news that Lucy and Philip had reached a big milestone in their recovery, and now our baby grandson was unwell. How could someone so motivated and eager become so introverted and disconnected from the world? We thought that the most appropriate place for him was with his parents. Edmund returned home within the week.

Lucy and Philip were pleased to have him, as it would help them to understand his condition more. David and I believed the best place for us, was to remain here in the hope that Edmund may one day return to us and continue his career. For us, it was clear we should look forward and not back.

From that day, Lucy would care for her son with relentless dedication. At times, the pressure became too much, and she too relapsed into a small quiet corner for hours at a time, as she too, had experienced the shock of seeing her son so incapacitated. Lucy eventually reclaimed her dignity and continued caring for Edmund to the best of her ability.

The two of us tried to, for their sake, distance ourselves from the events at Mandalong. I would often take a walk down by the foreshore. I looked out at the harbour. Lights streamed in from the pier beyond and danced across the ripples of water. The night sky appeared fractured as the wind played with the beams of light that projected from it. The ferry had started below me, its engine echoed across the bay. As the boat began its journey across to the other side, the rattle and churn became noticeable. The laughter of small children became absent as it chortled off into the distance. A bell was heard as the boat reached its destination a distance away, and then, complete silence.

I sat briefly to reflect on events leading up to this new set of circumstances. Later, David and I chatted on the small veranda outside our lounge. We remembered our first chance meeting with Lucy. She was twenty-three years old and had been sitting in the car outside our place, as she waited for Philip to check his mail. I came down to meet her and was noticeably impressed with her manner. As we got to know her, she struck both of us as having a sense of purpose and a substance of character. Lucy also loved to laugh, her sense of humour being evident in all her conversations. While her politics appeared slightly radical at first, she gravitated in time to the middle ground. Both David and I were quite pleased with this transition. Philip shared this same sense of purpose, and I guess that may have been the attraction at first.

One evening, David and I decided to take a short stroll along the beach. The small waves lapped softly against the sea wall. Seaweed tangled itself against the rocks below, while small crabs appeared, crawling sideways in search of food. The musical notes of the sea, played creatively with my mind, as I looked out to the horizon beyond. The sky had turned a deep violet, as the sun became obscured by cloud. In the distance, seagulls squawked as they battled for scraps, while wild pigeon observed the terrain from their perch in the Norfolk pines above. Children ran joyfully from the baths as they pulled at their costumes and slapped each other with wet towels. The smell of fish and chips came wafting across the concourse, as if to entice the observer.

It was late in the day, but I had arranged the travel that would take me up to Mandalong by the Friday of that week. David would remain at home, to manage the property and business deals he had the following week. I would catch the train into the city on Friday and arrange a plane from Mascot the following morning. Philip would then pick me up on Saturday from Katherine that afternoon, to then travel the distance to Mandalong by late evening.

Friday came, and I caught the train for 12.20 p.m. from St. Leonards station. The clunk of the railway carriages could be heard in the distance, with the occasional loud, ear-piercing screech as it grovelled to a halt. The strong smell of rubber caught my nostrils as I quickly passed. The startled traffic came to rest at the red traffic lights, and the loud blipping would push the vision-impaired in the right direction. From the other side of the pedestrian crossing, there stood a wall of scaffolding. The cranking of drills and the movement of cranes above introduced me briefly to the violent sound patterns experienced by those who live in our city. Sydney was ever evolving, twisting its way forward and never looking behind.

I became consumed by pedestrian traffic, the mania and determined resolve evident as I moved left to change direction. This procession of business suits and stiletto heels rivalled any European city, marking time with the capitalism that had made it. Then, as quickly as it started, all was quiet. The road ahead led out into a garden of flowers, the trees providing a canopy of green amongst a colourful spectacle. The air was cooler now, and the spell was real, as I melted into my new abode. It would be here that I would spend time to collect my thoughts, as I had hours to spare before catching the airport shuttle.

It had been months since my last visit to Philip and Lucy, but as I promised, I would get my three-year check-up before my return. The train ride was not eventful, although I always enjoyed riding in a carriage across the Sydney Harbour Bridge. It had been four years now since my operation, and this visit would mark my final check-up, so hopefully, I would be cleared and cancer-free. I was praying this would be the case, but it would be little steps before I could be free from worry. The month had been fraught with painful reminders of death as my friend's husband had recently lost his battle with the disease. During that time, I became reminded of my own ultimate demise.

I hailed a taxi and travelled the length of the city centre before alighting at Museum Station. From here, the walk was brief to the Macquarie Street surgery. Before entering, I quickly touched up my makeup before claiming a seat at reception. The consultation was brief, and I was delighted to hear that I was clear, and cancer was no longer my enemy. I was grateful for this result and was earnestly thinking how fortunate I had been. There were others in the waiting room, and I imagined their fate to be quite different to mine. We never know what is around the corner, but we must make the best of it. My mother always said that, *"A life lived, is a life spared."* She was right! I measured my steps down the flight of stairs to the ground floor entrance. David would be overjoyed. I would ring him from the phone booth below. Then I would make my way to Mandalong to give them the pleasing news.

My subsequent visit to Mandalong was brief but rewarding. I was able to have long chats with all my family, although Edmund was not too responsive. I believe the trip supported them as I was able to assist Lucy with the house duties, while she cared for Edmund. I was home after a fortnight and sat with my husband who, to my dismay, began to show signs that he too was unwell.

My husband, David, had spent four years since 2009 semi-retired and since that time, had enjoyed bike riding around the local streets and beyond. He participated in charity runs and challenged himself with worthwhile causes. Late in 2013, however, that began to change as he became diagnosed with a debilitating auto-immune disease. He then went on to suffer a crippling paralysis, culminating in loss of movement, so that in the end, his speech and appetite were seriously affected. David was hospitalised in November and so he spent Christmas at St. Vincent's, where he received the best of medical attention. In January 2019, Philip and Lucy joined me at David's bedside. We farewelled him early the following week, and grieved together the best part of the week after.

The family spent the rest of the month gaining strength from one another at the station. Uncle Rick joined us too. He was now in his late sixties and used a walking stick to get around. He still made us laugh, and his energy was noticeable at this time. Lucy and Philip were stronger than ever, weathering the battles that life had placed upon them. I continued to help where I could, cooking my Italian recipes for all. Eliza and Robyn would be arriving in a fortnight. This meant that Robyn would be cooking again, and I felt now was the time to return home. It was not that they did not appreciate me, but the staff loved their company, especially for an evening around the pool table.

Edmund was still the quiet soul, but he was becoming less introverted lately. Unfortunately, the family noted a dramatic and troubling change in his behaviour. He was becoming more manic, sleeping irregularly, barely having a conversation, and avoiding contact with others. He ate in his room and rarely ventured out, except to post papers or collect his mail. All of us were at the point of suggesting he should get more regular help.

Lucy was unsure about the direction she should take to help Edmund. Life had seriously taken an about turn, and she felt at times consumed by the enormity of the situation. She gravitated between one decision and another, as she supported her son through his sickness and adversity. Edmund would now sit for hours in front of his computer, rarely responding to loved ones. His fate was unknown, and all Lucy could do was wait it out. Doctors had assessed him, but there was no clear direction. In time, he had been placed on a cocktail of drugs to assist him to regain his former self. Life for Edmund appeared for the moment, empty and directionless.

Lucy spent hours contemplating her next plan but, in the end, she could do little, other than support his every physical need. The emotional and psychological response would need to be ongoing also, but she would not have answers quickly.

One morning, Lucy decided to spend some time riding. She

thought that this should help her gain perspective and think more clearly. She looked back at her reflection as she turned around in front of the mirror. Her body had retained the youthful physique she once shared with her sister, but her curves were more toned, acquired from the strict regimen she had practised in the saddle. Her eyes were still a pale blue, she told herself, and her skin still retained a youthful complexion. Lucy was careful to always wear a slouch hat now, as she was aware of the sun damage, if not protected.

Lucy braided her hair slowly and tied it up above her hairline. She had taken after her father and grandfather, as they had thick wavy hair which turned to a steely grey colour as they aged. She stooped carefully between the bed and side table to steady herself as she pulled her stirrups over her long legs. She laughed to herself as she remembered her friends calling her the 'praying mantis' as she ran in the playground at school. I guess she should be happy that she was not constantly dieting and spending her time with exercise regimens. She dotted her face with cream; forehead, cheeks, chin, and nose, and smoothed it over until concealed. She rarely wore makeup as her work made it an unnecessary exercise.

Lucy made her way to the outskirts of the property. She believed she had many things to consider. She sat on the tray of the utility. With her legs hanging from the edge, she kicked the box seat from below her. She would eat quietly and reflect on her options. Her lunch of cold chicken wings and mango were leftovers from the previous night's meal. She was not hungry but forced herself to consume some of the lunch before her. Lucy's decision to support Edmund came naturally, but it depended on her being available to him twenty-four-seven. This would conflict with her work on the property, but it seemed more favourable than sending him to a clinic in the city. She disposed of her lunch, throwing the contents below her for the menacing ants. She watched as they ran toward the feast, the frenzy continuing, until all was consumed but the naked bones.

She turned around to hear the *ki-ki-ki-ki* call of the goshawk. The melodious song of the honeyeaters could then be heard in answer until, all was quiet, and then, out of nowhere, the sound of wings swooping up past her from beyond the bough. A loud squawk dominated the air. Then feathers fell, spinning softly, as the breeze pulled them to the ground. The raptor had taken his prey, and the joyful song was quieter now.

Lucy's heart was in her mouth. The bush began fighting her, and it was all she could do to stay positive. Sometimes, she explained to herself, we do not get the support we need at critical moments in our lives. She needed the bush now, but it was not giving forth.

The heat was unusually intense now, and Lucy considered leaving, to manage some administration back home. She packed the box seat back onto the tray of the vehicle. She opened the door to the cabin and sat down. Lucy turned the ignition, but to her surprise, it would not start. She waited, knowing that if she tried again in quick succession, it might cause flooding to the carburettor. After a few minutes, she made a second attempt. The engine turned over, pushing out a steady stream of smoke from the exhaust. It was clear that the car needed 'the crew's' attention when she returned. Lucy made her way back to the open road and began her journey home.

The dark clouds assembled quickly above her and within minutes the heavy rains were deafening. The windscreen became a target, the water being so heavy that Lucy could not see the road. She stopped briefly for relief. Sitting cocooned in the cab, she removed her thoughts from the anxiety that had previously oppressed her. As she sat alone, she became quiet within, at peace within herself, and her surroundings. She began to breathe easier now, closed her eyes and said a heartfelt prayer. She was thankful and felt blessed.

The rains had come with great speed, so she opened her eyes, as she felt the cab move sideways. She held on carefully as she realised her vehicle had taken on a wall of water. Lucy held onto the passenger door, as she eased herself out of the window. Fortunately, the car was old and as the windows were not controlled by electrics, they could be wound down to support her weight as she climbed out. At last, her body became free of the vehicle, and she swam with the current, to finally find herself standing on a ridge above the calamity. The utility was still stirring upon the water as the engine had not been halted. It then coughed its last breath and sank into the brackish mud, which eventually claimed it completely. Lucy looked on, fearing that if she ventured forward, she too may sink below the sand. She later spoke of the flooding to Philip and her sons, and they were relieved that she had escaped certain death.

Sometimes, Lucy felt numb and knew that her desperate thoughts had only partially improved. In her heart, she was grieving, for those things that could have been, and were, it seemed, not possible. She performed her duties, but her body and mind were not at one. *'The orchestra played, but there was no music'*. She was too afraid to cry, but knew that if she did, she may not be able to stop. Her tears were not only for her son, but for her own recovery. She felt empty inside and found it hard to give the love he needed.

Lucy felt it was necessary to investigate Edmund's condition further and to ascertain whether it was hereditary. She had remembered Daniel telling her that Rebekah's sister Suzannah, had suffered a mental illness during her short life. She had been referred to as a 'lunatic' by the medical profession, which was the term given, at that time, to mean a behaviour that was not within the 'norm'. If it had not been for her mother, Suzannah would have spent her short life in an asylum, being subject to the brutal techniques of ice baths and electric shock treatment.

Suzannah was eventually diagnosed to be suffering from 'melancholia' or 'mania' which was characterized by violent outbursts. She was considered by medical 'experts' to have a hereditary predisposition to the disease at the time.

Her hallucinations were common throughout the eighteenth and nineteenth centuries, as female hysteria was one of the most diagnosed 'disorders'. **(23)** Lucy researched literature to find that there was a mistaken notion that women were somehow predisposed to mental and behavioural conditions, and this has had its origins as far back as Ancient Greece. **(24)** She learned that Suzannah, along with countless more patients, were given various treatments, including drugs to manage the condition. Recommended therapy for depression in the nineteenth century, included baths and massage, ferrous iodide, arsenic, ergot, strophantin, and cinchona. **(25)** While this information was important to her, it was somewhat confronting, as she knew there was a possibility that Edmund may have an incurable affliction, brought about through his birth. Again, she felt responsible, and this weighed heavily upon her.

For the next few weeks, Lucy turned her direction to her work on the station. Day after day, she had to make decisions, and with Philip at her side, she would systematically resolve them. She had little time to herself, as there was so much to do. Lucy would, however, take time to swim at the spring as she had when she was young. She knew that these moments were important, as this activity reinvigorated her and made it possible for her to continue to be strong.

"Though infinitely small and fragile in comparison with the powers of darkness, this place is still a light, my only light," she reminded herself.

It was on one such visit to the waterhole, that Lucy experienced what was to be the most memorable event of her life. She had been fortunate enough to have had a keen sense of the spirit world up until now, but today, it would be more remarkable than the last.

As Lucy stood waist-deep in water, the song of the bush became intense as nature played its melodic chant, announcing an arrival. It appeared from the East, bringing with it, the white light that illuminated her surroundings. Lucy shielded her eyes as she peered between her fingers. The Desert Star had revealed itself to her again. Then, as her eyes adjusted to its brilliance, below it, appeared a vision of white. Lucy beheld the glory of an angel who had unveiled herself to her.

Lucy could not describe it fully, but she felt at peace in the quietness. On this visit to the waterhole this Sunday evening, Lucy received the message that would change her life. She wrote these words to her sister Eliza, shortly afterwards.

"In a moment of indescribable joy, a piercing bright light appeared before me. It was translucent; a vision of white; a luminescence that surrounded all things. Such was this light, so blinding, but so satisfying. My eyes turned toward its source. There, with open arms draped in robes, my eyes became transfixed upon a face of glory. Without words, the message was that my son would, in his lifetime, fulfil a purpose, and that it

would follow a period of great uncertainty; God's grace would work through him."

The light dimmed and Lucy fell into a deep reflection. She had become touched by the light and given the courage to continue her journey in the steps of her ancestors. Lucy knew that with faith, she would witness immense joy at last, and that her son would not only recover, but follow his destiny.

Lucy sat for a time reflecting on these events after dark. She reminded herself of the advice once given to her by her mother. "An angelic revelation may not always be inspiring, transforming the soul into light, but sometimes it may reveal misgivings or omissions." Lucy opened her heart and found things she should change. She bent low and pledged herself in front of her creator.

The local Indigenous community believed that the spirit world was central to their existence. The surrounding mountains connect them with this spiritual place; a site where tribes for millennium have crossed over. The landscape of Mount Herbert has held the secrets and ancestral stories of the Tanami people. In her heart, Lucy knew that her mission to continue her spiritual journey was returning and the personal strength that she needed would now be found within.

The next morning, Lucy woke to a loud noise. She thought it must have been a tray of dishes, as it sounded like the entire load had smashed into pieces. She sat herself up on one elbow and looked at Philip.

"Insufferable!" Angus muttered angrily in the distance. Lucy volunteered to take no notice. Philip was still sleeping. Instead of investigating, she closed her eyes and tried to remember her encounter the day before. She knew something significant had transpired. Lucy kept her eyes closed, as she tried to remember the way the experience had made her feel. Her mind was clear, as she relived it again in her mind.

Edmund and his mother had always had a connection which Lucy could not explain. She had spoken to him about his ancestry and the passion she had for the land. He understood that his mother had a spiritual connection with the Tanami people, and it was stronger than her physical presence here at Mandalong.

Lucy stood up and made her way to Edmund's room. She stepped in to open the curtains. The sun was not yet up but sat on the horizon in anticipation. Edmund rolled over and then, realising his mother was present, sat up straight. His mood appeared different today, she thought to herself. He then spoke to her about a dream he had that night. He shared his thoughts with his mother as she sat at the end of his bed. He directed his gaze elsewhere as he tried to remember his dream, which he believed to be poignant, yet concerning. There was an old man in his dream, who sat down beside him and spoke. He talked of a gift; one that Edmund himself had received. The old man told him that he would continue the line of hope within the family, and would shortly engage upon a journey, one that had been prophesised by the ancients.

The old man, Edmund said, looked tired, but inspired by his message. Lucy wondered if this visit had been made by Daniel, or indeed Samuel. In any case, she reminded herself, this appearance was significant. She believed now that the journey was not complete, as the ancestors had extended their faith in her son. Lucy felt reassured, as she now knew that Edmund did indeed have a purpose.

Lucy bent over and hugged her son, and they both left the room together, convinced that from this day onwards, they were blessed by the ancestors. Edmund looked bright and flushed in his cheeks, an observation Lucy had not made about him for a time. She felt she understood those two great old men, better now than ever. They had handed the baton on to her in the past, and it was now time for her to do the same. The next generation, born from Edmund would learn to listen to their father, who would, like the chosen before him, interpret the message of the spirit dancers of this great land.

Edmund retired to his room at last to pack his belongings and leave for future study and reflection. His spirit was refreshed and the passion for living which he had recently obtained, allowed him to plan for his future. There seemed to be possibilities, she thought to herself. His mother and father waved farewell as he boarded his flight for a new position in Canberra. It took some time for Lucy to begin her work again at the homestead. Now she must reclaim her life and begin to recover what she could.

Philip had often spoken to Lucy about his pleasure in seeing Angus develop so well at the station. He had observed that he had improved his skills in the saddle as, he watched carefully and learnt from 'the crew'. His father relied on him also, as both had attended cattle auctions to increase their stock. Angus had a good eye for cattle and appeared to get a decent price per head each time he attended. His skills of negotiation were also noticeable, as he traded the Mandalong stock for export. He was ambitious like his father, and they spoke for hours about building their investment.

Angus had become a noticeable asset on the property; however, his personal life had been for the moment, a well-kept secret. Angus was developing a strong personal attachment to a young lady from the local community. Her name was Ruth, and her father was a leading hand at Mandalong. Ruth and Angus had formed an attachment, and he enjoyed spending time with her when he had completed his day's work.

Ruth was the local teacher at the school. Her wish was to have a large family and the two of them regularly spoke about their future together. The time came when Angus thought it was appropriate that he shared his personal decision with his family. He introduced his fiancé and prepared for the upcoming wedding that Christmas.

Before long, Angus and Ruth celebrated their engagement with the Stanford-Roddick family and the wider community. The locals were excited that their teacher had found herself a husband, and enthusiastic about the up-coming nuptials. The celebration had gone according to plan and the couple prepared to leave. As Ruth and Angus walked towards Lucy, she opened her arms and hugged them. She held Ruth as she slid the gold leafed brooch into her hands. She then explained its significance, and that it belonged to the next matriarch of Mandalong. Lucy then stepped aside to quietly thank Millie, for she knew without her, all of this would not be possible.

For all the initial plans regarding their education and future, Lucy realised that her sons would master their own destiny. She was proud of them, and satisfied that the nurturing they had received, made them both feel an attachment to Mandalong and the community.

The day was clear, and Lucy knew this date would mark a new chapter in the Stanford-Roddick history. She lifted her head up high as she threw the rose petal leaves over the newlywed couple. No doubt, the family tree would soon receive additional members. Lucy knew Daniel and Jack would be equally proud of her family, as she had been of them.

The Tanami Desert Star beamed down upon Lucy as she

looked up at the heavens and thanked her forebears for their gifts. Mandalong and all those who lived within this great community, she believed, were safe as the future looked bright.

I too, knew that my family did not need me as often now, and for that reason my job was complete. I turned and faced the water's edge.

The view from the harbour caught me by surprise, as the words of James Taylor rang out in my ears, *"The secret to life is enjoying the passage of time."*

The End

References

(1) This story is known as the Napaljarri-Warnu Jukurrpa: The Seven Sisters – Dreamtime Story
https://www.kateowengallery.com/

(2) The Story of the Aboriginal People of the Central Coast of NSW. F.C. Bennett

(3) Brolga (An Excerpt from Corroboree)
What is Brolga about?
https://www.Bangarra.com.au

(4) Aboriginal Land Rights Act (Northern Territory) 1976
https://www.legislation.gov.au/Details/C2016C00111

(5) The Secret Sites Act
https://legislation.nt.gov.au/en/Legislation/NORTHERN-TERRITORY-ABORIGINAL-SACRED-ITES-ACT-1989

(6) The Central Land Council
https://www.clc.org.au/the-alra/

(7) Lives that shaped Australia's history: Obituaries Australia, Davidson, Allan Arthur (1873-1930) News (Adelaide), 9 January 1930, p 12 (view original); Advertiser (Adelaide), 11 January 1930, p 21, by Michael Terry https://oa.anu.edu.au/obituary/davidson-allan-arthur-21568

(8) Tourism and Gold in Kakadu: The Impact of Current and Potential Natural Resources Use in the Northern Territory Economy, Australian National University; North Australia Research Unit, Darwin, 1991
Tanami: The Newmont projects.
www.newmont.com

(9) Mina Mina and the Tanami Desert; Nadia Phillips, Jan 17, 2020
Laws to protect the rights of Indigenous communities and their claim to 'Aboriginal Knowledge' or Sacred Sites.
www.wentworthgalleries.com.au

Since 1972 serious efforts to acknowledge the Aboriginal peoples' ongoing land and cultural rights have taken place. The Aboriginal Land Rights (NT) Act of 1976 gave the Indigenous communities limited protection, but it was not until the following year that the Aboriginal Land and Scared Sites Bill (NT) of 1977 that these custodians continued to protect sites on Aboriginal freehold land or sites.

In 1978, Indigenous communities obtained self-government, eventually culminating in the establishment of the Sacred Sites Authority of 1979. Unfortunately, the notion of sacred sites at this time not understood by the broader community, and it was not until 1988 the NT government introduced the Aboriginal Areas Protection Bill (NT). This law was instrumental in creating a balance between the protection of Sacred Sites and the development of the Territory, its people, and resources. The Aboriginal Sacred Sites Act of 1989 gave further protection to

these sites.
www.austrade.gov.au
Australian Trade and Investment Commission

(10) Mining and Indigenous Tourism in Northern Australia by D Brereton · 2007 · Cited by 17 — Project Aims and Benefits csrm.uq.edu.au https://www.csrm.uq.edu.au ›

(11) Manning, I., 1997. 'Native Title, Mining and Mineral Exploration: The Impact of Native Title and the Right to Negotiate on Mining and Mineral Exploration in Australia'. Canberra: Aboriginal and Torres Strait Islander Commission.

(12) Doppelganger, German, CG Jung Memories, Dreams and Reflections, translated by Richard and Clara Winston (New York: Parthenon,1963) pp.16-17, 87-88

(13) Six years after the discovery of an ancient rock art site in the Katherine region, a team of researchers have found evidence the art dates to 36,000 years ago which makes it the oldest site of its kind in Australia. Katherine Times Ancient rock art uncovered. https://www.katherinetimes.com.au › ...

(14) Munanga, 'white person' is widespread among the languages of the Arnhem Land region, as Jay Arthur (1996:161) notes in her compilation of written Aboriginal English, supported by citations from the northern NT 1977-1995.4 Oct. Source: What is the correct term for Aboriginal people? - Creative Spirits, retrieved from
https://www.creativespirits.info/aboriginalculture/people/how-to-name-aboriginal-people

(15). Blackfella: Blackfella (also blackfellah, blackfulla, black fella, or black fellah) is an informal term in Australian English to refer to Indigenous Australians, in particular Aboriginal Australians, most commonly among themselves. Blackfellas, whitefellas, and the hidden injuries of race, National Library of Australia Cowlishaw, Gillian K. (Gillian Keir), 1934- https://www. nla.gov.au/

(16) Bunji means friend/mate, cooee: An Aboriginal word that is often unknowingly used by non-Indigenous people. 5 Jan 2021
Source: What is the correct term for Aboriginal people? - Creative Spirits, retrieved from https://www.creativespirits.info/aboriginalculture/people/how-to-name-aboriginal-people

(17) 'Aborigine' comes from the Latin words ab meaning from and original meaning beginning or origin. It expresses that Aboriginal people have been there from the beginning of time. 'Aborigine' is a noun for an Aboriginal person (male or female). The media, which is sometimes still using this term, has been called on to abandon it because its use has 'negative effects on Aboriginal and Torres Strait Islander peoples' self-esteem and mental health'.
Source: What is the correct term for Aboriginal people? Creative Spirits, retrieved from https://www.creativespirits.info/aboriginalculture/people/how-to-name-aboriginal-people

(18) Laws to protect the rights of Indigenous communities and their claim for recognition and protection of the development of land including mining sites in the NT.

The Tanami gold mine is the second-largest underground gold mining operation in the country. Since 1976, the Central Desert Aboriginal Lands Trust has managed the property on behalf of the Aboriginal people. One of Australia's most productive gold mining areas, in the remote Tanami Desert, a five hundred kilometres north-west of Alice Springs in the Northern Territory. The site is situated 563km north-west of Alice Springs and 949km south-west of Darwin. The Granites and Dead Bullock Soak mines owned by one of the world's leading gold producers. The mines have produced around eight million ounces of gold over the past twenty years and have reserves to sustain production for another ten years. These Dead Bullock Soak mines and associated the Granites milling plant are located on Aboriginal freehold land owned by the Warlpiri people (Yapa).

Returning land to country: Indigenous engagement in mined land closure and rehabilitation; Australian Journal of management; May 31, 2020; The University of New South Wales.

(19) The Minnamurra Boating Tragedy, 21; In remembrance of those citizens of Kiama who by their lives and their deeds deserve to be noticed by visitors. To the Kiama General Cemetery at rest 1860-1987, K & DH Society Inc's Cemetery committee 1989

(20) Adapted from 'Kingswood Public School Centenary 1892-1992; Mr Bert Evans, Penrith City Library, 1992, pp 20,21

(21) The Bogey Man; Arnhem Land, in Australia's north, is the abode of malevolent shades and vampire-like Wind and Shooting Star Spirit Beings. There are also murderous, humanoid fish-maidens who live in deep waterholes and rock holes, biding their time to rise, grab and drown unsuspecting human children or adults who stray close to the water's edge. Certain sorcerers gleefully dismember their victim's limb by limb, and there are other monstrous entities as well, living parallel lives to the human beings residing in the same places. The existence of such Evil Beings is an unremarkable phenomenon, given that most religious and mythological traditions possess their own demons and supernatural entities.

Monstrous beings Dreaming's' and place – Aboriginal monsters and their meanings

Christine Judith Nicholls, Australian National University; Published: April 30, 2014

(22) https://www.gettyimages.com.au/photos/jillaroo

(23) Alexander, F. G., Selesnick, S. T.: The History of Psychiatry. New York: Harper & Row, 1966.

(24) Female hysteria: The history of a controversial 'condition' https://www.medicalnewstoday.com ›

(25) Historical notes on the therapy of depression - PubMed https://pubmed.ncbi.nlm.nih.gov